Praise for *When I Was You*

"*When I Was You* doles out twists and turns at the perfect pace, leading up to a fantastic conclusion... A gripping psychological barnburner."
—*Shelf Awareness*

"Fans of tricky tales of obsession and revenge will be well satisfied."
—*Publishers Weekly*

"Amber Garza has upped the game on the classic stalker novel! *When I Was You* is a fast-paced, beautifully plotted book that will keep you reading until the last page. You won't want to put this one down."
—Samantha Downing, *USA TODAY* bestselling author of *My Lovely Wife*

"Exhilarating, page-turning, shocking, this is one of those rare psychological thrillers that really is the whole package. An electric, raw, emotional story that will leave you breathless... *When I Was You* is a dark and twisty delight."
—Christina McDonald, *USA TODAY* bestselling author of *The Night Olivia Fell*

"A compulsive read about a friendship and maternal instincts gone awry, with a twist you won't want to miss."
—Karen Cleveland, *New York Times* bestselling author of *Need to Know*

"Garza's debut thriller packs a wallop of intrigue... The unpredictable twists and turns culminate in an explosive, shocking ending. A definite must-read!"
—Samantha M. Bailey, author of *Woman on the Edge*

Look for Amber Garza's next novel
Where I Left Her
available soon from MIRA.

WHEN I WAS YOU

AMBER GARZA

mira

ISBN-13: 978-0-7783-1207-9

When I Was You

First published in 2020. This edition published in 2021.

Recycling programs
for this product may
not exist in your area.

This edition published by arrangement with Harlequin Books S.A.

For questions and comments about the quality of this book, please contact us
at CustomerService@Harlequin.com.

Mira
22 Adelaide St. West, 40th Floor
Toronto, Ontario M5H 4E3, Canada
www.Harlequin.com

Printed in Spain

For Andrew—with love, always

WHEN I WAS YOU

PART ONE

"Sometimes we want what we want
even if we know it's going to kill us."
—DONNA TARTT

CHAPTER ONE

It was a Monday morning in early October when I first heard about you. I was getting out of the shower when my phone rang. After throwing on a robe and cinching it, I ran into my bedroom, snatching my cell off the nightstand.

Unknown number.

Normally, I let those go. But I'd already run all the way in here, and I thought maybe it was a call from Dr. Hillerman's office.

"Hello?" I answered, breathless. Goose bumps rose on my pale flesh, so I pulled the robe tighter around me. My sopping wet hair dripped down my back.

"Is this Kelly Medina?"

Great. A salesperson. "Yes," I answered, wishing I hadn't picked up.

"Hi, Kelly, this is Nancy from Dr. Cramer's office. I'm calling to remind you of your well-baby appointment this Friday at ten a.m."

"Well-baby?" I let out a surprised laugh. "You're about nineteen years too late."

"Excuse me?" Nancy asked, clearly confused.

"My son isn't a baby," I explained. "He's nineteen."

"Oh, I'm so sorry," Nancy immediately replied. I could hear the clicking of a keyboard. "I apologize. I called the wrong Kelly Medina."

"There's another Kelly Medina in Folsom?" My maiden name had been Smith. There are a million other Kelly Smiths in the world. In California, even. But since I'd married Rafael, I'd never met another Kelly Medina. Until now.

Until *you.*

"Yes. Her child is a new patient."

It felt like yesterday when my child was a new patient. I remembered sitting in the waiting room of Dr. Cramer's office, holding my tiny newborn, waiting for the nurse to call my name.

"I have no idea how this happened. It's like your numbers got switched in the system or something," Nancy muttered, and I wasn't sure if she was talking to me or herself. "Again, I'm so sorry."

I assured her it was fine, and hung up. My hair was still wet from the shower, but instead of blow-drying it I headed downstairs to make some tea first. On my way, I passed Aaron's room. The door was closed, so I pressed it open with my palm. The wood was cold against my skin. Shivering, I took in his neatly made bed, the movie posters tacked to the wall, the darkened desktop computer in the corner.

Leaning against the door frame of Aaron's room, my mind flew back to the day he left for college. I remembered his broad smile, his sparkling eyes. He'd been so anxious to leave here. To leave *me*. I should've been happy for him. He was doing what I'd raised him to do.

Boys were supposed to grow up and leave.

In my head I knew that. But in my heart it was hard to let him go.

After closing Aaron's door, I headed down to the kitchen. The house was silent. It used to be filled with noise— Aaron's little feet stomping down the hallway, his sound effects as he played with toys, his chattering as he got older. Now it was always quiet. Especially during the week when Rafael stayed in the Bay Area for work. Aaron had been gone over a year. You'd think I'd be used to it by now. But, actually, it seemed to get worse over time. The constant silence.

The phone call had thrown me. For a second it felt like I'd gone back in time, something I longed for most days. When Aaron was born everyone told me to savor all the moments because it went by too quickly. It was hard for me to imagine. I hadn't had the easiest life growing up, and it certainly hadn't flown by. And the nine months I was pregnant with Aaron had gone on forever, every day longer than the one before.

But they were right.

Aaron's childhood was fleeting. The moments were elusive, like a butterfly, practically impossible to catch. And now it was gone. He was a man. And I was alone.

Rafael kept encouraging me to find a job to fill my time, but I'd already tried that. When Aaron first left, I applied for a bunch of jobs. Since I'd been out of work for so long, no one wanted to hire me. That's when Christine suggested I volunteer somewhere. So I started helping out at a local food bank, handing out food once a week and occasionally doing a little administrative stuff. I enjoyed it, but it wasn't enough. It barely filled any of my time. Besides, I was one of many volunteers. I wasn't needed. Not the way Aaron had needed me when he was a child.

When he left, the Kelly I'd always known ceased to exist. Vanished into thin air. I was merely a ghost now, haunting my house, the streets, the town.

As the water boiled, I thought about you. Thought about how lucky you were to have a baby and your whole life ahead of you. I wondered what you were doing right now. Not sitting alone in your big, silent house, I bet. No, you were probably chasing your cute little baby around your sunny living room, the floor littered with toys, as he crawled on all fours and laughed.

Was your child a boy? The lady on the phone didn't say, but that's what I pictured. A chubby, smiling little boy like my Aaron.

The kettle squealed, and I flinched. I poured the boiling water in a mug and steam rose from it, circling the air in front of my face. Tossing in the tea bag, I breathed it in, leaning my back against the cool tile counter. The picture window in front of me revealed our perfectly manicured front yard—bright green grass lined with rose bushes. I'd always been particular about the roses. When Aaron was a kid he always wanted to help with the pruning, but I never let him. Afraid he'd mess them up, I guess. Seemed silly now.

Heart pinching, I blew out a breath.

I wondered about your yard. What did it look like? Did you have roses? I wondered if you'd let your son help you prune them. I wondered if you'd make the same mistakes I had.

Bringing the mug to my lips, I took a tiny sip of the hot tea. It was mint, my favorite. I allowed the flavors to sit on my tongue a minute before swallowing it down. The refrigerator hummed. The ice shifted in the ice maker. My shoulders tensed slightly. I rolled them out, taking another sip.

Shoving off the counter, I was headed toward the stairs when my cell buzzed inside my pocket. My pulse spiked. It couldn't be Rafael. He was a professor and his first class had already started.

Aaron?

Nope. It was a text from Christine.

Going to yoga this morning?

I'd already showered. I was about to tackle my latest organization project. Today was the kitchen pantry. Last week I'd bought a bunch of new containers and bins. Friday I'd spent the day labeling all of them. After taking the weekend off since Rafael was home, I was anxious to continue with it. I'd already organized several closets downstairs, but my plan was to work my way through all the closets and cabinets in the house.

Usually I loved yoga, but I had way too much to do today.

No, I typed. Then bit my lip. Backspaced. Stared at the phone. My own reflection emerged on the slick screen—disheveled hair, pale face, dark circles under the eyes.

You need to get out more. Exercise. It's not healthy to sit in the house all day. Rafael's voice echoed in my head.

The organizing would still be here tomorrow. Besides, who was I kidding? I'd probably only spend a couple of hours organizing before abandoning my project to read online blogs and articles, or dive into the latest murder mystery I was reading.

I typed yes, then sent it and hurried to my room to get ready.

Thirty minutes later, I was parking in front of the gym. When I stepped out, a cool breeze whisked over my arms. After three scorching hot summer months, I welcomed it. Fall had always been my favorite season. I relished the festiveness of it. Pumpkins, apples, rustic colors. But mostly it was the leaves falling and being raked away. The bareness of the trees. The shedding of the old to make room for the new. An end, but also a beginning.

Although, we weren't quite there yet. The leaves were still green, and by afternoon the air would be warm. But in the mornings and evenings we got a tiny sip of fall, enough to make me thirsty for more.

Securing the gym bag on my shoulder, I walked briskly through the lot. Once inside, it was even colder. The AC blasted as if it was a hundred-degree day. *That's okay.* It gave me more of an incentive to break a sweat. Smiling at the receptionist, I pulled out my keys for her to scan my card. Only my card wasn't hanging from my key ring.

I fished around in my bag, but it wasn't there either. Flushing, I offered the bored receptionist an apologetic smile. "I seem to have misplaced my tag. Can you look me up? Kelly Medina?"

Her eyes widened. "Funny. There was another lady in here earlier today with the same name."

My heart pounded. I'd been attending this gym for years and never had anyone mentioned you before. I wondered how long you'd worked out here. "Is she still here?" My gaze scoured the lobby as if I might recognize you.

"No. She was here super early."

Of course you were. I used to be too, when Aaron was an infant.

"Okay. You're all checked in, Kelly," the receptionist said, buzzing me in.

Clutching my gym bag, I made my way up the stairs toward the yoga room, thoughts of you flooding my mind. A few young women walked next to me, wearing tight tank tops and pants, gym bags hanging off their shoulders. They were laughing and chatting loudly, their long ponytails bouncing behind their heads. I tried to say excuse me, to move past them, but they couldn't hear me. Impatient, I bit my lip and walked slowly behind them. Finally, I made it to the top. They headed toward the cardio machines, and I pressed open the door to the yoga room.

I spotted Christine already sitting on her mat. Her blond hair was pulled back into a perfectly coiffed ponytail. Her eyes were bright and her lips were shiny. I smoothed down my unruly brown hair and licked my dry lips.

She waved me over with a large smile. "You made it."

"Yep." I dropped my mat and bag next to hers.

"I wasn't sure. It's been a while."

Shrugging, I sat down on my mat. "Been busy."

"Oh, I totally get that." She waved away my words with a flick of her slender wrist. "Maddie and Mason have had a bazillion activities lately. I can barely keep up."

"Sounds rough," I muttered, slipping off my flip-flops. This was the problem with getting married and having a kid so young. Most of my friends were still raising families.

"I know, right? I can't wait until they're adults and I can do whatever I want."

"Yeah, it's the best," I said sarcastically.

Her mouth dropped. "Oh, I'm sorry. I wasn't talking about you…" Her pale cheeks turned pink. "I know how much you miss Aaron. It's just…"

I shook my head and offered her a smile "Relax. I get it."

Christine and I met years ago in a yoga class. She's one of those women with almost no self-awareness. It's what first drew me to her. I loved how raw and real she was. Other people shied away from her, unable to handle her filterless statements. But I found her refreshing and, honestly, pretty entertaining.

"I remember how busy it was when Aaron was younger," I said. "One year he signed up for baseball *and* basketball. They overlapped for a bit, and I swear I was taking him to a game or practice like every day."

"Yes!" Christine said excitedly, relief evident in her expression. "Sometimes it's all just too much."

"Yeah, sometimes it is," I agreed.

The class was about to start and the room was filling up. It was mainly women, but there were some men. Most of them were with their wives or girlfriends. I'd tried getting Rafael to come with me before, but he laughed as if the idea was preposterous.

"Remember when there were only a few of us in this class?" Christine asked, her gaze sweeping the room.

I nodded, glancing around. There were so many new people I didn't know. Not that I was surprised. Folsom had grown a lot in the ten years I'd lived here. New people moved here every day.

Staring at all the strangers crowding around us, I shivered, my thoughts drifting back to you. We hadn't even met, and yet I felt like I knew you. We had the same name, the same gym, the same pediatrician for our child.

It felt like kismet. Fate had brought you here to me. I was certain of it.

But why?

CHAPTER
TWO

The wine was dark red as it swirled in the glass, leaving stains like spiderwebs up the sides. Christine lifted it to her lips and took a long sip.

"You're not gonna order a drink?" She raised her eyebrows as if it was bizarre that I wasn't drinking at noon on a Monday.

I wasn't even sure why I let her talk me into going out to lunch after yoga. I still had errands to run today, and I was desperate to get out of my sweaty workout clothes.

"No, I actually can't stay long. I have to hit the grocery store after this," I said.

"Go tomorrow," she said, a hint of impatience in her tone. "C'mon, have a drink with me."

"I can't go tomorrow. I have to get stuff for dinner tonight." I glanced at the menu in front of me, scanning the lunch items. A burger and fries sounded good. I was starving. Glancing down at my stomach lapping over the band of my pants, I frowned. *I probably shouldn't, though.*

When Rafael and I met, I was thin. It wasn't until after I had Aaron that my body changed, got softer, rounder. It didn't bother me, though. I looked motherly. The added weight only confirmed the miracle that had happened in my body. Besides, it happened to all women, right? Shortly after Aaron's birth, Raf started making snide comments and remarks. He began scrutinizing what I ate and urging me to work out more. I listened to him, slimmed back down and kept the weight off. But recently I'd put a little back on.

I decided on the Santa Fe chicken salad. Dressing on the side.

"Oh, please," Christine said. "No one's gonna be home tonight. Just pop some popcorn and pour some wine. That's what I'd do if I had the house to myself."

Christine acted like I lived some glamorous life. Like being alone was something to covet. It wasn't. I'd give anything to go back in time. To have a full house and busy schedule like she did. But instead of saying any of this, I simply smiled. "Yeah, maybe I'll do that." Honestly, it didn't sound like the worst plan.

We were sitting at a table outside, and I glanced over as a young woman jogged past pushing a stroller. It was covered, so I couldn't see the child inside. I glanced back up at the woman's face. She was dark-haired, pale skin, probably in her twenties.

For a moment, I wondered if she was you.

I had no idea what you looked like or how old you were. Since I knew you had a baby, I'd been picturing you as a young woman, but I supposed lots of women had babies later in life. Also, I had no reason to believe this baby was an only child.

Did you have a whole brood or just one?

Were you married?

Did you live near here?

Questions swirled in my mind.

One thing I was pretty sure of was that you weren't contemplating having popcorn and wine for dinner.

You were probably planning to make a nice meal for your family. Something simple like pasta since you had an infant. You'd have to bide your time, sticking him in his swing or, better yet, cooking while he napped. Then you and your husband would take turns eating, passing your baby between the two of you.

Smiling to myself, I remembered doing that nightly while Aaron was a newborn. I don't think I ate a hot meal for two years. It was actually annoying at the time. Not sure why the memory made me feel all warm and fuzzy now.

After ordering, Christine finished off her glass of wine and eyed me suspiciously. "What's going on with you? You're so quiet today."

I hadn't planned to tell her about you. It just came out. "There's another Kelly Medina in Folsom."

Her face scrunched up. "What do you mean? Like a doppelgänger or something? You know they do say that everyone has a twin."

I didn't know if that was true. I didn't even know who "they" were. "No, not someone who looks like me. I mean, there's another lady with my exact same name."

"Oh." Her face fell. "Well, I mean, Kelly's a pretty common name. I meet other Christines all the time."

"But have you ever met someone with your same last name too?"

She shook her head. "I guess not, but I'm sure they're out there."

"Well, yeah." I shrugged. "But they're not in your same

town, working out at your same gym and taking their kid to your same pediatrician."

"Huh?" Her forehead bunched together and she pursed her lips.

"Yeah." I nodded. Finally, a reaction from her. "I got a call this morning from the doctor's office reminding me of my well-baby appointment. Then they said they called the wrong Kelly."

"Or maybe there was a glitch in the system," she surmised. "When I used to work at that dental office, one time we sent out appointment reminders from like years earlier."

I shook my head. "No, that wasn't what this was. They said she was a new patient."

"Oh, so Kelly Medina's the baby?"

I paused. For a second I wondered if that was true. I'd been picturing you as an adult, but had I gotten it all wrong? Was it possible that you were the child, not the mom? My vision blurred slightly, a headache pricking behind my eyes.

No. That's not right. The nurse, Nancy or whatever, said that your child was the patient. And the girl at the gym said you were a woman. Hadn't she?

Blinking, I cleared my head. Yeah, I was sure she had.

"Kelly? You okay?" Christine frowned. "The phone call upset you, huh?" She waved over the waitress. "Let me order you a drink. Just one. It'll help you relax."

I meant to say no, but found myself nodding. I'd been trying to cut back. It was empty calories I didn't need. But one glass wasn't going to make much of a difference. Besides, I had ordered a salad. I just wouldn't have any more wine tonight.

When the waiter set the wine in front of me, I had planned to sip it slowly. But instead, I ended up drinking greedily like a dog lapping up his bowl of water after running around in the heat. My body warmed almost instantly, my mind blurring at the edges. I shouldn't have drank so fast. I hadn't eaten anything today. When my salad arrived, I picked up my fork with a shaky hand and shoveled in a few bites, hoping to steady myself a little.

It tasted like paper.

I eyed the dressing.

Oh, screw it. After generously pouring it on, I continued eating. *Way better.*

"So, wait until you hear about the fight Joel and I got into the other night," Christine said, picking at her own salad. I noticed she hadn't put any dressing on hers. "He was all over me about how much money I spend on food," she said before taking a tiny nibble out of a piece of lettuce. "Food," she repeated, louder this time. "Can you believe that? It's not like I'm out buying a bunch of shoes or something."

I looked up at her, cocking my head to the side.

She offered me a knowing smile. "Well, okay, I mean, maybe I am. But that wasn't what he was mad about. He was mad about food. And I was like, 'Look, I buy food for our entire family.' And he was like, 'You don't have to shop exclusively at Whole Foods. Other families shop at Costco or WinCo.' And I was like, 'So, you're upset that I'm feeding our family healthy food? Is that what I'm hearing? You'd rather me feed them soda and chips, or what?'"

I nodded like I understood, but I kind of didn't. On Rafael's teaching salary, we'd never been able to afford to shop at Whole Foods.

I reached for my wineglass, but it was empty. *Huh. That went fast.*

"Oh, hang on." Christine bent down, fishing through

the purse by her feet. "I just missed a call." Sitting up, her eyes widened as she stared at the screen. "It's Maddie's school. They left a message." She threw me an apologetic look. "I'm sorry. Give me a minute."

"No problem." My mouth was dry. I reached for my water. Squinting, I wished I'd remembered my sunglasses. The sun was getting brighter by the minute. It was warming up too.

"Oh, no. Maddie got hurt in PE." Christine pushed back her chair. "I'm really sorry, but I gotta take off."

I waved off her apology. "No worries. I totally get it. Remember, you were with me when Aaron dislocated his finger."

"That's right. Let's hope she didn't do that." Flinging her purse over her shoulder, she looked down at the table. "Crap. We haven't even paid yet. Let me see if I have any cash on me."

"No, it's fine. I got it."

She hesitated. "You sure?"

I nodded. "Yep."

"Okay. Thanks. I'll text you later. Okay?" She still wore that concerned look, but I had no idea why. I felt fine. Maybe it was about Maddie this time, not me. *Yeah, that made sense.*

As I watched her leave, my mind flew back to the day Aaron dislocated his finger. I was out with Christine and some of the other moms having a mimosa brunch. It was Christine's birthday month (yes, she celebrates the entire month), so she insisted I have a drink with her. I was on my second mimosa when the school called. All they told me was that Aaron hurt his finger playing basketball during lunchtime. I was irritated until I saw Aaron. His face was ashen, his teeth chattering, his body trembling. His pinky finger was bent at a grotesque angle, and it was way longer than it was supposed to be.

The wait at the doctor went by so slow, I could barely breathe. It was heartbreaking to see him in all that pain. I tried everything to make him laugh or smile, to take his mind off of it. But the pain was too great. Still, he was brave.

A trouper, the doctor said.

"Can I get you anything else?" The waitress appeared by my side, cutting into my memory.

I opened my mouth to ask for the check. Then the vision of my empty house filled my mind. Sitting back in my chair, I said, "Another glass of wine, please."

I didn't think about you again until that night.

The afternoon was a blur. I'd drunk more wine than I intended, and eventually made my way home. Then I'd fallen asleep for a few hours and missed Rafael's call when he got off work.

He sent me a text saying he was going out with some of his coworkers and he'd try again later.

Christine texted also. Maddie was fine. Just a sprained wrist.

As the sun disappeared and darkness blanketed the sky, I headed into the kitchen to eat something. My head pounded. My throat was scratchy, my tongue cottony. After guzzling some water, I pulled out a box of crackers and bit down on one.

The faint sound of children's voices reached my ears, and I turned toward the window. A woman was chasing her two little kids around the neighbor's front yard across the street. The woman who lived there was in her seventies. This had to be her daughter and grandchildren.

And that's when my thoughts drifted to you.

I wondered if you had family in town. I figured you must've moved here recently, since our paths had never crossed until today. Maybe it was to be closer to family.

We'd initially moved here to be near my parents, but they were gone now.

My gaze landed on my laptop sitting on the table in the breakfast nook. The little flashing light told me it was charged. My heart rate picked up speed.

I was certain you were on social media. Everyone seemed to be. Even I had a Facebook and Instagram account. I'd started them to stalk Aaron, but then ended up getting sucked in. Now I probably posted more than I should.

Water in hand, I made my way over to the table. I opened my laptop. It zoomed to life, heat emitting from it. After logging on to Facebook, I searched for Kelly Medina. Dozens of accounts came up.

Who knew this many people in the world had my name?

Man, this could take a while.

I scrolled through all of them, but didn't think any of them were you. For starters, none were in this area, and only a couple of them had young families.

Next, I tried Instagram, but that was even harder to navigate.

Frustrated, I sat back. Surely, you were on here somewhere. Why couldn't I find you?

CHAPTER THREE

In the distance a song played. Something familiar. I couldn't place it exactly, but I knew I'd heard it a million times before. The title was right on the tip of my tongue. Nostalgia enveloped me, all cozy and warm like a big bear hug. But there was a conflicting feeling too, an urgency, like hands on my back pushing me forward against my will.

When I forced my eyelids open, everything was blurry. Dark. My cheek was sticky. Sitting up, I wiped my skin with the back of my hand. I glanced down at the dark wood of the table. The laptop. My gaze scoured the dimly lit kitchen.

The song got louder. Closer. Clearer. Oh, yeah. "I Know You Want Me" by Pitbull. Rafael thought it was the funniest thing ever when he programmed that song in as his ringtone on my phone.

Quickly, I shot my hand out and picked up my cell.

"Hello," I answered swiftly before he hung up. My voice was gravelly like I'd eaten a pile of sand.

"Sorry. Did I wake you?" His words were low and thick, slightly slurred.

I squinted, peering at the clock on the microwave. It was after midnight. "Are you just getting in?"

"Yeah, it was Frank's birthday, so the guys and I went out to celebrate," he said. "What about you? You weren't around when I called earlier."

"Oh. Sorry." No way was I telling him I'd been napping in the middle of the day. He'd never let that go. "I was out with Christine."

"Good." There was hope in his voice. "Did you guys have fun?"

"Yeah," I said, yawning.

"Sounds like you're tired," he said.

"Well, it is the middle of the night," I answered sarcastically, and then instantly felt guilty. It was like I was trying to pick a fight, and lord knows I didn't need to do that. The fights found us easily. No reason to go looking for them.

"Sorry. I guess I'll let you go, then."

"No, I'm up now," I said, trying to smooth things over. "Is there anything you wanted to talk about?" It was out of character for him to call this late. Usually, if he missed me he'd just try again the next day.

"No, not really. I guess I just wanted to hear your voice before I went to bed."

It was the kind of thing he used to say. Back when we were dating or right after we got married. It caught me off guard. Now I really felt bad for my sarcastic comment. My heart softened toward him in a way it hadn't in months. I wasn't sure if it was his words or the wine. Probably a mixture of both. I opened my mouth, wanting to respond with something sweet back, but the words didn't come. It had been so long since we'd been romantic or loving, it was like

I'd lost the ability to be that way. Disheartened, I mumbled a swift good-night and hung up.

After setting the phone down, I wrinkled my nose and glanced around.

Had I really fallen asleep at the kitchen table?

Everything felt fuzzy. After forcing myself to stand, I headed upstairs. The last thought I had before falling asleep was that I never told Rafael about you.

My car was stolen.

It wasn't in the driveway or garage or parked along the curb. I even walked up and down the street.

As I stood on my porch, staring at the empty driveway, my gaze tracing the misshapen gasoline stain on the concrete, panic took root inside my chest. It fluttered against my insides until I felt shaky.

With trembling fingers, I pulled my phone out of my pocket and called Rafael. When it went to voice mail, I groaned.

I scrolled up my contacts, my hand hovering over Aaron's name and picture. His smiling face stared up at me. My heart pinched. I clicked on his name. The phone rang and rang, and then finally his voice mail came on. I listened all the way through up to the beep and then hung up.

He couldn't help me.

Neither of them could.

They weren't here, so I'd have to deal with it myself. Not like that was anything new at this point. I was about to dial the police when a knock on the door startled me. Heart rate spiking, I flung it open.

Christine stood on my front porch wearing skinny jeans,

ankle boots, a flowy white top and a cheery smile. "Morning," she trilled.

Relief swept over me, easing my nerves a little. The knot in my chest slightly loosened. "Oh, thank god you're here." Grabbing her by the arm, I tugged her inside and slammed the door closed.

"What's going on?" she asked, her eyes wide.

"Someone stole my car."

She laughed. "No, they didn't."

What kind of response was that? "Yes, they did. It's not here."

"Of course it's not, silly. You Ubered home from the restaurant yesterday. That's why I'm here. You texted last night and asked me to come get you this morning, so we could pick it up."

I froze, my gaze traveling back to the kitchen where the laptop sat open, my cup of half-drunk water next to it. My mind reeled back as I tried to piece together the events of yesterday.

Oh, right.

The wine. The buzz. The dizziness. The Uber.

Now I remembered.

God, I couldn't believe I'd almost called the cops. They would've thought I was crazy. Thank god Christine showed up when she did.

"Are you okay?" Christine stepped closer, wearing a frown. I was so tired of her looking at me like that.

Laughing, I shook my head. "Yeah, I was totally joking. Of course I remembered taking an Uber. I was just messing with you."

"Oh. Okay." She smiled, but it didn't quite reach her eyes. She still wore that concerned expression.

The one I knew all too well.

"Well, let's go get my car." As I walked out the front door, I rubbed my palms together.

But Christine didn't follow. "Kel, you're still in your pajamas."

If I was trying to convince her I was okay, I was doing a terrible job. I raced upstairs to change quickly. My fingers were stiff from falling asleep with them resting on the laptop keyboard. And my eyes were tired from staring at the bright screen for hours in the dark last night. I couldn't remember the last time I'd stayed up late on the computer. It was probably back when Aaron was in high school. When he'd go to homecoming or prom, I'd spend the entire night perusing his Facebook page and his friend's Facebook pages to see what they were posting throughout the night.

But this was different.

This time I'd been searching for you.

And I'd learned that our name wasn't unique. In fact, it was pretty popular. A couple of the other Kelly Medinas out there were even guys.

Having the same name didn't mean anything.

You were a stranger.

Nothing more. Nothing less.

As I got dressed, I made a pact with myself to let this whole silly obsession go. Just move on. Stop looking for you. Stop thinking about you.

Just stop.

I emerged from my room feeling lighter than before. Air flowed freely through my lungs. My car wasn't stolen. You weren't crowding my thoughts. All was right in my world again.

"Ready?" Christine asked when I got to the bottom of the stairs.

"Yep."

"Awesome." She headed toward the front door. "I thought we could stop for lattes on the way. I'm dying for a coffee. Literally."

I smiled. "Coffee sounds great."

We picked up lattes at Peet's and then headed toward Old Folsom to where my car was parked. Christine held her cup with one hand and the steering wheel with the other as she drove. If I did that, my coffee would end up in my lap. But she'd always been more graceful and coordinated than me. That was never more apparent than when we did yoga together.

"So, I have to tell you the weird thing Rafael said to me last night."

"Yeah?" She shifted her body toward me slightly, cocking one eyebrow.

"Raf called me at like midnight after he'd gotten home from hanging with friends."

Her forehead dipped. "What kind of friends?"

I knew what she was asking. The same thought had crossed my mind. But I simply shrugged, as if I wasn't worried at all. As if I was as naive and in the dark about Raf's extracurricular activities as he thought I was. "Just the other professors." He hadn't said which ones, other than Frank, but I assumed it was the usual suspects—Jon, Adam, Mark, maybe even Keith. But Christine didn't need all these details. It's not like she knew any of them. "It was one of their birthdays. Anyway, he was kinda sweet. Said he just wanted to hear my voice before he went to bed."

"And that's weird?"

"Well, I mean, it wouldn't have been years ago. But now it is. He never says romantic things like that anymore."

"Had he been drinking?"

I nodded.

"Well, there you go. Guys get like that when they're drunk. If he'd been home, he would've stumbled into bed with you and tried to get his freak on."

Frowning, I stared at the hands in my lap. She was right. I was stupid to think any different.

"But I'm sure he meant it," Christine added, like she was reading my mind. "You know Raf loves you, Kel. You're just going through a rough patch." She paused, pressing her lips together. We came up on a red light and she stopped, turning her head toward me. "What happened..." She swallowed hard. "Well, it's gonna take some time to heal from. Are you still seeing that therapist?"

Shifting in my seat, I took another sip of my coffee. My hands trembled slightly. I rarely had caffeine anymore. "Of course. I don't have a choice. It's a requirement, remember?"

"But that's good, right? 'Cause it's helping you?"

"I guess." Staring out the window, I thought about Dr. Hillerman's stale office and his bushy brows. Was he helping? I mean, I was getting better, but I didn't think I'd give him the credit.

We turned the corner and I spotted my car. I sat up as she pulled up to the curb behind it. Once she was parked, I unlatched the door and stepped outside.

"Thanks, Christine. I appreciate it," I said before closing the door and hurrying to my car. Inside it smelled like damp earth. I turned on the engine and cracked a window to let in some fresh air.

Christine waved as she drove past, and I waved back.

As I was about to pull away from the curb, my phone pinged from where it sat faceup on the passenger seat. I glanced over at the screen to see a Facebook notification.

Kelly Medina accepted your friend request.

What?

My arm shot out to snatch up the phone.

I thought maybe I had found you after all.

But when I clicked on the app I realized it wasn't you. It was a *guy* named Kelly Medina. I must have accidentally clicked on "add friend" when I was scrolling his page. *Shit.*

I hadn't kept the promise I'd made to myself at lunch. Not only did I have more than one glass at the restaurant, but I had ended up downing a couple more glasses at home in the evening.

This was why Aaron always said not to drunk Facebook. I couldn't tell you how many girls posted random things on his page late at night or accidentally liked a photo of his from months ago. He'd have a good laugh, but I'd warn him not to tease the girls about it. I was certain they were mortified enough already.

I deleted the strange man from my page and tossed my cell back onto the passenger seat. It was good that I had decided to stop searching for you. Clearly, it was causing me to act impulsive and reckless.

Two of the things I'd been trying so hard not to be.

For the next couple of days, I kept busy. Went to the gym, the library, shopping. I didn't search for you. In fact, I hardly even thought about you.

That's why you have to believe me when I say I never meant to show up at the pediatrician's office looking for you. It wasn't premeditated. I'd made a pact to leave all thoughts of you behind. And I fully intended to do it.

But then Friday morning hit, and everything changed.

I'd been planning to meet Christine for yoga at ten. But I couldn't stop thinking about the phone call from Dr. Cramer's office about your appointment. The receptionist's words played on repeat in my mind.

I'm calling to remind you of your well-baby appointment this Friday at ten a.m.

Her child is a new patient.

I have no idea how this happened. It's like your numbers got switched in the system.

The only reason I'd stopped seeking you out was because I'd been worried that I was being obsessive, stalkerish, unhealthy or whatever other words my therapists had used about me in the past. But it wasn't like that.

You were the one who'd come to me. Not the other way around. You went to my same gym. Took your child to my same pediatrician. Moved to my town.

It was *you* who had inserted yourself into my life.

I was simply curious. I wanted to see what you were like. I mean, you had my same name, my same likes, my same doctor. It was like you were copying me.

Didn't I have the right to be curious?

Seriously, what would it hurt for me to simply show up at the doctor's office and get a glimpse of you? I mean, what if we even looked alike? Wouldn't that be wild? Also, I'd been dying to know if your baby was a boy or girl.

It was simple curiosity, that's all.

Nothing sinister or odd.

This was normal.

Completely normal.

Yeah, I'd just show up in the parking lot, get a little look and take off. No harm. No foul.

At least, that was the plan.

CHAPTER
FOUR

I knew it was you the minute you got out of your car. You were oddly familiar. I almost felt like we'd met before, but that was impossible. I'd been sitting here for over thirty minutes. I'd seen multiple moms go into the pediatrician's office, but none of them had babies. A couple of them had elementary-aged kids; one had a teenager. So, when I saw a young woman in a minivan pull up, a car seat visible in the back, my pulse spiked. I glanced at the clock on my dashboard. It was almost ten.

This had to be you.

My car was parked a few spaces over from yours. I sat in the driver's seat, watching you through the dark lenses of my sunglasses.

You walked swiftly around your minivan, then slid open the back door. I could hear it squealing all the way from inside my car. Seriously, how old was that van? Was it safe to drive your child around in?

I inhaled sharply as you leaned into the back seat. When you lifted the baby out, I blew out the breath I'd been holding. *A boy.* I smiled as he kicked his chubby little legs underneath his blue onesie. Then I thought about how cold it was this morning, and my smile slipped. *Shouldn't he be wearing pants?*

I always made sure Aaron was bundled up when he was a baby. Their skin isn't as developed as ours. Their poor little bodies get cold fast.

You nestled your son closer to your body and an ache spread through my chest. There's nothing quite like cuddling a baby. I conjured up the powdery baby scent. Imagined the feel of his silky soft skin.

After securing a diaper bag on your shoulder, you closed the van door and started walking. I glanced down at your son's feet, and was glad to see that even though you forgot his pants, you remembered to put socks on him.

Too bad that with all the squirming and kicking he was doing, one was starting to slide off. It had already moved down to his toes and was dangling precariously. I waited for you to notice and fix it, but you never did. You kept walking, not looking down at your son at all, while his sock slid farther and farther. My heart squeezed in my chest, my body buzzing.

You were nearing my car. His sock was almost off, and you still weren't noticing. His foot was going to be frozen by the time you got inside. I mean, he wasn't even wearing pants and it was a cool fall morning.

Oh, screw it. I opened my car door, jumped out and picked up the sock just as it fell to the ground. You had already walked past without even seeing it drop.

"Miss?" I called to your back. "Your son lost his sock."

When you turned, I held it out. Smiling broadly, you snatched it from my fingers. "Oh, wow. Thank you so much."

You seemed surprised, almost shocked, at my kindness.

It endeared me to you a little. I knew that feeling. I often felt like everyone around me was my enemy, not my friend. Rarely did people stop to help each other. It was like everyone was too into themselves to notice when someone was in need. At first, I thought I'd made a mistake by jumping out of my car, but now I was happy I did it. Warmth spread through me as I watched you cover his tiny foot.

I did the right thing.

"He's adorable," I said, staring into your son's bright blue eyes and perfect tan skin. His hair was dark just like Aaron's, and he had the same big cheeks and heart-shaped lips.

"Thanks." Your smile deepened as you glanced down at him. Now that I was up close, it was obvious how young you were. Your skin was impossibly smooth, devoid of the wrinkles that had creeped into the corners of my eyes. If I had to take a guess, I'd say you were in your early twenties. Glancing down at your left hand, I didn't see a wedding ring. "Well, I better get inside. Sullivan has an appointment in a few minutes."

"Sullivan? What a cute name," I said. "Different. When we had our son, I had lists of really cool, unique names, but my husband wouldn't go for them. We ended up naming him Aaron after my husband's father."

"Aaron," you repeated. "I like it. It's cute."

You were wearing a pair of black overalls, a black-and-white-striped shirt and gray ankle boots. Your brunette hair appeared windblown and messy, but it was obvious you had styled it that way on purpose. My son would most likely describe you as a hipster. I was certain you'd never name your son something as traditional as Aaron, but I appreciated your compliment. You were clearly gracious. Friendly. I was starting to like you more and more.

"How old is your son?" you asked me, your gaze shifting around the parking lot. "Is he here?"

I shook my head. "He's nineteen. In college."

"Oh, wow." You leaned in, your eyes crinkling, as if you were studying my face intently. "You so don't look old enough to have a nineteen-year-old."

"I'm not," I joked, and you laughed along. "How old is Sullivan?"

"Seven months."

I glanced down at the baby. "Really? He's tiny. I was going to guess younger."

"Well, he's a preemie, so I guess if he'd been born on time he'd only be like five months or something."

You glanced at the building then, and I knew our conversation was winding down. I felt a twinge of desperation in my gut. Talking to you had been nice. Different than with my other friends. You reminded me of a younger version of myself, even down to the brown hair and hazel eyes. You still hadn't told me your name, but I was certain I had the right person. I could feel it.

"Well, it was cool talking with you. I've been kinda lonely. I just moved here and you might be the first person I've had a legit conversation with," you confessed.

"Really? Where'd you move from?"

Your smile faltered a little then. You took a step back, throwing me an apologetic look. "I really have to get inside or we'll be late for our appointment."

"Of course." I waved away your words in a nonchalant way. "It was nice to meet you…" My voice trailed off, allowing the unspoken question to linger. I waited for you to answer, praying I hadn't got this all wrong.

"Oh. I'm sorry," you said. "I'm Kelly."

Relief washed over me, thick and refreshing like an ocean wave. How ridiculous would it have been if I went to all this trouble, and I'd been talking to the wrong person? I felt like it had been you the whole time, but now I was certain. I fought to keep my face neutral, to mask my elation. Instead, I faked a laugh. "How funny. My name's Kelly too. Kelly Medina." I never added my last name when meeting someone, but I couldn't resist this time.

Your reaction was priceless. Your mouth dropped, your eyelids shooting clear up to your forehead as if you'd just been injected with Botox. "No way. Kelly Medina? Are you serious? That's my name too."

"No, it's not," I said as if I thought you were yanking my chain.

"I'm dead serious," you said firmly. "My name really is Kelly Medina." Sullivan wiggled in your arms, letting out a tiny cry. You shushed him, gently bouncing him up and down. Then you dipped your other arm into the diaper bag. "I can totally show you my ID." Sullivan's cries intensified.

"No, no. It's fine." I winced as he got louder. You needed to worry less about proving your identity to me and more about your son being upset. "I believe you."

"It's okay, baby," you said soothingly, rubbing your son's back. He started to calm a little. "I still can't believe we have the same name. What are the chances?"

I wanted to point out that our name wasn't as unique as I thought it was a few days ago, but then I'd have to admit I'd been looking for you online. So, I just smiled. "I know. It's really strange."

"Yeah. Totally."

We were running out of time. You were already late for your appointment. But I couldn't leave until I knew there was a way to see you again. "Hey. If you ever want someone to show you around, I'm happy to do that. I've lived here awhile."

"Oh, man, that would be awesome," you said, your face lighting up. "Do you have your phone? I can give you my number." Your gaze flickered once again to the doctor's office.

With shaky fingers, I hurriedly pulled out my cell. After clicking into my contacts you rattled off your number and I plugged it in.

"Okay. Just send me a text, so I'll have your number too. I'll talk to you later." You backed away and spun around, walking swiftly toward the building.

"No problem. Nice meeting you," I said.

My phone buzzed in my palm. I glanced down. It was Christine.

Where are you? Class already started.

I frowned. What class? *Oh, crap.* That's right. I was supposed to be at yoga.

I looked back up at the building. You and Sullivan were gone. You must have already been inside. I smiled, happy to have finally met you. It was funny. You were exactly like I thought you'd be.

By the time I got to the gym, class was winding down. I caught the last ten minutes.

Once it was over, Christine turned to me wearing a frown. "Where were you?"

"Sorry. I had a bunch of stuff to do and lost track of time," I said. "Remember, it's Friday? I actually have to cook tonight."

Her face softened a little then. "Oh. Right. What time will Rafael be home?"

Raf and I had hardly spoken this week other than that odd conversation in the middle of the night, but he was usually home by four on Fridays, so that's what I told her.

"That means you still have time to grab a quick workout." She smiled.

"But you just finished your class."

"That was yoga. I could definitely use a little cardio. Friday night is pizza night at our house, so an extra workout is always necessary."

I smiled. "Yeah, when Aaron was younger we got pizza a lot on Friday nights too."

She chuckled. "Because by Friday we're too exhausted to cook anything else. Am I right?"

Nodding, I laughed lightly. "When I think back on it, I like to believe it was some cool family tradition. But you're right. It was probably just because I was tired."

"I've given up on even pretending I'm doing anything for a reason. Let's be real. I'm just trying to survive." She winked.

We made our way over to the elliptical machines, and Christine climbed onto one. I got on the one next to hers. After taking a generous swig of my water, I turned on the machine.

"So, what are you making for dinner?" Christine asked, moving her legs swiftly back and forth in time with the machine.

"I have no idea," I said, my breath already coming out labored.

Her head snapped toward me. "Weren't you shopping this morning? Isn't that why you missed class?"

"Yeah, no, I went shopping. I just still don't know what sounds good for dinner."

"Oh, girl, I go through that every night. Just order take-out. Save yourself some trouble." She gave me a teasing grin. "Go buy yourself some lingerie instead. Then Rafael won't even care what's for dinner."

Rafael had been uncharacteristically sweet the other night on the phone. Maybe new lingerie was the way to go. I could slip it on, do my makeup and hair, shave my legs, light some candles, order takeout. It had been a long time since we had a romantic night. We used to spend hours languishing in bed together.

"How long have we been in this bed?" I pressed my cheek into Rafael's bare chest, my fingers drawing circles on his skin.

"Not long enough." Without even looking up, I could picture his devious smile.

My insides warmed.

"Is that so?" I lifted my head, my lips meeting his. A few strands of hair brushed over my cheek, bringing with them the scent of vanilla. The sheets rustled as Rafael shifted on the bed, angling his body toward mine. His arm swept upward as his hand cradled my head, massaging my skull.

He kissed me hard, but not too hard. Firm is maybe a better word for it. I melted into him, our bodies fusing.

Minutes turned into hours. Time was hazy. Gray. Blurry at the edges.

It no longer mattered.

My body was slick with sweat, my hair matted, my cheeks flushed. When I caught sight of myself in the mirror over the dresser, I cringed.

"Oh, god, I look awful." Frantically, I reached up and

smoothed down my hair with my palm. We'd been married only a few weeks, and I wasn't used to him seeing me without my hair and makeup done.

"Stop." He grabbed my hand, weaving our fingers together. "You look amazing. Don't change a thing."

Smiling, my heart rate picked up. I glanced toward the window. The curtains were closed but I could tell it was getting darker. We'd been holed up in our apartment forever. My stomach made a funny noise.

"We should probably get dressed and go get something to eat," I said.

Rafael shook his head. "Bed. Naked. Good." He winked. "Clothes. Outside. Bad."

"When did you turn into a caveman?"

"I'm not a caveman," he said, tugging me toward him. "I just have all I need right here. I never have to leave."

"Really?" I raised my brows. "Pretty sure that's not how science works. Eventually you'll have to eat and drink."

He flashed me an amused smile. "It's sexy when you speak smarty-pants to me."

My stomach rumbled again. "Seriously, though, I'm starving." I sat up, reaching for my clothes.

Raf shoved me back down on the bed. "So am I." His mouth covered mine.

Frustration momentarily sparked, and I attempted to wriggle out of his grasp. I needed food. But then I looked into his eyes, and I relented. Rafael had a way of doing that. Of making me forget about everything but him.

"Maybe I will." I smiled now, biting my lip.

"Good for you." Christine leaned over and nudged me gently in the side. "I think that's great, Kel. Honestly, I was a little worried about you the other day at lunch. All that stuff about the other woman with your name, then the thing with your car."

"I told you I was joking about the car, and there is another woman with my name. I met her this morning."

"What are you talking about?" She turned to me, her eyes wide.

"The other Kelly Medina. I just met her."

Christine slowed down, wiped her face with her workout towel and stared at me pensively. "Where did you meet her?"

I opened my mouth and then shut it again. I couldn't tell her I ran into you at the pediatrician's office. Then she'd know I'd been following you. There would be no reason for me to go there otherwise.

"The store," I lied.

"Kel, have you told Rafael about this?"

I shook my head.

"Well, maybe you should." Her tone had switched from "friend Christine" to "concerned-mother Christine." I bristled. "And while you're at it, maybe you should call your therapist."

Frustration sparked, hot and sudden, like a lighter igniting. I shut off my machine and hopped off. "Why would I need to call my therapist just because I made a new friend? That doesn't even make any sense." I grabbed my towel and water. "Why are you wigging out over this?" Understanding smacked me in the face. "Oh, I get it. You're jealous."

Christine stopped her machine and sighed heavily. "No, Kel, I'm not jealous of your imaginary friend."

I felt the strength of her words like a slap in the face.

"She's not imaginary!" I shouted, and a few people glanced over.

Christine's hand flew to her hair and she fluffed it with vigor. She always did this when she was nervous. Well, good. I didn't care that I caused a scene. She was being ridiculous. How dare she accuse me of something like this?

"I met her this morning. Her name is Kelly Medina. She has a son named Sullivan and she just moved here. And she's 100 percent real."

"Okay, okay." Christine spoke gently, holding up her hands like she was afraid I'd strike her. "I believe you."

But she didn't. I could tell. And I wasn't going to stand here one more minute with her looking at me like I was crazy.

"I gotta go. I still have a lot of stuff to do before Raf gets home."

"Kel, wait. Don't leave mad." She reached for my arm. "You know why I had to ask."

But I shook her hand off and stalked out of the gym. I'd told her things in confidence, and now she was using them against me. And it wasn't fair. It wasn't even accurate. I mean, yeah, maybe I had imagined things in the past, but that was before I started seeing Dr. Hillerman. My brain was all muddled then. It wasn't now. Couldn't she see that?

Things were clearer now.

You were real.

Right?

I blinked against the harsh light of the sun and licked my lips.

Yes, you had to be real. I talked to you. I touched your son's sock.

I put your number into my phone.

Your number! That's it. Heart pumping, I yanked my phone out of the little side pocket of my yoga pants. I opened my contacts, and at first I didn't see your name. My stomach dropped. I scrolled back up...and there you were. I had put you in as KELLY M.

I exhaled slowly, my heart rate slowing.

You were real.

I wasn't imagining things.

Not this time.

CHAPTER
FIVE

Lola was my best friend growing up. She had strawberry-blond hair, and a smattering of freckles across her nose and pale cheeks. Her scent was a mixture of roses and popcorn, sweet and salty to match her personality. She was fun, adventurous and followed me around for years like my shadow. She was the best friend I'd ever had, which is sad because she was imaginary.

Her existence worried my parents. When I kept insisting she was real, they made me see a psychiatrist. He concluded that I was a lonely kid with an overactive imagination. I didn't have any siblings, and was so shy I had a hard time making friends.

The strange part is that even to this day it's hard to wrap my brain around the fact that she wasn't real. To me she was as real as I was. As my parents were.

She'd always been there in my memories, a reminder of love and friendship. Her face was still etched in my mind— breathing, living, active.

Christine's words follow me home from the gym. They rattled around in my brain, sinking into my gut.

Was I imagining you, the way I'd done with Lola?

You seemed real. Then again, so had Lola.

She's not the only person you've ever imagined, though, right? Dr. Hillerman's voice echoed in my head.

When I got home from the gym, I logged on to my laptop. The sun was bright today and as it leaked in through the window, it bathed the table in lemon-yellow light. My browser was still open to Facebook. I refreshed the screen and then typed in our name on the search bar. Scrolling down, I looked for your face—your dark hair, bright eyes and smooth pale skin. I thought now that I'd seen you in person, perhaps you were one of the many Kelly Medinas on social media. Turns out, you weren't.

I still found it so odd that you weren't on any social media platforms, especially at your age. But maybe you were staying hidden to protect Sullivan. Social media wasn't a thing when Aaron was a baby, but when I perused Facebook now I often shook my head at these women who posted incessant pictures of their kids. They're practically handing their children to predators.

After giving up my social media search, I decided to shoot you a quick text.

It was nice meeting you today.

And you responded almost immediately.

You too.

See? If you weren't real, you couldn't text me back. I almost screenshotted the conversation to send to Christine, but decided against it.

She'd been a good friend to me, especially in the past six months. She'd taken me to doctor's appointments, held me when I cried, spent the night when Raf was gone and I was too scared to be alone.

Her husband told me once that she always needed a hobby. Maybe that's what I was to her right now. Perhaps she wanted me to be needy, desperate for her to fix me.

But I wasn't.

I was fixed.

If only she could see that.

I could hear the garage door opening, and Rafael's car pulling inside. My heart arrested. Quickly, I lit the candles on the nightstand and tossed the lighter into the top drawer. I scanned the room. Everything was in place.

Smiling, I flung myself down on the bed. My boobs fell out of the flimsy red lace cups of my new lingerie. I shoved them back in, then shifted on the bed, bending one leg and placing a hand on my hip in what I was hoping was a seductive way.

A car door slammed from inside the garage.

I rubbed my lips together. They were sticky from the red lipstick I'd put on.

The door from the garage into the kitchen opened and closed. I could hear Rafael walking around downstairs. "Kelly?" His tone was laced with concern.

"Up here!" I called, my gut twisting.

Fluffing my thin, limp hair, I took a deep breath as I listened to Rafael's footsteps ascending the stairs. My body shook a little. I couldn't remember the last time I wore lingerie for Raf.

"Kel?" Rafael stepped into the bedroom. I froze. He smiled. "Wow."

My face heated up. His gaze roamed over my body, and I instinctively raised my arms with the intent of covering myself. Rafael shook his head sharply, and that's when I noticed the way he was looking at me. Like he was desperate for me. It had been so long since he'd reacted this way toward me. Until now, I hadn't even realized I wanted him to. "Yeah?"

"Yeah." He nodded, climbing onto the bed. A panicked look crossed his face. "Wait. I didn't forget our anniversary or something…"

"No." *Not this time.*

"Then what's the occasion?" Grinning, he reached out to lightly finger the edge of the lace, one fingertip lightly skimming my thigh.

I shivered.

"No occasion." Our eyes met. His grin deepened.

I sat up and scooted toward him, my eyes never leaving his. When I got close enough, I grabbed his face in my hands and pressed my lips to his. Rarely was I the one to initiate things. His body stiffened, and I worried that maybe he didn't like me taking the lead. But then he kissed me hard, his arms coming around my body. Within seconds he'd flipped me over on my back and was on top of me. His hands were in my hair, on my skin, his lips on mine, and then traveling down my chin, neck and chest. We rolled on the bed like a couple of teenagers, greedily tearing off each other's clothes, touching and kissing with desperation.

When it was over, we lay on our backs, breathing hard and staring up at the ceiling.

"If that's how you're planning on greeting me after work

from now on, maybe I need to come home more often."
Rafael laughed.

It was supposed to be funny. A joke. So, I laughed along
with him. But my chest tightened. When Rafael left his job
at Folsom Lake College to teach at UC Fallbrook, our plan
had always been to let Aaron finish out high school here
and then move to the Bay Area. But as soon as we started
looking for a house near the university, it was clear we'd
never be able to afford to move there. So I'd begged Raf to
find a job closer to home, or at the very least come home
sometimes during the week. I knew other women whose
husbands worked in the Bay Area and they came home a
lot more than Raf did.

Raf insisted it was impossible for him to make the com-
mute any more than he already did, reminding me that it
was a two-hour drive one way. But I knew that wasn't the
only reason.

I'd gotten pregnant a few months into our marriage, and
that was when we first started having problems.

*"How did this happen?" Raf asked me, his lips quiver-
ing, the vein in his forehead pulsating.*

*"Well, when two people really love each other," I said
with a smile, trying to lighten the mood, "sometimes
they—"*

"This isn't a joke, Kel," he said, cutting me off.

My smile faded. "I know that."

"You're on the pill, right?"

I nodded.

"Then how did you get pregnant?"

*My gaze shifted around the small room. This used to be
Raf's apartment. It still looked more like him than me. I'd*

*tried doing little things to make it mine, but often it felt like
I was staying over at his house.*

*"I don't know. I think I forgot to take the pill a couple
of times."*

His eyes flashed. "You did this on purpose."

"No, I didn't."

It was the truth. I hadn't done it on purpose. I just wasn't
careful about taking the pill. We were married, and I'd always wanted kids. I was an only child, raised by an unkind
mother and a passive father. Growing up, I dreamed of one
day having my own family. A house full of kids I could
raise with all the love I never got. He didn't get it. He'd always had the perfect family. It was part of what drew me
to him. I knew he was the person who could give me the
thing I'd wanted most for my entire life. Still, it was a mistake. An oversight. It wasn't calculated the way Rafael was
making it out to be.

*"What's the big deal anyway? We're married. Isn't this
what married people do? Start families?"*

*"I just wanted you to myself a little longer," he con-
fessed, and my heart softened.*

*I went to him, taking him in my arms. "Well, you still
have me all to yourself for another seven or eight months."*

But he didn't. Not really. Pregnancy was hard on me. I
suffered from horrible morning sickness, and my sex drive
dwindled to nothing. I was tired all of the time, and every
single part of my body swelled so bad I hated going anywhere. Rafael said I'd changed. That I wasn't the woman
he married. That I was boring now.

I talked to my mother-in-law about it, and she assured me
that this happened in all marriages, and that things would
get better once the baby came. But she was wrong. After

Aaron was born, things only got worse. I was even more tired, and Raf was constantly frustrated with me. It was like I could never live up to his expectations. I was never horny enough. Or sexy enough. Or wild enough.

The relief on his face wasn't hidden from me when he escaped Aaron and me on Monday mornings. And I could hear the lie in his tone when he couldn't make it home some Friday evenings.

Things had only gotten worse in the past six months. Now it seemed like coming home was unbearable for him.

I swallowed down the familiar feelings of resentment and anger. This wasn't the time to bring it up. Raf and I were finally connecting. I wouldn't screw that up. Forcing a smile, I shifted my body so it was facing Raf. "You hungry? I ordered takeout."

Raf leaned over to lightly kiss my lips. "Starving," he said against my mouth.

At first I thought maybe he was going for round two, but no, he was actually hungry for dinner. Drawing back, he slid off the bed and put on a pair of boxers.

I headed over to my dresser and started perusing my pajama drawer. Before I could pull on one of my old T-shirts, Raf's arms snaked around my naked middle. He planted a kiss on my forehead. I breathed in his familiar scent, which always reminded me of the air right after it rained.

"Put that little red thing back on. I liked it."

The thought of forcing my body back into that getup was not appealing, but once I looked up into Raf's eyes I knew I wouldn't say no. I'd never been able to. He'd had the ability to unravel me with just one look from the moment we met.

After putting the uncomfortable lingerie back on, I followed Raf downstairs. The Chinese takeout was on the counter. I opened the boxes and grabbed a couple of plates and forks. As I scooped chow mein noodles, chicken and vegetables onto our plates, Raf kept staring at my chest and grinning. I shivered, hugging myself. When I sat down at the table, one of my boobs slipped out. This negligee was clearly meant for someone with younger, perkier breasts. Mine needed a lot more support than this.

"Nice." Raf nodded, cocking one eyebrow.

I was an animal on display at the zoo.

Readjusting my top, I shifted in my seat. I hadn't realized how hungry I was until this moment. I couldn't remember the last time I'd eaten. Breakfast, maybe? This morning I'd been so fixated on meeting you. After that the rest of the day was kind of a blur.

I took a few bites, eating faster than usual.

"We really worked up an appetite, huh?" He was doing it again. Looking at me like he was the predator and I was the prey.

Swallowing, I shifted in my seat. It's what I wanted, right? I went to all this trouble to try to reignite our sexual spark. And it seemed like I was succeeding.

So, why was I so uncomfortable?

I twirled chow mein noodles on my fork for a minute and then took another bite. It was by far the best thing I'd eaten all week. I hadn't cooked since last weekend when Raf was home and I made a pot of spaghetti. Usually, I cooked every night, even if it was only soup or grilled cheese. It was a habit I hadn't been able to break after Aaron moved out. But when Christine suggested popcorn as a dinner option the other day, I realized that cooking every night was pointless. I was alone now. That may not have a lot of perks, but it did have one—not having to cook. I could live off of crackers, cheese and popcorn, and I had proved that the past few days.

Looking up from my plate, I asked, "How was your week?"

"Fine." He took a bite.

"That's it?" I pressed, remembering how I used to do the same thing with Aaron at dinner time. *How was your day? Good. How was school? Good. How did you do on your test? Good.*

"Yep." He shrugged. "Same old, same old. Nothin' really to share."

Seriously, throw me a bone. "What about Frank's party or whatever? How did that go?"

"Wasn't really a party. Just a few guys grabbing beers at a pub."

How was it that a few minutes ago we were so connected in the bedroom, and now out here we were miles apart?

"What about you? Sounds like you've had a good week. Been hangin' with Christine and working out a lot." I cringed at his belittling tone. It was the same voice he used to use on Aaron when he was a little boy. *Sounds like you've had a big day. I heard you've been going pee-pee in the potty.*

"Yeah." After setting my fork down, I wiped my mouth with a napkin. The AC vent above me clicked on and cool air whisked over my bare flesh. I shuddered. "We've been going to the gym and lunch. It's been fun."

"That's great." The genuine smile Raf flashed me eradicated my earlier annoyances. He loved me; that's why he was worried. I shouldn't be so hard on him.

Buoyed by his compliment, I kept going. "Yeah, I even made a new friend. A young woman with a baby who's new to Folsom. I'm gonna kinda show her around and…" The words trailed off as Raf's smile vanished.

"Do you think that's wise, Kel?" he asked.

God, he sounded like Christine. "Making a new friend? How would that be unwise?"

"No, I didn't mean…" His lips came together into a hard line. He paused, drawing a breath in and out through his nostrils. "I'm sorry. That's great, Kel. I'm glad you made a new friend. Just… Well, just be careful."

Just be careful? Really? That's rich coming from him.

"Careful about what?"

"Well, I mean, what do you even know about this woman?"

"I think I'm a little old for the stranger-danger talk, Raf," I said drily. "Trust me, she's harmless."

"That's not what I'm worried about," Rafael said, "and you know it."

Bitterness swam up my throat, and I choked it down, moisture filling my eyes. "You're worried about her, then? What? I'm some kind of monster now?"

"Kel." Rafael reached across the table to touch my hand, but I yanked it back. "You know that's not what I think."

"Then what do you think?" My voice rose. Rafael shrank back. I was losing him now. He'd shut me down. Call me crazy. It had been a tactic of his our entire marriage. The only difference was that recently I'd given him some ammunition to use against me.

"I think it's too soon."

Too soon? As if time was really going to change anything.

I shoved back from the table. "I'm gonna go put on some clothes."

"Kel." His eyes pleaded with mine. "Come on. Sit back down."

"I'm fine. Just cold." I glanced at his half-eaten plate. "Finish eating. I'll be back in a minute."

Rafael stared at me as I walked from the room. I almost expected to hear the scrape of his chair on the hardwood floor, his feet as he hurried after me. But when I peered over my shoulder, his back was to me, his body hunched over his food. The sound of chewing reached my ears.

Who was I kidding?

He wasn't going to fight for me. He'd made that abundantly clear.

When we connected in the bedroom I'd mistakenly believed that things would get better. That we could bridge this gap between us. But clearly that was wishful thinking.

There was no way to repair the damage we'd done.

I awoke to a man standing at the foot of my bed. He hovered over me, large and imposing, wearing dark clothing. His arms were outstretched, his fingers spreading out wide as he reached for me. Clutching my covers tightly, I let out a scream.

"Kel, it's just me," the man said, but it took me a minute to register the voice.

I froze, the scream dying on my lips. "Raf?"

"Yeah." Slowly, he came toward me, his hand lighting on my arm. "I didn't mean to scare you."

Shivering, I breathed out. "I forgot you were home." I'd gone to bed after our argument at dinner. The alarm clock revealed it was now two thirty in the morning.

He crawled into bed beside me. "I'm sorry about what I said."

The mattress gave underneath me as he shifted his weight. I clutched my blanket in an attempt to secure my-self.

"I worry about you."

"I'm not going to break," I said. "I'm stronger than you think."

He released a long, slow breath before speaking. "I used to think that." Wrapping his arms around me, he drew me into his chest.

"What does that mean?"

"I don't know, Kel. I guess…when we met I thought you could handle anything. But now…you're just not the same."

How dare he? I shoved away from him, prying his arms off my body.

"C'mon, babe. Don't do that. Stay so we can talk this out. We never talk anymore."

"Gee, I wonder why." Scooting to the edge of the bed, I rolled over and faced him. It was dark, but moonlight fil-tered in through the window, casting Rafael's body in a bluish hue.

"Can you honestly say that you haven't changed in the last six months, Kel? That you haven't done things that are worrisome?"

My chest was so tight it was hard to draw in a breath. "Of course I've changed. We both have. How could we not? After the way you—" My lips quivered. I couldn't bring myself to say the words. I didn't want to talk about it. I wouldn't.

"Kelly?"

I shook my head.

"What were you gonna say?"

"Nothing. I'm tired. I just wanna go back to bed."

"Don't do that. You were gonna say something," he said, pleading with me. In his eyes, I could see how badly he needed this. I thought I did too. Earlier today I'd been desperate to connect with him. I thought that if the two of us could move past this, maybe I'd find some healing. "Please, let's talk about it."

I opened my mouth, imagining the relief I would feel at spilling out all of the pain that I kept locked inside. But then I clamped it shut, remembering all of the other times Rafael had tricked me into doing this only to twist my words or shift blame. I never felt better after confiding in him. He always made me feel worse.

"No," I said firmly, one last time.

In the moonlight I watched Rafael's face fall, harden. Without another word, he turned his back on me and fell asleep. It felt cold and empty on my side of the bed. My heart sagged. If I had given in and said something, would this time have been any different?

First thing Monday morning, I threw the red negligee in the trash.

Rafael and I had sex several more times over the weekend. Every time Raf insisted I wear the stupid thing. By Sunday, I'd regretted buying it.

Slamming the lid down on the garbage can, I glanced down at my arm. Bruises bloomed, dark purple and grey, puke yellow, against my pale skin. When Rafael's hands had gripped me tightly, his fingernails digging into my flesh, I told myself it was for pleasure. Now I wondered if it was for pain.

After Friday, things were rougher, almost violent. Like he was punishing me. My fingers fluttered over my neck, remembering how he'd slid his hands around it Saturday night. I'd immediately torn his fingers off, throwing him a harsh warning look.

"Relax. I'm not going to hurt you." He'd laughed it off as if the idea was preposterous.

But it wasn't. He had hurt me once.

Aaron was around two years old. In the afternoon I'd dropped him off at my in-laws' house. Then I went home to take a shower and get ready for our kid-free night. As I stood under the hot spray of the shower, I imagined what we'd do. Dinner out. Dessert in. Maybe rent a movie.

I was leaning back to wet my hair when I heard a noise. I froze. Leaned forward to listen.

Footsteps.

My heart stopped.

"Hello?" I called out, then chastised myself. Oh, my god, I'm one of those fragile women from a horror movie.

"Hey," Raf's voice responded. I gasped. My heart hammered.

When I peeked out of the curtain, Rafael stood in the steaming bathroom wearing jeans and a collared shirt.

"You scared the crap outta me," I told him.

"Sorry." He smiled, looking anything but.

"What are you doing here?" I wasn't expecting him for two more hours.

"Got off early." There was a twinkle in his eyes. "Anxious to get date night started."

I smiled. "Okay, well, I'll be out in just a minute." After dropping the curtain, I stepped back under the water.

"No, stay in," Raf said. "I'll join you."

There was a quiver low in my belly when Raf stepped naked into the shower. My gaze immediately fell to his tanned, taut chest. He'd always been fit. Working out was something he'd prioritized since the day I'd met him.

Reaching around me, he grabbed a bar of soap. After lathering his hands, his palms found my skin. He ran them over every inch of my flesh until I was weak in the knees. Until my insides trembled. Biting my lip, I squealed softly in my mouth.

Raf's face came close to mine, his breath against my mouth. "You don't have to be quiet."

Oh, that's right. We were alone. I'd gotten so used to keeping it down for Aaron's sake.

He handed me the soap. My turn, then.

As I worked the soap over his muscular arms and chest, his mouth covered mine. Water cascaded down my back, pelted my head. Rafael wrapped his arms around my middle and spun me around, so my back was to the wall. At the time I'd thought it was sweet. His way of protecting me from the water.

But then he shoved me up against the tiles so hard, I bit my tongue.

It was a mistake, I told myself. He was excited. Passionate. He didn't know his own strength.

Ignoring the beginning of a headache, and the metallic taste in my mouth, I focused instead on the places he touched me. Kissing me slowly, his hand slid up my body and curved around my neck. The kiss deepened, the pressure on my neck becoming firmer.

It felt good...until it didn't.

When the pressure got to be too much, my eyelids flipped open. Rafael wasn't kissing me anymore. He was watching me.

And he was cutting off my air supply.

It took me a moment to register what was happening.

Surely, my own husband wasn't choking me, was he? I felt
trapped. Scared.

My mind flew back to the last time I'd felt this afraid.
And suddenly Rafael's face was replaced by another man's.
A man who had caused me harm. A man I'd spent years
trying to forget.

No air was coming out of my mouth. My head spun, my
throat ached and my lungs started to burn. Desperately, I
reached up to grab at his fingers and pry them off my neck.

Rafael stopped then. I shoved him back.

"I'm sorry." His tone was apologetic.

"What the hell was that?"

"Just spicing things up." That was his explanation. I
hadn't even realized we needed things spicier.

It was the first of many fights about our sex life. Over
the years he'd accuse me of being a prude. Sometimes I'd
give in, try something new. But never the choking.

Shaking my head, I left the kitchen, abandoning all
thoughts of Rafael and our weekend, leaving them in the
trash with the lingerie.

The house was quiet and empty. Mondays were usually
hard for me, but this week I was glad to have the place
to myself again. Heading upstairs, I took a shower and
changed into my favorite jeans and fuzzy sweater. It felt
good to be dressed and warm. Covered up.

As I walked back downstairs to make some tea, I shot
a text off to Aaron.

Just wanted to say good morning. I love you, son.

Rafael always accused me of smothering Aaron.
Wait for him to text you, he'd say.

But what did he know anyway. I snorted bitterly. No one would accuse Raf of being father of the year.

After pouring some steaming hot water into a mug, I dropped in a tea bag and thought about you. I wondered what you did all weekend. You were in a new town with a new baby and didn't know anyone. You were probably going stir-crazy.

Even though you weren't wearing a wedding ring, I didn't want to assume your baby daddy was completely out of the picture. A lot of young people didn't get married nowadays. Maybe you two were still dating, or living together even.

There were so many things I didn't know about you.

Curiosity got the better of me, and I sent you a text.

Hey! I'm heading out to do some shopping. Want to come with? I can show you around.

Biting my lip, I stared down at the phone.

Minutes ticked by and nothing. No response.

Hmm. What could you be doing? Surely, not sleeping. Not this late. I glanced at the clock. It was already nine. When Aaron was an infant he was up by five a.m. like clockwork.

I reached for my tea and took a sip. Then I checked the phone again. Still nothing. I tapped my fingernails on the counter. They were chipped on the edges. I needed to get them done. *Ooh, that gave me an idea.*

With shaky fingers, I texted again.

Actually, scratch the shopping idea. I need to get my

nails done. Want to hit the salon with me? I'll pay for yours.

When I saw the little dots pop up on the screen, my chest expanded. It was the salon that did it, huh? Shopping was boring. Why had I even suggested that?

That sounds amazing, but there's no way I can do that with Sullivan.

My heart sank. Of course. Why hadn't I thought of that? It had been so long since Aaron was a baby. It was hard to imagine what life was like back then.

We'll take turns. I can keep him occupied while you get your nails done.

Several minutes passed, the screen remaining blank. The house creaked. A bird chirped from outside. I leaned against the counter, sipping my tea in silence. The lady with the kids was back across the street. She propped one child on her hip, while holding the other one's hand as he tugged her up to the front door.

I wondered why I hadn't seen her before last week.

She shifted the baby higher up, and the familiar pang of longing cut into my chest. When the front door opened, the older one let go of her hand and ran inside. Even from this vantage point, I could see her shoulders soften with relief.

I remembered that feeling. For years, my body was used as a jungle gym. Aaron would jump on me, pull on me, hit me and hang on me. Sometimes all I wanted was one minute where my body was mine and mine alone.

Being so far removed from that time of my life, I saw it all through different lenses. Rose-colored ones.

The phone buzzed in my palm.

You sure?

I typed back with my thumbs.

Of course. It'll be fun.

Then I added, I won't take no for an answer.
Your response came quick.

Doesn't sound like I have a choice then.

I laughed.

Nope. You don't.

You texted me your address, and I said I'd be there in a half hour. Then I tucked my phone into my pocket and took my tea upstairs to fix my hair and makeup. As I got ready, I felt happy.

I guess that's how it felt when you were doing something good. Helping someone.

Staring at my reflection, I smiled, thinking about how excited you were probably feeling. I know I would've loved for someone to do this for me when Aaron was little.

Wasn't it lucky that you met me?

CHAPTER
SIX

You were waiting outside, standing on the sidewalk, when I pulled up to the address you gave me. In your hand, you held Sullivan's carrier. A diaper bag was strapped to your shoulder. I parked along the curb directly in front of you. Getting out, I glanced down at Sullivan sleeping soundly, seat-belt straps holding him in, slightly cutting into the flappy skin folds of his neck. His head was bent to the side, his lips parted and his eyelids fluttering.

"He's gorgeous," I told you, reaching out to adjust the straps.

"Thanks," you said, pushing a strand of hair off of your cheek with your free hand. It was in a side braid, but wavy tendrils framed your face. You wore ripped jeans, a white T-shirt and slip-on shoes. I felt old and stuffy next to you in my boot-cut jeans and turtleneck sweater. At least my brown boots were sort of youngish looking.

"He has the longest eyelashes," I mused, staring at them resting against his porcelain skin. "That must be a boy thing, 'cause Aaron did too."

You laughed. "Yeah, it's so not fair. I have to wear falsies to get mine that long."

I'd never worn fake eyelashes, but I nodded and smiled as if I knew exactly what you were talking about. Then I fleetingly wondered if I even remembered to put on mascara today.

Opening the back door, I ushered you forward with a sweep of my arm. "I'll let you get him situated," I told you, unsure of what the new laws and regulations were. They were changing all the time.

"Sure." You hoisted the carrier into the back seat and leaned inside.

I peered up at the white house with the wraparound porch and large windows.

"Your house is so adorable," I said, then gasped when an older woman appeared in the window. She smiled and waved, and I did the same. "Do you live with your parents or something?"

"Oh, no." You ducked your head as you got out of the back seat. After standing straight, you closed the door. Your cheeks were splotchy, a slight sheen gathering along your brow bone. "That's Ella, the owner of my apartment."

"Apartment?"

You nodded. "Yeah, I live in an apartment behind this house. I guess technically it's like a guesthouse or in-laws quarters or something."

"Ah, okay." *Yeah, that made more sense.* I had been wondering how someone your age could afford this quaint little house in Old Folsom. "That's cool. You like it?"

"Oh, yeah. It's super cute, and Ella's the best."

When I glanced back, Ella was no longer in the window. Disappeared like a ghost. A breeze whisked over my body and I shivered. A few leaves skittered along the sidewalk, fast and prickly, like tiny spiders.

Hugging myself, I hurried back to the driver's side and hopped into the car. Sullivan was lightly fussing. After you got in, you handed him a toy and he immediately stuck it in his mouth. A lot of slobbering ensued.

"Thanks for this," you said as I drove to the salon. "I can't even remember the last time I got my nails done."

"I didn't get mine done either when Aaron was a baby."

"Yeah, I mean, I don't really have anyone I can leave him with. But sometimes I just need a break, you know?" You looked at me expectantly, like you wanted me to agree.

But I wasn't sure I could. I didn't leave Aaron until he was nine months old and only because Raf made me. It wasn't even like we left him with a sitter. He was with Rafael's parents, but I still spent the entire date night worried about him.

"Do you have family nearby? Anyone who could help?" *A partner or boyfriend perhaps?* The last question was on the tip of my tongue, but I couldn't bring myself to ask it. We'd just met and I didn't want you to think I was nosy.

"Nope." You looked out the window, so I couldn't make out your expression, but your tone was dark, kind of sad.

I felt bad for you, all alone in a new town. "What brought you here, then? A job or something?"

You shook your head. "I'm not working right now. Just focusing on being a mom."

There were so many questions I wanted to ask you. My mind was spinning so fast it was like one of those rides at the fair that made me puke. But before I could say anything more, we pulled up to the salon. You barely gave me a chance to park before hopping out.

If I didn't know better, I'd say you were trying to get away from me.

My insides knotted when you showed me the red you'd picked for your nails. I tried to talk you into something more tasteful. French manicure. Maybe a subtle nude, or shimmery pink. But, no, you were adamant about the red.

It reminded me of that damn negligee.

I glanced down at my own nails. I'd chosen a tasteful peachy nude.

Sullivan had been asleep in his carrier since we got here. I thought it was strange that he took a nap so early in the morning, but you assured me this was his normal nap time. I couldn't remember Aaron's nap schedule when he was this age. I do know that I took him places all the time—to stores, restaurants, long walks—and it was likely he slept through some of it.

When Sullivan stirred, I pitched forward. *Finally*. I'd been waiting for him to wake up since we'd gotten here. My fingers were itching to touch him, my arms practically begging to wrap around his squishy little body.

His eyelids popped open and he stared up at me for a few seconds. Then he let out a little cry, his face scrunching up. I smiled, understanding. Patience wasn't one of my strengths either.

"Is it okay if I take him out?" I asked you.

"Of course," you responded, barely glancing over.

I bent over and unhooked Sullivan from his carrier. Even before picking him up I felt the weight of him in my arms. The ache was strong. Heavy.

It subsided once Sullivan was settled on my chest, his head on my shoulder. I bounced him gently with my hand resting on his bottom, the way I used to do with Aaron. He quieted.

My insides warmed.

I've still got it.

Catching a whiff of his milky scent, my body relaxed. There was something euphoric about that scent, like a contact high. Plus, it sure beat the smell of nail polish and remover. I closed my eyes, breathing him in. Lowering my head, my nose lightly brushed his soft, smooth skin.

He started whimpering, his body wiggling.

"Shh, it's okay," I murmured, bouncing him a little more. But this time it didn't work. "You think he's hungry?" I asked.

You glanced over your shoulder. "Probably. There's a bottle and some formula in his bag."

Formula? "You don't breastfeed him?" God, I sounded like one of those judgmental, holier-than-thou moms Christine and I always made fun of.

"No," you said without offering any explanation. A part of me was repulsed. I had breastfed Aaron until he was a year old because it was good for his health. But a small part of me was envious of your confidence. You didn't feel the need to defend your decision to me. To explain ad nauseam why you'd chosen not to breastfeed, as if it was any of my business. Truth is, I didn't love breastfeeding the way other women seemed to. It was inconvenient and uncomfortable. Many times I wanted to quit, but I'd been shamed into continuing by my own mom. I'll never forget the look of horror on my mom's face when I confessed my feelings about breastfeeding to her. I'd been so honest, sharing how my boobs had gotten so engorged I no longer fit in any of my shirts. And how I was in constant back pain.

"You've always been so selfish, Kelly," she'd snapped, disgust in her voice.

Her words had sealed the deal. There was no way I could stop breastfeeding after that.

I didn't have the confidence back then that you had now.

"Oh. Okay. Well." I glanced down at the diaper bag, unsure of how I was going to make him a bottle here. My gaze scoured the room. There was a sink in the back. But would I be able to balance him and make the bottle? I wasn't sure. It'd been so long since I was in this predicament.

His cries increased. Holding him flush against my chest, I reached out with my free hand, fumbling around in the diaper bag. My fingers trailed over some washcloths, keys, wipes. But where was the formula and bottle?

"All done," you announced, standing up.

Oh, thank god you'd gotten a gel manicure. Regular polish would've taken forever to dry.

Relieved, I handed him over to you the minute you reached me.

As you scooped him up, my gaze landed on your lacquered nails. The splashes of red against Sullivan's white onesie looked like that stupid red lingerie cutting into my skin.

CHAPTER SEVEN

After leaving the salon, we stopped for lunch. I hadn't asked if you wanted to before pulling into the parking lot of the café. It was already twelve thirty, so I assumed you'd be hungry.

But your brows furrowed. "What are we doing?"

"Oh, I thought we'd grab a bite to eat."

You bit your lip, your gaze flickering to Sullivan in the back seat. "Um… I'm actually not that hungry. I ate a big breakfast."

I was famished. I hadn't even eaten breakfast. All I'd had all day was a cup of tea. And I hardly had anything left in my fridge. "You can just get an appetizer or salad or something. My friend Christine goes on fad diets all the time. Sometimes she even goes on juice cleanses, but we still go to lunch." I winked at you. "It's more about the company anyway."

You nodded, flashing me what could only be described as a forced smile. "Yeah, but…you see, it's almost Sullivan's afternoon nap time…" Your gaze shifted out the side window as if plotting your escape.

Why were you so desperate to get home? I was having a good time, and I thought we were connecting. Besides, the idea of going back to my empty house chilled me to the core. When I first texted you, I'd assumed we'd spend the day together. I'd paid for your nails. Was joining me for lunch really too much to ask?

That's when I noticed you fishing through the diaper bag, your fingers lighting on your wallet. It was tattered and old.

It reminded me of a wallet I'd had early on in my marriage. We were young and poor, so buying diapers, formula and food took precedence over things like wallets.

"It's on me," I assured you.

Your face relaxed a little. "You sure?"

I nodded. "Positive."

You hesitated for one second and then said quietly, "Okay."

My stomach uncoiled. I smiled and we both got out of the car. After walking into the restaurant, I asked the hostess for a table outside. It had been cool this morning, but now it was warming up to a perfect fall day. Plus, there was hardly anyone sitting on the patio, so I figured it would be easier for you since you wouldn't be so worried about Sullivan making noise.

We both ordered sandwiches, and I was grateful to finally have a friend who ate something other than salad. Sullivan started fussing a little. I offered to take him and you gratefully deposited him into my arms.

"He's been so fussy lately," you confessed. "I can't figure out what's wrong."

"Did you mention it to the pediatrician last week?" I shifted Sullivan until he was nestled onto my shoulder.

His hand brushed against my arm, his fingers tickling the skin through my shirt.

You nodded. "Yeah, but they didn't have any answers, really. Just that babies cry."

"Well, that's true." I bounced Sullivan up and down gently, patting his bottom the same way I'd done in the salon. It had the same effect. He offered a pudgy smile, and I laughed.

"Was Aaron fussy?"

I had to think a minute. It had been so long since anyone asked me about Aaron as a baby. "I mean, he wasn't colicky or anything. But he cried when he needed something. To be changed or fed or held."

You laughed. "This one always wants to be held."

"Aaron did too," I said. "But, trust me, one day you'll want nothing more than to cuddle your little boy, and it'll be too late." I blinked. "So, enjoy it now while you can."

"Everyone says that, but right now time seems to be going at a snail's pace. It's hard to imagine being able to sleep through the night, let alone having him all grown up or something."

They say hindsight's twenty-twenty and I guess they're right. It's impossible to get someone else to see a reality that's different than their own.

"I get that," I said. "I felt that way when Aaron was a baby. But, seriously, that feels like yesterday." Sullivan rubbed his face on my shoulder. It must've been wet because I felt the dampness through my shirt. I'd forgotten how slobbery babies were.

A doubtful look crossed your face. "Yesterday totally feels like a hundred days ago."

I laughed as the waitress appeared with our food.

For not being hungry, you sure ate like someone who was. Once you'd downed half your sandwich, you finally looked up as if just remembering Sullivan and I were there. But I understood that. I used to joke after Aaron was born that I'd forgotten how food tasted when it was still fresh and hot. "Oh, I'm so sorry." Pink spots appeared on your cheeks. "Want me to take him?"

"Don't you dare," I said teasingly.

"You're like an angel or something. Like my fairy godmother," you joked, before reaching for the second half of your sandwich. "Only instead of turning into a pumpkin, I'm going to turn into a single mother at midnight. Oh, wait. I guess I'm that all the time." You laughed bitterly before taking another bite of your food.

Ah-ha. So, the dad wasn't in the picture.

I picked up a French fry and popped it into my mouth. Sullivan wiggled, his feet kicking. I touched one of his tiny toes, savoring the silkiness of his skin.

"It must be hard, huh?" I hedged. "Raising him alone?"

You swallowed down a mouthful of sandwich. My stomach gurgled. I prayed you didn't hear it. My desire to hold Sullivan was stronger than my desire to eat at the moment.

"A lot harder than I thought it would be." You wiped the side of your mouth with a napkin. "You know, before Sullivan was born I thought of giving him up. I wasn't sure I could handle raising him on my own."

My insides seized. I gripped Sullivan tighter. What were you saying? "Do you wish you had?"

"No, of course not," you said vehemently, and my body relaxed. "I don't regret my decision… I guess I just wish I had someone to help."

When your gaze met mine, I smiled. *My mission was*

clear. "You do now. You have me." A loud rumble came from Sullivan's diaper, followed by a strong odor. My hand on his bottom grew suddenly hot. I winced, turning my head away from him.

"Oh, jeez." You leaped up from your chair and yanked him from my arms. "I'll go get him changed. I'm so sorry."

"No worries." I waved away your apology, but did inspect my shirt, lap and hands to be sure I was clean. "It happens. One time when Aaron was about Sullivan's age, we were at Disneyland…" My words trailed off. You had already walked away, hurrying to the bathroom, the diaper bag in one hand and Sullivan in the other. He was crying now, not that I blamed him. That was pretty gross.

After you disappeared inside, I bent over, dipping my hand into my purse. The scent of dirty diaper was still pretty strong. Holding my breath, I fished around for my antibacterial lotion. After finding it, I squirted some on my hands and rubbed it between my two palms.

When I sat up, I spotted Christine walking swiftly down the sidewalk, clutching a shopping bag. She wore a pair of oversize sunglasses, a black hat that was a sharp contrast to her white-blond hair, a gauzy black shirt and skinny jeans. When her gaze caught mine, her eyes widened. I waved and she walked toward me.

"Kelly?" She glanced down at my plate. "What are you doing here?"

I thought it was pretty self-explanatory, but answered anyway. "Having lunch."

"By yourself?"

"Actually, I'm here with the other Kelly Medina," I answered smugly.

Christine scrunched up her nose, her gaze sweeping the table. "Where is she?"

"Oh." I glanced toward the restaurant. You were nowhere to be seen. "She's changing her son's diaper. I'm sure she'll be back any minute."

"Where is her food?" Christine furrowed her brow.

I looked across the table. Huh. Your plate was gone. I hadn't even noticed the waitress come by to take it. But maybe it was when I was putting on my antibacterial lotion. "She ate it already."

"But you haven't touched yours." Christine nodded toward my plate.

"That's 'cause I was holding Sullivan," I said. "You know how it is when you have a baby. You never get to eat right when your food comes. So I thought I'd help her out."

She was giving me that look. The same one my mother used to give me when I told her Lola was sitting at the dinner table with us. Her gaze flickered toward the restaurant, her chest rising and falling, her face lifting, then sagging.

She bit her lip, peering down at the watch wrapped around her wrist. "Maddie has a doctor's appointment in a half hour, but it's just a checkup. I can reschedule and stay here with you if you want."

"Why would you do that?" I laughed. "I'm fine. Just having lunch with a friend."

"And her baby." Christine said slowly, her head bobbing up and down.

I heard the door to the restaurant open. Chest expanding, my head snapped in its direction. But it was a busser. He headed to a nearby table and started cleaning it with a rag. Christine glanced down at her watch again, drawing in a slow breath.

"Kelly will be back in just a minute," I assured her.

In her eyes, I saw pity mixed with concern.

My chest tightened.

"She's right here, Mommy. Can't you see her?"

"No, Kelly. Of course I can't see her because she's not real."

"Okay, well, then I guess you don't need me to stay." Christine offered a shaky, forced smile. "I better go get Maddie, then."

"She is real, Mommy." I stomped my feet. "She is!"

"Okay, okay. Fine. Calm down." Grabbing my arms, she held me tight. "It's okay. Yes, I see her now. I believe you," she assured me. "Hi, Lola." I frowned. She was looking in the wrong direction.

Desperation bloomed in my chest. The door to the restaurant remained closed. "Wait just a minute. I want you to meet Kelly."

"Sorry, Kel, but I really have to go."

"But she'll be out in a second, I'm sure." *What was taking you so long?*

"I'm late. I have to go." Christine gently touched my arm. "I'll call you later, okay?"

"Okay." I nodded as her hand slipped from my arm.

Sighing, I watched her leave.

"Mom, Lola's not over there. She's right here." I pointed to my right side where Lola stood wearing red overalls and a striped shirt. When I pointed her out, she offered Mom a silly smile. I giggled.

"Of course. My mistake. Hi, Lola," she repeated, thrusting out her arm.

"Mo-om." I gasped. "You just hit her in the face."

"Oh, for god sakes." Mom groaned, throwing her arms up in the air. *"I give up."*

"Sorry that took so long." Your voice startled me. "Mr. Wiggle-butt here made it pretty difficult to change him."

My head snapped over my shoulder, searching for Christine. Crap. She was too far away to catch now.

"Everything okay?" you asked.

"Yeah." I turned back around. "I just saw one of my friends." My stomach full-on growled.

"You haven't even touched your food yet," you pointed out.

"No, I guess I haven't." Smiling, I reached out and picked up my sandwich. We were the only ones out here. It was such a nice day. Odd that no one else would want to sit outside.

Leaning over, I took a bite. The chair creaked beneath me. Sullivan was silent now. No more crying or fussing. It was eerily silent, almost as if I was all alone.

"Why are you playing out here all alone?" Dad asked.

"I'm not alone. I'm with Lola."

He looked around. "Where is she? I don't see her."

"You don't?" I glanced at Lola, sitting cross-legged in the grass. Why was I the only one who could see her?

CHAPTER EIGHT

My mom wasn't much of a cook. When I married Rafael, I could make simple, easy dinners like tacos, spaghetti, lasagna, baked chicken. And nothing was made completely from scratch. All my sauces were from a jar or can, all my crusts and doughs from a package.

But Rafael's mom was a great cook. Even to this day, my culinary skills would never compare to Carmen Medina's, a fact my husband has never ceased to remind me of. Carmen spent hours with me in the kitchen, attempting to teach me how to make her beloved family recipes. And she never made me feel stupid the way Rafael did when I'd ruin the tortillas or botch the tamales. Despite what a great teacher she was, I only mastered one recipe of hers before she passed away—her homemade enchilada sauce.

Over the years, Carmen's chicken enchiladas had become a staple in our home. And, like clockwork, I always made a batch on the first cold, rainy day of fall. Rafael grilled a lot in the summer, but during the first rain, we all craved comfort food. Something hot coming from the oven.

So, when I woke up this morning to the sound of rain

pounding down on the roof, I immediately went downstairs and rummaged through the kitchen. I was surprised to find that I had most of the ingredients, since I hadn't been expecting to make enchiladas this early in the season. Usually, rain held off until we were deep into winter. Even then, it was no guarantee we'd get much. Summer droughts were more common around here than rainy winters.

After getting ready, I'd headed to the grocery store to get the items I was out of.

Now I was standing barefoot in my kitchen, stirring homemade enchilada sauce on the stove while rain pattered against the kitchen window. Aaron and Rafael wouldn't be home to enjoy the enchiladas tonight, but that wasn't going to stop me from making them.

I'd sent them both texts earlier, though, to make them wish they were home.

Rafael had responded with a sad-face emoji.

Leaning over the stove, I caught a whiff of the red chili sauce and nostalgia filled me. The house was no longer silent. It was filled with the noise of my family. Of Aaron's baby squeals as he played on the floor near my feet, and the sound of sports blaring from the television as Rafael sat on the couch, heels propped on the coffee table.

The sauce bubbling over yanked me back to the present. To the empty house, quiet save for the rain rhythmically pounding against the roof.

No, mija. *You've got to keep stirring.* I heard Carmen's voice in my head.

Lowering the heat, I gently stirred the sauce to keep it from burning. The scent told me I may have scorched it a tad. If Rafael was here, I'd probably throw this batch out and start over.

Burning the sauce wasn't a mistake Carmen made.

As the spoon swirled in the red sauce, spinning it like a whirlpool, my thoughts drifted to you. I wondered if your mom was a good cook. Did she teach you? I didn't know anything about your parents, other than that they didn't live here. We hadn't talked any more about them the other day.

Honestly, we hadn't talked about much at all. I still didn't know what happened to Sullivan's dad, or why you moved to Folsom.

My phone dinged, signaling a text. I spun around. My cell sat faceup on the island. Wary of abandoning the sauce for a mere second, I hurriedly snatched it up and then resumed the stirring. I held the phone with my free hand and checked the message.

It was from Christine. Hey, girl. What are you up to?

I finished up the sauce before responding. Cooking.

What are you making?

Enchiladas, I typed back.

On my way.

Usually, I would think this was a joke, but Christine had been acting so clingy lately that I wasn't sure. And, really, it wouldn't be so bad if she was on her way. I'd made enough sauce for two pans of enchiladas. I'd never be able to eat that many.

My thumb hovered over the letters, ready to text Christine back and invite her over. But then I stopped, your words from the other day flying through my mind.

I just wish I had some help.

Biting my lip, I stared out the window at the darkened, rainy sky. The wind was so fierce the tree in my front yard was bent at a funny angle, leaves being torn from it and tossed into the air by invisible hands.

I imagined you and Sullivan snuggled up together in your little guesthouse. The walls were probably thin. A lot of those older homes didn't even have central air and heat. And who knew what kind of amenities a backyard apartment had.

Were you cold and scared?

How was Sullivan handling the storm?

Aaron hated them. They always made him wail, especially when he heard thunder.

"God, no wonder he won't stop crying." Rafael chuckled, but there was an undercurrent of frustration in his tone. "I'd cry too, if you kept singing to me like that."

Cradling Aaron's head in my hands, I pressed him into my chest, shielding his ears from the clap of thunder that rang out. "What are you talking about? I thought you liked my singing. That's what you said when we were in choir together."

Laughing again, he shrugged. "Of course. I was trying to get in your pants."

"What?" I recoiled. It was like he'd slapped me in the face. We'd met in choir. The first thing he'd ever said to me was "you have a beautiful voice."

"Come on, you had to know that was a line."

"I didn't," I answered honestly. Aaron was still crying in my arms. I swayed side to side. He'd been crying for hours. I'd tried everything. Sometimes my singing soothed him even if it was apparently awful.

"Here, let me take him." Rafael reached out, and I reluctantly placed his screaming son in his arms.

"So, you lied to me?"

"It wasn't a lie. It was a way to talk to you. That's all." He swayed with Aaron exactly like I had done. If it hadn't helped when I did it, why did he think it would help when he did? My chest tightened as I watched him. "I mean, the whole reason I was in choir was to meet girls."

Heat worked its way up my spine. "Girls, plural?"

Swaggering in my direction, he offered a pitying smile. "I ended up with you, didn't I?"

Stepping back, I crossed my arms over my chest. "You didn't answer the question."

"It's true, Jeans and I had to take an elective and we chose choir to meet chicks." Jeans was his best friend from high school. Got his nickname for wearing a pair of supertight jeans in middle school that split in the butt crack at lunch one day. "But once I saw you, you were the only girl I was interested in. You were definitely the prettiest girl in the class."

He knew the right thing to say. It's why I'd fallen for him. He was always complimenting me. "You're the prettiest. The best." But now I wasn't so sure I believed him.

"Look," he suddenly burst out, wearing a triumphant smile. "I got him to stop crying."

"How did you do that?"

"Don't know." He shrugged. "I guess I'm Super Dad."

"Yeah, I guess so," I muttered, feeling a mixture of irritation and gratitude. It was a feeling I'd grow very accustomed to over the years.

My phone pinged, catching my attention. It was another text from Christine. I felt bad about not inviting her over.

She was my best friend, but she didn't need me the way you did. She had a house full of people. Her kids still lived with her and her husband was home every night.

I sent Christine a laughing-face emoji, hoping she'd take the hint. Then I set my phone down. Purpose renewed, I grabbed a couple of pans out of the cupboard and started assembling the enchiladas.

An hour later, my entire house smelled like melted cheese and chili sauce. I set the fully cooked enchiladas on the counter, allowing them to cool for a few minutes while I went upstairs to change since my top was now painted with red splatters.

After getting into warm clothes, I packed the car up with enchiladas and hopped inside. Luckily, I'd been smart enough to park in the garage last night. When I pulled out of it, wind whisked over my front window, rain sprinkling the hood.

A flash of lightning strobed across the dark blue sky. I tightened my jacket around me before backing out of the driveway. The air from the vents was still heating, so cool air spilled from them. A chill shuddered down my spine. None of my neighbors were outside. Lights glowed from the windows. I spotted kids and spouses, eating dinner or watching TV.

An unexpected lump formed in my throat. Swallowing hard, I returned my attention to the street in front of me. The windshield wipers squeaked along the glass. I squinted to see through all of the moisture streaking the windows.

It wasn't very late, but it was so dark it felt like the middle of the night. Part of me wondered why I wasn't at home snuggled on the couch under a throw blanket where it was warm and safe.

Then I thought about you and Sullivan, alone and in need across town and I pressed harder on the gas. My tires hit a slick patch, and my car pulled to the left. Letting out a tiny gasp, I righted the car and slowed down.

As I rounded the corner, a pair of headlights shone directly in my eyes.

Jeez, buddy, turn off your high beams.

I was grateful when he passed me. Although, now I was seeing spots. *Great.*

Reaching out, I touched the warm enchilada pan on the passenger seat, making sure it was still secure. The last thing I needed was food all over my nice leather seats. This car wasn't brand new exactly. I'd bought it when Aaron got his license, so he could have my old car. It seemed fitting that he had to drive the minivan. It was him who'd stained the leather with grape juice and wrote on the seat with permanent marker.

When I neared your part of town, I had to pay close attention to the street names. I wasn't familiar with the older part of Folsom. Most of my friends lived in Empire Ranch or one of the newer subdivisions. Aaron's friends all lived near the high school.

Finally, I found your street.

The houses over here had their own unique style. I liked it. When I was younger, I always thought I'd buy an older home. One with history. A story. But then Raf reminded me that they also came with problems. Ones that cost a lot of money to fix. So, that's how we ended up buying a brand-new home.

The stories had started with us.

Our ghosts were the only ones that haunted it.

I thought I'd recognize your house immediately. I'd

stared at it the entire time you strapped Sullivan's car seat into my car. But now I couldn't figure out which one it was. And for the life of me, I could not remember the address.

Keeping one hand on the wheel, I reached down into my purse with the other one, trying to locate my phone. When my fingers lighted on it, I yanked it out. Glancing down quickly, I turned it on and went into my texts.

Scrolling down to your name, I clicked on it. Our last text thread came up. I had to scroll upward a little way to find it... Ah-ha! There it was.

Your address was—

A flash of light cut through my vision, a loud honk piercing through the air. My tires skidded on the slick asphalt, my car sliding out of my control. A stunned gasp leaped from my throat. My phone thudded down near my feet. Grabbing hold of the steering wheel with both hands, I swerved back into my lane. The car that had honked at me drove past. I couldn't see the driver through the darkness and rain, but I was sure he was yelling expletives or flipping me off or something. Not that I blamed him. I knew better than to be on my phone while driving. How many times had I cautioned Aaron against that?

Too many to count.

I pulled my car over to the curb. Sitting there, I breathed in and out, in and out, attempting to slow down my racing heart.

Blue-and-red lights flashing in the window.

Rain thundering on the roof like a herd of deer.

Two policemen standing on my front porch.

"Mrs. Medina?"

Shaking my head, I forced myself back to the present.

Everything was okay. Touching the handle of the door, I grounded myself.

Once I'd calmed down, I bent over and picked my cell back up. Then I scrolled through until I found your address.

Squinting, I stared out the window but couldn't even make out the numbers on the house in front of me. It did look similar to yours, though, so I was probably close. Wind howled, screeched, like an animal in pain. Leaves marched across my front windshield. Sitting forward, I peered at the houses. Light glowed from the kitchen window in the house to my left. An elderly woman stood in front of it staring outside, while her arms moved as if she was doing dishes. When she glanced in my direction, my heart lifted. I recognized her. She was your landlord.

Ah-ha. I found you.

The rain and wind were vicious, attacking me as I hopped out of the car and walked toward the passenger door. Strands of hair slapped me in the face, catching on my eyelashes and sticking to my lips. Wiping them away, I struggled to open the side door. Leaning inside, I relished the warmth. Taking a deep breath, I picked up the casserole dish, cradling it in my arms. Heat seeped through the sleeves of my jacket.

It was useless to put my hood back on. The wind kept shoving it down like a toddler desperate for attention. Hurrying toward the house, I clutched the enchilada pan tightly. The older woman was no longer in the kitchen window. The lights had been turned off, giving the illusion that no one was home. Passing it, I made my way along the side yard. It was dark, but a sliver of light shone a path for me to follow.

By the time I reached the door to the guesthouse, my hair was soaked, dripping down my back. I shivered, my teeth chattering. The thin jacket I'd worn wasn't enough to stave off the cold. I'd always been a California girl at heart. I was never prepared for colder weather.

As I knocked with my free hand and waited, a chill snaked down my back. A flash of lightning cut through the sky, bright like a firework. Thunder boomed through the air, causing me to flinch. I heard a baby's muffled cry from inside.

"I'm scared, Mommy." Aaron looked up at me, his eyes wide and trusting. Blue light illuminated his porcelain cheeks. His hair was mussed from sleep, his eyes red. He was wearing his favorite Spider-Man jammies.

"It will be okay." I drew him to me and gently stroked his hair.

The crying continued. I knocked again.

There was no awning, so rain continued to pelt me. I pulled my hood over my head, praying it would stay this time.

"Kelly!" I hollered, knocking once again.

Where were you?

Sullivan's cries intensified. Surely, you were in there with him. What kind of mom would leave their baby alone?

The door opened a crack, your head poking out. Your eyes widened. "Kelly? What are you doing here?" Your hair was plastered to your head and your eyes were watery and bloodshot as if you'd been sleeping. Sullivan still cried in the background.

Why weren't you going to him?

I held up the enchilada pan, desperate for you to let me in, so I could help with Sullivan. "I brought you dinner."

"Oh." Your mouth froze around the word. "Well, um…

that was nice of you, but I wasn't really expecting company."

"I'm not company. I'm here to help." Impatient, I shoved open the door with my hand and forced my way inside. "Sorry," I said in response to your shocked expression. "I needed to get out of that storm and you need to go get Sullivan."

"Right." You nodded, closing the front door, "I'll go get him. I guess…um…just make yourself at home." Hugging yourself, you left the room.

I could see why you were hesitant to let me in. The place was tiny, the little kitchen area part of the living room. Dirty dishes filled the sink, trash lining the counters. The floor was littered with Sullivan's blankets, pacifiers and empty and half-drunk bottles.

But the most striking thing of all was that you had no furniture. Just a few fold-up chairs and a small flat-screen TV that was sitting on top of what appeared to be a nightstand. Boxes lined the far wall as if you still hadn't unpacked.

How long had you lived here?

Were you planning to stay?

The walls were stark and white, not one picture or painting.

I walked over to one of the kitchen counters and pushed a few things out of the way to make room for the casserole dish. It felt good to finally put it down. My arms instantly started to cool. Peeling off my jacket, I hung it on the back of one of the folding chairs.

You reentered the room, Sullivan in your arms. His crying had ceased. Rain pounded against the roof. It kind of smelled like dirty rags in here. My gaze dragged along the walls up to the ceiling, as I wondered if this place was riddled with mold.

A moldy house is no place for a baby.

Looking back at Sullivan's innocent little baby face, unease settled into my gut.

"Sorry about the place," you said as if reading my mind. "It's been a rough day."

My heart softened at your tired tone.

"We'd been trying to sleep when the storm started," you added.

I nodded, feeling bad for how judgmental I was being. "I remember napping when Aaron did. I was so exhausted when he was a baby."

You bit your lip. "Being a single mom is just so much harder than I thought it would be."

Your vulnerable statement reminded me of why I'd come over in the first place. "Well, tonight you have help." I pointed to the casserole dish. "I made you my famous enchiladas. Why don't you hand me Sullivan and you can fix yourself a plate?"

"Really?" You studied me a moment, your forehead crinkling.

"Really." I smiled.

Smiling, your shoulders relaxed. You'd pulled your hair up into a bun since I'd gotten here. There wasn't a stitch of makeup on your face, and your skin was shiny, your cheeks bright. You looked like a child.

"You are seriously a godsend." Stepping forward, you dropped Sullivan into my waiting arms and headed over to the counter.

I drew Sullivan in like a relieved sigh. The squishiness. The sweet scent. I breathed it all in.

When you opened the kitchen cabinet, I noticed there were only a few dishes inside. As you started scooping out enchiladas to put on your plate, I looked around your tiny living space.

The lamp in the corner flickered. "Need a new bulb?" I asked, eyeing it.

"No. It's weird. All the lights kind of do that sometimes," you answered. "Maybe because of the storm."

"Yeah, maybe." When it happened again, I frowned. *Or maybe this place has faulty wiring and is about to go up in flames.* "How long have you lived here?"

"About a month."

A month was long enough to unpack and decorate. "Funny, it looks like you just moved in," I joked.

"Yeah, well, Sullivan keeps me so busy I haven't really had time to unpack and everything," you said around a mouthful of food. A tiny dab of red enchilada sauce stained the side of your lip. "This is the bomb, by the way."

"Thanks." It felt good to have someone enjoying my enchiladas. Even though I still wasn't entirely comfortable in your home, it sure beat eating alone in my big empty house.

Walking around the small space, I bounced Sullivan up and down in my arms. He rubbed his face into my shoulder and chewed on his fingers, making little suckling noises. Saliva dribbled on my shirt, mixing with the rain splatters. My hair was still damp, causing a chill to settle into my bones. Boxes lined the side wall. One of them looked like it had thrown up a pile of your clothes. When Rafael and I had moved into our house, my clothes were the first thing I unpacked. No way was I going to rifle through boxes to get ready in the morning.

"I'm happy to help you unpack and get settled," I offered.

"Oh, I couldn't ask you to do that," you answered. Your mouth was partially full, so you subtly covered it with your hand.

"You're not asking. I'm offering," I said.

Thunder cut through the sky, and we both flinched. Sullivan whimpered. I held him tighter, swaying back and forth.

"It's okay," I said soothingly.

"I was the same way," you said, your gaze landing on Sullivan. Your fork was suspended over your plate, and only a few bites were left. "My mom said I cried through every storm when I was a baby."

"Yeah. Aaron wasn't a fan either." I gently stroked Sullivan's head.

"What about you? Were you scared of storms as a kid?" you asked.

"I don't know," I answered honestly. "I never really talked to my mom about it. We didn't really…talk." I had no idea why I was sharing this with you. I never opened up about my parents. Not with anyone. Taking a deep breath, I walked forward, continuing to bounce Sullivan. Peeking into the one bedroom, my heart sank. One lone mattress sat in the center of the room. Beyond that, an old playpen was set up in the corner. This was no way for a baby to live.

"I'm sorry," you said compassionately, and my insides melted. It had been a long time since someone acknowledged my feelings without making me feel shame or guilt.

My eyes filled with tears, but I swallowed hard and blinked them back. I was here to help you. Not the other way around. "It's fine." I waved away your words. "It sounds like you and your mom are close, though." I was fishing. But you being here was puzzling. In this town where you knew no one. Even more so now that I knew you had a close relationship with your mom.

"We were. It was always just the two of us. She raised me all by herself. I never knew my dad," you explained. "But she died about five years ago."

Once again I felt like a total jerk. What was it about you that made me so suspicious? "Oh, I'm...so...so...sorry." My desire to help you grew exponentially in that moment. You were all alone in this world. There was no way I could turn my back on you now. "I know from experience how hard it is when your parents are no longer around."

Nodding, you frowned, your eyes softening around the edges.

Trying to lighten up the mood, I said, "I guess our name isn't the only thing we have in common."

"Yeah, I guess you're right." You forced a shaky smile, then reached out your arms. "I can take Sullivan now. Have you eaten?"

"No." Turning around, I handed him back to you. When you took him into your arms and held him tightly, you smiled contentedly.

I knew you loved him. That much was obvious.

But it took a lot more than love to be a good parent.

CHAPTER NINE

I hadn't shopped for a baby in years. *What did a baby need?* I stared around at the massive baby section, at the playpens, high chairs and bouncy seats, trying to remember what I'd had for Aaron. But his stuff looked a lot different. Everything was more high-tech now. Baby monitors with screens, toys that hooked up to Bluetooth.

I shook my head.

It was overkill. Sullivan simply needed the basics. A crib. A high chair. Diapers. Blankets. Washcloths. What else? When my gaze landed on a baby swing, I smiled. Aaron spent hours in his swing. It was the only thing he seemed to like as much as my arms. It was my saving grace, allowing me to get stuff done—showers, cleaning, fixing my hair.

This morning I'd thought about calling you. Making sure you were okay with me purchasing a few things for your son. But surprises are so much more fun, right?

As the saleswoman rang up the items I'd chosen, I tried to imagine the look on your face when all of it arrived at your house. Giddiness rose up inside of me. You were motherless. Alone. And, clearly, in need of some serious help. You'd said so yourself.

You're so lucky you met me, Kelly.

When Aaron was a baby, I had Rafael. His parents. My friends.

You had no one.

Until now.

Smiling, I handed the saleswoman my credit card. After swiping it, she bagged everything up, except for the larger items. Those would be delivered. I made sure to get the date and time of delivery, so I could be there to direct them. Your guesthouse was tucked back away from the street and might be hard to locate.

Hands full, I stepped out of the store. The straps from the multiple shopping bags cut into the skin on my fingers, turning them a sickly shade of white. I tried to shift them, but it was impossible. Squinting, I located my car. It wasn't that far away, so I walked faster, desperate to put the bags down.

When I reached it, I hit the button on my keys to open up the back. As I started tossing the bags inside, I heard a familiar voice calling my name.

"Kelly?"

I turned. Susan walked swiftly in my direction, wearing workout pants, a sporty jacket, her hair pulled up in a tight ponytail. It swung behind her head like a pendulum. Her eyes fell to the diapers I clutched against my side.

"Hey, Susan," I answered as brightly as possible, but secretly wishing I'd left the store two minutes earlier. Susan used to do yoga with Christine and me, and every once in a while, we'd hang out socially. But we hadn't hung out with her recently. Actually, I hadn't spoken to her in months. I swallowed hard, remembering our last conversation. The way she'd looked at me with pity and then stepped away as if tragedy was contagious. As if she were afraid to get too close because she'd catch my bad luck as easily as a cold or flu virus.

"What are you doing?" she asked.

"Shopping," I answered, slightly annoyed. *Wasn't it obvious?*

"But you're buying baby stuff." She peered into my car, studying the bags intently. Then she looked at my stomach. "You're not...?"

Her words evoked memories of the glorious swell of my belly, the little flutter kicks in my belly. "Of course not. This is for a friend."

"Wow. You bought a lot of stuff."

I was glad she couldn't see the crib, swing and high chair. "She needs a lot," I answered, picturing you in your empty guesthouse. Susan opened her mouth like she was about to say something else, but I cut her off. "Anyway, I need to get going. Say hi to the family for me."

"Yeah, you too," Susan said, offering a limp wave before walking off.

She didn't even ask me how I was, or how Rafael was. Not that I was surprised. She'd always been pretty self-involved. It didn't matter. I didn't need her. You were my purpose now, Kelly.

Your address was now etched in my brain, the route becoming familiar. After parking along the curb, I hopped out. Crisp air whisked over my face, carrying with it the scent of damp earth. The sun was deceptive, sitting high in the sky—bright and radiant—yet offering no warmth.

Tugging my jacket tightly around my body, I walked to the back of the car.

After rounding up all of the bags, I headed down the walkway toward the guesthouse. The strong, pungent smell of weed filled my nostrils. It reminded me of my college days.

Funny that Rafael became a professor, because when we were in school together he was the troublemaker. The partier. The bad boy. The player. He was the boy all my friends warned me to stay away from.

Maybe I should have listened.

Deep down I knew they were right.

But he was magnetic. The pull he had on me was strong. All-consuming. Even now I sometimes felt it.

Glancing around, I wondered where the smell was coming from. Surely not the old woman who owned the home. A neighbor, perhaps?

The smell blossomed the closer I got to your front door. Was it you? *No way.* I shook my head. It couldn't be coming from the guesthouse. You were a responsible single mom. I was certain you knew better than that.

Then I pictured your undecorated house, dishes in the sink, clothes on the floor, wrappers and soda cans piling up in your garbage can. My stomach twisted.

Setting the bags at my feet, amid a pile of multicolored leaves, I knocked. A dog barked in the distance. A car drove by, its tires buzzing on the asphalt. Faint music played from somewhere along the street, spilling through an open window. It was a '90s song that I recognized and I found myself humming along, nostalgia pecking me swiftly on the cheek.

Once it passed, I looked around.

Where were you?

Stepping forward, I attempted to peek through the tiny opening in the blinds. But I couldn't make anything out.

After knocking again, and getting no response, I walked back out to the street and scoured the curb. And there it was across the street. The van you'd been driving the first time we'd met. So, you had to be home.

Why weren't you answering the door?

With large strides, I made it back to your front door and tried again. This time I heard movement inside. My pulse quickened. The door opened slightly, one eye peeking out, just like last time.

It alarmed me. In a town where you knew no one but me, why were you always so shifty about someone knocking on your door? Surely, visitors weren't a frequent thing.

"Oh. Kelly. Hi." Your words were choppy, uneven. You didn't immediately open the door or usher me inside. You held it partially closed, only one eye visible.

Why weren't you happy to see me, Kelly? I thought we were friends. I thought you needed me. What was it you called me the last time? *A godsend.*

So, why were you acting like this now?

"I brought you some stuff," I said cheerily, not allowing your odd behavior to deter me.

Your one eye peered downward. Was it just my imagination or was it red?

Bending down, I picked up a few of the bags. "Why don't you help me carry them inside?"

A beat of hesitancy on your part. Worry grew inside of me like weeds taking over a flower garden.

"Okay," you finally answered, not exactly the tone of someone excited to have me over. I chose to not let it of-fend me. "Just give me a minute to go grab Sullivan." The door closed firmly, shutting me outside.

I was struck then by the wrongness of all this. You were a mystery to me. A stranger who'd appeared out of nowhere. Our shared name was the most I knew about you. That didn't make us friends. It didn't make you safe.

Suspicions played in my mind, dark and haunting, like a minor chord.

I was about to hightail it out of there when the door popped open. I still contemplated leaving. It was Sullivan's fault I stayed. You held him around his middle, facing him outward. His large eyes looked around, taking everything in. The baby items screamed at me from inside their bags.

This was about him, not you.

Staring up at me, he flashed a smile and broke through my resolve.

"He's so animated," I mused as I stepped inside, bags dangling from my fingers.

The place looked worse today than it had last night. How was that even possible?

"Yeah, he's been animated all night," you said in a tired voice.

That's when I noticed the circles under your eyes, the sallowness of your complexion. You weren't high. You were exhausted.

"He kept you up all night, huh?" I offered you a knowing smile. "That's rough. I remember when Aaron would do that. Just about killed me."

"Right? I think it has." You let out a stilted laugh, but it kind of sounded like a cry.

Trustworthy or not, the mother in me felt a connection to you. I dropped the bags on the ground. "Here. I'll take him."

He was warm. Soft. Perfect.

You were staring down at the bags as if you weren't sure what to do next. The look on your face—that mixture of tension and naivete—softened me.

"You can go ahead and look through it," I told you.

Sinking down to the floor, you tore through the bags like they were presents and this was Christmas morning.

"You didn't have to buy all this stuff." You pulled out a can of formula and a couple of blankets. Your gaze scanned the diapers and onesies.

"I wanted to," I answered, my smile growing. "And, actually, this isn't all. Tomorrow at two in the afternoon, a few more items will be delivered."

I expected you to get excited. Maybe squeal. Possibly hug me. Instead, your face fell.

What's wrong with you now?

God, it reminded me of when Aaron was going through puberty. How he'd be happy one minute and crying the next.

I distinctly remember one night he stood in front of me, frustrated tears raking down his cheeks, screaming, "I don't even know what I'm crying about!"

Hormones can be a bitch.

But you weren't a teenager anymore. It was time to grow up. Rein in those mood swings.

"Kelly, I can't accept all of this," you finally said, your lips quivering.

"Why not?"

"It's too much."

"No, it's not," I assured you. "I wanted to do this. For you. For Sullivan." Our gazes met. "Please. Let me do this for you."

"It's just that it's so nice… I, um… I just…well, I don't deserve all this."

You came at me then, surprising me by giving me a side-armed hug, careful to do it on the side that Sullivan wasn't on. When you were close, I caught a whiff of your floral scent. I think it was your hair.

You smelled clean. Good. Relief flowed through my chest.

The alarm bells hadn't completely subsided, but they were faint.

"Thank you," you whispered.

"Of course," I said. "Now, why don't you go get some rest and I'll take care of Sullivan? Then we can tackle the unpacking and cleaning."

"I really don't need help with the unpacking and stuff," you said. "I can do it myself."

"Nonsense." I waved away your suggestion. "It'll be way faster with two of us."

You stared at the ground. Nervously, you pushed your bare toe along the carpet. The nails were painted blue, chipped around the edges. "It's just that I have a lot of my mom's and my grandma's stuff. I kinda wanna go through it alone."

"Your grandma's?" You'd never mentioned a grandma before.

Your lips wobbled. You didn't look up. "I lived with her after my mom died, until she passed away recently."

You poor thing.

God, I was the worst. Here I'd been thinking all these terrible things about you just moments ago. You were so young, and yet you'd lost everyone who mattered to you.

I knew that feeling.

Loss.

Loneliness.

I knew it all too well.

There was a shed in my backyard. To the naked eye, it was filled with junk. Boxes of old stuff. But it was magical. It was all my memories, tucked into one place.

My mom's old Christmas ornaments. My dad's old records. Carmen's recipe books. Photo albums filled with pictures of Rafael's family. Aaron's school papers, certificates, awards. Baby blankets and clothes. Old toys.

I'd spent hours going through those boxes. Reminiscing about my time with Carmen, the good times I'd had with my dad, the few happy memories I had of my mom, Aaron's childhood. I didn't even want to do it in Rafael's presence. He'd probably laugh at me for getting so choked up.

I understood the need to do that kind of reminiscing alone.

"Okay. Yeah, I get that." I gently rocked Sullivan in my arms, but he was wiggly and restless. Sun crept in through the blinds in the window. "Do you have a stroller?" That was one item I hadn't thought to buy. "It's so nice out, maybe we can take Sullivan on a walk."

"Yeah, I have one." You pointed to the door where a stroller was folded up against the wall. "But I don't feel like going outside." Yawning, you stretched your arms high above your head, your fingers spread wide.

"That's okay. I can take him on a walk, if you want to stay and nap." I bit my lip, trying not to appear too eager.

Smiling, you emphatically nodded. "Oh, that would be awesome."

It was the fastest you'd taken me up on an offer before.

"Are you ready to go for a walk?" Holding Sullivan up,

he kicked his little legs, swimming through the air. "Yeah, you like walks, huh?" I giggled, nuzzling his face.

"Thank you so much. Seriously. You're an angel," you gushed.

Aaron sat next to me on a blanket in the backyard, staring up at the blue sky. We were having a picnic lunch of peanut butter and jelly sandwiches. Reaching out, his tiny fingers trailed up my spine. Goose bumps rose on my skin.

"Where are they, Mommy?"

"Where are what, sweetie?"

"Your angel wings," he said.

I laughed. "Why would you think I have angel wings, silly?"

"Because Daddy said angels are the people who protect us, and that's you."

I wrapped my arms around him and drew him close, planting a kiss on his button nose. "I'm not an angel, but you're right. I will always protect you."

It wasn't the first or last time I would lie to my son.

"I'm not an angel," I said to you now, irrationally frustrated that you'd brought up an unwanted memory.

"Maybe not, but you act like one," you said. "There's a bottle already made in the fridge for when Sullivan gets hungry." After yawning one last time, you shuffled out of the room.

I unfolded the stroller and set Sullivan inside. After getting him all bundled, I put on my jacket and we headed out the front door.

"Looks like it's just you and me, buddy," I said in a singsong voice. His cheeks pushed up as he offered a toothless grin. My insides turned to mush. Baby smiles were my favorite. I'll never forget the first time Aaron smiled.

I'd immediately pulled out his baby book and jotted down the date.

Then again, I chronicled everything he did back then.

Aaron's first word: *mama.*

The first time he crawled: seven months.

The first time he walked: ten months.

His first haircut: two years.

There was nothing I left out. I even wrote letters for him to read when he was older. When he had a family of his own.

I wondered if Sullivan had a baby book, and if you did the same for him.

It was quiet as I pushed Sullivan, the rickety wheels of the stroller groaning along the sidewalk. Leaves crunched beneath my feet. Sullivan's eyes were wide as they stared up at the blue sky. The street was gorgeous, like something out of a painting, with trees lining it, bowing into the center as if reaching for the ones on the other side.

We made it all the way down to Sutter Street, where we passed antiques shops and restaurants. I used to take Aaron here all the time when he was little. There weren't many people out today, which was surprising given how nice the weather was.

When we got to the end of the street, my phone buzzed in my pocket. My first thought was that it was you. Panic surfaced swiftly and I yanked the phone out.

But it was only Christine.

It was like the tenth time she'd called me today.

Sighing, I answered. "Hey, what's up?"

"Oh…" A breath blew through the line. "I wasn't expecting you to pick up."

"Well, you've called a million times. I thought maybe it was an emergency."

A motorcycle drove past. It was so loud I couldn't hear Christine's response.

"Where are you?" She finally spoke once it was quiet again.

"On Sutter Street."

"What are you doing there? Shopping or something?"

"Nope." I turned Sullivan's stroller around and headed back toward your house. "I'm taking Sullivan on a walk."

"Sullivan?"

"Yeah, Kelly's baby. She's at home taking a nap."

"Right." She dragged out the word in an uncomfortable way. "Well, um… I…ran into Susan at the kids' school."

Oh, yeah. I'd forgotten they had kids the same age.

"She told me she saw you yesterday."

"Yeah, I was at the store buying some stuff for Sullivan."

"And now you're taking him on a walk." She was doing that weird, talking slowly thing again. "So, you're out with him? On Sutter Street? Alone?"

I swallowed hard, continuing to push Sullivan. He hadn't made a sound since we started walking. He simply stared upward, content to watch the clouds.

Babies were lucky. For them everything was simple.

"Yep," I said, my tone clipped.

"Does she… I mean, your friend knows you have him, right?"

Heat rose to the surface of my skin. "Of course she knows. How could you ask me something like that?"

"Come on, Kel. You know why I have to ask."

"Ma'am." The man held out his arms, his voice stern,

and his expression grim. "He's not yours. You have to hand him over."

I swallowed. "This isn't like that."

My head spun. I pinched the bridge of my nose.

I was better.

Healthier.

Right?

"Okay," Christine finally answered. "I believe you."

"You do?" I waited for the catch.

None came. "Yeah, I do. I just…um…well, I just want you to know that I'm here for you…you know, if you ever want to talk or whatever."

I passed a couple and they nodded, their hands raised. I nodded too, since both my hands were occupied. Sullivan cooed in the stroller.

"I know that." Rounding the corner, I left Sutter Street and headed back toward your house. Too bad that meant I had to climb a pretty steep hill. Based on how out of shape I was, it would've been hard for me regardless, but pushing Sullivan's stroller up it was killer. My breath became more labored, my one arm burning. "Hey, Christine. I'm heading up a hill, and I kinda need both hands. Can I call you back later?"

"Sure. We'll talk later." Not sure if she meant it to, but it sort of sounded like a warning.

After hanging up, I tucked the phone back into my pocket. Gripping the stroller with both hands, I struggled to reach the top of the hill. When I finally did, I stopped to take a couple of deep breaths. A woman jogged past me, glancing over curiously. As if she was so much more in shape than I was.

I mean, didn't she see the stroller? That made it twice as hard.

Sullivan whimpered, and puckered his lips.

I recognized that look.

"Are you getting hungry?" I asked as if he could answer me.

He cried a little louder now.

I guess he could.

"Okay. We're almost back home," I assured him, moving faster as his cries intensified.

He was screaming pretty loudly by the time we arrived back at the guesthouse.

"It's okay. Mommy said there's a bottle in the fridge," I said to Sullivan while pushing the stroller into the kitchen. I continued pushing the stroller back and forth with one hand, while opening the fridge with the other. The motion seemed to be working for the moment. I found the bottle you'd told me about, but when I opened it, it smelled sour. Frowning, I was glad I checked it. Had you been feeding him spoiled bottles?

Oh, Kelly, it's a good thing we met. I have so much to teach you.

After making Sullivan a new bottle, I unhooked him and carried him into the family room. Then I sat down on the couch to feed him. Your heavy breathing traveled from the bedroom. You were out, and by the time Sullivan finished his bottle he was out too. He lay in my arms, lips parted, eyes closed. I stared down at his pale face, so soft it was hard not to reach out and run my fingers over it. But I didn't want to wake him.

I understood your need for some privacy while you unpacked, but I couldn't sit here and do nothing the entire time you slept. At the very least I could organize and clean. Carefully, I set Sullivan down on a blanket spread out on the floor. Arms numb, I stood up, shaking them out.

The kitchen needed the most attention, so I started there. I scrubbed the dishes in the sink and cleaned Sullivan's bottles. Once those were drying, I organized the few dishes in the cabinets. I folded back up the stroller and put it by the door.

Then I decided to tackle the family room. Baby rattles, blankets and pacifiers littered the floor. As exhausted as I had been when Aaron was a baby, Rafael never would've allowed our house to get like this.

"Shit, Kel," Rafael snapped. "Seriously?"

"What's going on?" I hurried into the family room.

Rafael held a toy car in his hand. "I just tripped over this."

Welcome to parenting a toddler, I wanted to say, but knew better. "Sorry. I must've missed that one." While Raf was at work, I'd allow Aaron to play freely. Set up his toys wherever he wanted. He'd create an entire village in our living room. And sure, I'd trip over the occasional toy, get stabbed in the sole of my foot. But it was a small price to pay to see my son's imagination take flight. He had the freedom to play, to create. I never had that as a kid and I wanted that for mine.

But I'd become good at rapidly cleaning everything up during Aaron's afternoon nap. I thought I'd gotten everything. But leave it to Raf to find the one toy I'd missed.

"Aaron!" Rafael hollered, still holding the offending toy.

My heart seized. I held out my hand, palm up. "Just give me the toy. It's no big deal."

"Is that your parenting philosophy? Oh, it's no big deal." Rafael rolled his eyes. "That's great, Kel."

"Hey, Daddy." Aaron ran in, his smile open and trusting.

My breath caught in my throat as I watched Rafael, awaiting his response.

Aaron ran right up to his dad, lifting his arms.

My gaze met Rafael's. I nodded as if to say, "Pick him up. Hold your son. Let the toy thing go." And maybe he would have if I hadn't been so blatantly asking him to.

"Do you see this toy?" Rafael asked Aaron firmly.

Aaron's smile slipped.

"I just tripped over it," Rafael said, and clearly not getting the right response added, "I could've hurt myself." He shoved the toy into Aaron's hand. "You need to pick up your toys after you play with them."

"Mommy says I don't have to," Aaron said stubbornly, his forehead creasing, his bottom lip protruding.

Rafael's head snapped toward me, his expression one of betrayal.

I bit my lip. "He's only four."

"I cleaned up after myself at four," Rafael said.

Of course he did. I sighed.

"You just got home from work, Raf. Why don't you hug your son?" I prompted.

He paused and for a second I thought he would. But instead, he said, "Go put away the toy, Aaron." As Aaron shuffled out of the room, Rafael looked up at me. "I'll leave the coddling to you."

My eyes filled. I blinked.

"And you might want to pick up that sippy cup that's spilling milk all over the couch." His head bobbed in the

*direction of our new leather couches. The ones he insisted
on buying even though we had a toddler in the house.*

*"Crap. The little spill-proof thing must've come off in
the dishwasher." I snatched it up, sticky milk dribbling
onto my arm.*

*"I thought you had to hand wash those," Rafael mut-
tered before leaving the room.*

*Exhaling in frustration, I plunked down on the couch.
There wasn't one thing out of place. The house was pris-
tine. Dusted. Swept. Mopped. I killed myself trying to keep
up with all of it. And yet, it was never good enough.*

*"Mommy." My head whipped up at the sound of Aar-
on's voice.*

"Sorry." His eyes were red and sad.

*"Oh, honey." I drew him to me. "It's fine. You didn't do
anything wrong."*

"I didn't mean to hurt Daddy."

"You didn't." I rubbed his back in reassurance.

It seemed neither of us were good enough for him.

Blowing out a breath, I stepped into your family room.
I never had anyone to help around the house when Aaron
was younger. It felt good to be able to do this for you. After
picking up the assorted baby supplies I headed toward the
corner where a pile of clothes sat. Picking them up, I took a
whiff to see if they were dirty. They smelled clean enough,
which was surprising. You didn't have a washer or dryer.
Where did you clean your clothes? Surely, you didn't go to
a Laundromat. That was no place for a baby.

I made a mental note to tell you that you could use my
washer and dryer anytime.

Since the clothes smelled clean, I folded them into neat
stacks on the floor. When I got to the last shirt, my face

heated up. For a moment, I thought I must be mistaken. But when I held it up, it was clear that I wasn't.

I knew that logo.

I knew that shirt.

Why did you have it?

"What are you doing?" Your voice startled me.

Dropping the shirt, I spun around. You stood in the doorway, your eyes puffy, and your hair flipped haphazardly to one side. I thought about our shared name, about how familiar you seemed, about how much I cared for Sullivan. My mouth dried out. There was a reason I'd felt so connected to both of you from the beginning.

You weren't a stranger.

Not really.

I knew you. Or at least, I knew of you.

And now I knew why you were here.

CHAPTER
TEN

Rafael called me early that evening. I'd been expecting to hear from him all day. I thought about ignoring it, but I knew that would only make things worse.

Taking a deep breath, I picked up the phone.

"Hello," I answered in my most normal voice. It was the same voice I'd used with you when you walked in on me going through your clothes. With my foot, I'd shoved the telling shirt under the others, and I'd offered you a blank, innocent smile. Then I'd explained that I was only trying to help you clean up a bit. You gazed down at the floor, but the offending shirt was nowhere to be seen. You seemed visibly relieved, which puzzled me. Why didn't you want me to know who you were?

"Kelly, I just checked our bank statement. What the hell is going on?"

"Nice to hear your voice too, Raf," I said drily.

"C'mon, Kel," he practically growled, his tone thick with impatience.

I sighed. Coming clean was my only option. There was

no other way to play this. "I bought some stuff for my new friend. Remember I told you about her?"

"Seriously? That's what this is about?"

"It's not about anything," I said through gritted teeth. At least, it wasn't when I first purchased everything. "I'm helping out a friend."

"You should've consulted me first."

"You mean, I should've asked permission," I shot back. We hadn't always been like this. There was a time when I'd bragged about our partnership. Bragged about how forward thinking Rafael was.

Those days had passed.

"We don't have that kind of money to be spending on strangers."

"She's not a stranger." *Ha. Wasn't that the truth?* "She's my friend."

"Well, whoever she is, why did she need so much baby stuff? Doesn't she have all that?"

"She's young. Alone. Poor."

"Kel, the baby is with his mom, right? He's not at our house, is he?"

"What are you accusing me of, exactly?" I asked through gritted teeth. My hand was gripping the phone so hard, my knuckles were a sickly shade of white.

A heavy sigh floated into my ear. "I worry that maybe you're doing it again."

"Doing what again?"

"You know what I'm talking about, Kel. This baby… He's not yours."

"I know that," I snapped. "God, I'm doing a good thing here. Isn't that what you and Dr. Hillerman are always saying to me? Find a hobby, Kelly. Find a purpose. Serve people. Get outside of your own head. Now I'm doing that and you're getting all upset."

"Yes, I'm glad to see that you've been making your appointments." His tone was sarcastic.

"It was two weeks ago, and I only missed one appointment. Let it go."

"And your next one is tomorrow, right?"

"Yes," I grumbled. It would be so hard to keep silent about who you really were. Dr. Hillerman had a way of making me open up even when I didn't want to. But it was too soon for me to go blabbing about it to anyone else. Besides, I didn't technically know anything. It was merely a suspicion right now. I had to wait until you came clean. Why hadn't you yet? Did you not trust me? Were you scared?

"That's great, Kel. I've been so worried. And I know Christine has been too."

Betrayal stung me. "You talked to Christine?"

"She cares about you, Kel."

"I'm fine," I hissed. "I've been helping out a woman in need. That should be celebrated, not picked apart."

You're an angel. Your words floated through my mind.

You were starting to trust me. We were getting close, I could feel it. Maybe soon you'd open up, tell me what I'd already figured out.

I smiled, my insides cozy. This whole time I'd thought you were the one who needed me. Turns out, I might need you too.

"How did your last weekend with Rafael go?" Dr. Hillerman narrowed his eyes, pegging me with a challenging stare.

"Fine," I answered.

"Just fine?"

"Yeah." As I gazed past Dr. Hillerman's shoulder and out the window, a memory surfaced.

When I was in middle school I went with a group of friends to the state fair. We ate corn dogs, drank slushies, looked at the animals and rode the rides. I'd gone a few times before with my parents but had never had this much fun. They always limited my sweets and would only let me go on the Ferris wheel. With my friends I had a freedom I'd never experienced before.

I felt bold, empowered.

Until I got lost.

To this day, I'm not sure how it happened. One minute I was talking with my friend Heather and the next I was standing in the middle of a crowd of strangers. I spun in circles, frantically scouring the area around me. My heart pounded, sweat forming along my forehead and across my shoulder blades. It was hot out that day, but the sweat had nothing to do with the heat and everything to do with the panic that was unfurling inside of me.

My mom had rattled off a list of instructions that morning. And one of them was to stay close to my friends. To not get separated.

Way to follow instructions.

If I hadn't been so freaked out, I might have been proud of myself for finally doing something rebellious.

The scent of fried food and sticky candy wafted under my nose, but it didn't excite me the way it had earlier. In fact, I came dangerously close to puking. I closed my eyes, wishing there was a way I could magically transport myself back home.

When I opened them, my stomach plummeted. Nope. Still at the fair. Still alone.

"Kelly?" A male voice interrupted my internal freak-out.

My head snapped up. It took me a minute to recognize the teenage boy standing in front of me. When I did, relief flooded me. "Jeremy?"

Smiling, he nodded.

Oh, thank god.

I exhaled, every muscle in my body unclenching. Jeremy had been a counselor at a local summer camp program Heather and I had gone to together. We'd both had a little bit of a crush on him, actually. Not only was he cute, but he didn't treat us like little girls.

"Are you here all alone?" The crowd moved around us steadily like ocean waves. But we were the rocks, holding steady despite the current.

"I was here with some friends. Actually, Heather's one of 'em. But I guess I kinda got separated from them."

"Okay, well, I'll help you look for them," he offered without hesitation.

"You will?"

He nodded.

"Who are you here with?"

"Some friends too. They're over at the carnival games."

"Why aren't you with them?" Had he wandered off and got lost too?

"Had to use the restroom." His cheeks reddened.

I giggled. See, he didn't treat me like a kid. He treated me like a friend.

We walked side by side, weaving through the crowds, keeping our eyes out for my friends. After about a half an hour of looking, he suggested we go look in the buildings.

Said maybe they'd gone in one. It seemed like a long shot, but I would've followed him anywhere. Plus, he was older and wiser. What did I know? I was the one who got lost in the first place.

We rounded the corner and came up on a couple of buildings. Jeremy grabbed my hand and guided me around the back. Goose bumps rose on my skin at his touch. I couldn't wait to tell Heather about this. As we entered a small opening between two buildings, I stared down at our entwined fingers, feeling a rush of excitement pulse through me. It was dark and cold in the small space Jeremy had led me to, and I shivered. His fingers released mine and disappointment sank in my gut. It didn't last for long, though, because before I knew it, he'd pressed me up against the building, his hands touching me in other places. Places that had never been touched. Places that didn't make me feel excited or special.

I tried to escape. Turn my head. Push him away.

But his hand slid up my neck, his fingers closing around it, holding me in place and stealing my breath.

When it was over, he took off and I was alone again.

Why had I chosen to tell him that story?

It was strange. I hadn't thought about that in years. I was a child. It was only a blip in my life. I'd been through much worse things since then.

"I have no idea why I shared that," I said once I was finished.

"I think it speaks to the trust issues you have, Kelly," Dr. Hillerman said, rolling his pen between his forefinger and his thumb.

"I don't have trust issues," I bristled.

"Really?" His forehead became a mess of squiggly lines.

"Because the last time you were here we talked about the issues you were having with Rafael. Have those issues been resolved?"

I shrugged. "Kind of."

"Your weekend was good, then?"

"Great," I answered firmly, lifting my chin.

"Because when I asked you about your weekend earlier you said it was fine. And then you chose to tell me about a time when you felt violated and trapped. Is that how Rafael made you feel last weekend?" One bushy eyebrow cocked. When I first started coming here, almost six months ago, I couldn't even focus on what he was saying. Instead, I stared at his incredibly bushy brows the entire time. I often had the intense urge to give him my aesthetician's number on the way out. But I doubted he would ever go.

"I mean..." I paused, squirming in my chair. I'd worn a skirt and for the life of me couldn't figure out why. I guess I'd wanted to look professional, put together. But now my skirt kept riding up my legs and I felt like a mess. Exposed. Cheap. Pulling down my skirt, I swallowed. "I don't know." But I did know. He'd gotten it exactly right. His ability to do that was annoying.

"You don't know if he made you feel violated?"

I forced a laugh. "He's my husband. Of course I didn't feel violated. The weekend was actually good. We connected in a way we hadn't in a long time." It was partially true. There were moments. But so much had changed since last weekend. My thoughts drifted to you. To Sullivan. To my conversation with Rafael last night. "We're not really fighting about the same things we were last time I came in. We've sorta moved on to new stuff."

"What kind of stuff?"

"Well, I recently made a new friend, and I've been doing a lot to help her."

"In what ways have you been helping her?" Dr. Hillerman stopped spinning the pen. He leaned back in his chair, tenting his hands. I knew what his body language meant. He was intrigued.

Why had I brought you up? I hadn't meant to. Then again, maybe it wasn't so bad. I'd been doing a good thing. Helping you proved that I was making progress. I assumed Dr. Hillerman would be proud of me.

And it's not like he had to know anything about your real identity.

"Just, you know, hanging out with her," I said, careful to keep it vague. "Helping with her baby. Making her meals. Buying stuff she needs for her baby."

"She has a baby, huh?" I didn't like the way he was looking at me.

"Yes." I shifted again in my seat. "She needs a lot of help with him. It's like she knows absolutely nothing about being a mom."

"I see." Dr. Hillerman wrote something on his pad of paper and then turned his narrowed eyes back toward me. "And how did you two meet?"

I clamped my mouth shut, unsure if I should answer that. The conversation wasn't going in the direction I thought it would. I uncrossed my legs and then crossed them on the other side. The chair creaked. I'd never liked this chair. Dr. Hillerman could really use an interior decorator. Everything in here was old. Stale. Uncomfortable. It even smelled musty.

"Kelly?"

My head jerked upward. "Sorry." I scratched the back

of my neck. "It's just that this chair is super uncomfortable. Have you thought about redecorating your office? I have a friend who does interior design. I could give you her number."

"I'm actually quite happy with my office. Thank you." He offered a bland smile. "Is there some reason you're uncomfortable sharing with me how you and your new friend met?"

Shit. Again, I'd miscalculated. By not telling him the story I'd made it obvious I was trying to hide something.

"It's kind of funny, actually. We both have the same exact name," I blurted out.

"Kelly? That doesn't seem so uncommon, now does it?"

"No. She actually has my entire name—Kelly Medina."

"Interesting," he said, and I worried he would have the same reaction that Christine had had. But he surprised me by saying, "You know, there actually used to be another Dr. Hillerman here in Folsom years ago. He was a general practitioner, but still it got to be quite confusing. We were always getting each other's mail and phone calls."

"Yeah," I said excitedly, relieved that he understood. "That's how I first heard of the other Kelly. I got a phone call that was meant for her."

"Is that so?" He waggled his eyebrows in a conspiratorial manner as if we were two girlfriends gabbing about boys or something. "The good thing for me was that the other Dr. Hillerman was a bit younger, so it's not like anyone would confuse us if they met us."

I thought about how you and I might look similar if it weren't for our glaring age difference. "Yeah, it's the same with the other Kelly. She's like twenty years younger than me." I smiled, picturing Sullivan. "And she's got this adorable little boy."

"Huh. Almost like a younger version of yourself," he mused. "Weren't you in your early twenties when you had Aaron?"

The implication slammed into me. I shrunk in on myself like a folded-up piece of paper. With my head bent down into my chest and my arms wrapped around my body, I swallowed hard and nodded.

"In our last session you mentioned how you wish you could go back and start all over."

My mind spun. How had I let it happen again? He was twisting my words. Making it sound bad. Sinister.

Like I was crazy.

"Isn't that what you said?" he pressed.

"I don't remember that," I lied.

"You don't? We'd been talking about—"

"Stop!" I pressed my hands to my ears. I wouldn't let him say it again. He wanted me to face the truth, but I wasn't ready. Not yet.

It was a mistake to bring you up.

A huge mistake.

CHAPTER
ELEVEN

I was leaving Dr. Hillerman's when I got a text from you.

Thank you for the crib, high chair and swing. You really didn't have to do all this.

My heart sank. Crap. I'd wanted to be there when the furniture arrived. When I'd scheduled the delivery, I'd completely forgotten about my therapy session.

When I hit a red light, I hurriedly texted back.

You're welcome.

I'd barely gotten down the street when another text came through.

I appreciate it so much. I have no idea how I'll ever repay you.

I smiled to myself, and texted back: No need to repay me. It was my pleasure.

You seemed to like me. To be comfortable with me. And I'd never given you any reason not to trust me. So, why the secrecy?

My phone buzzed. I assumed it was another text from you, but it wasn't. It was Christine.

I've hardly seen you this week. Wanna come over?

Pausing, I bit my lip. I'd wanted to head to your house and see all the furniture set up, but Christine was my best friend and I did feel bad that I'd been avoiding her. She didn't deserve it. I mean, yeah, her words had hurt my feelings, but I knew she was only trying to be a good friend.

Sure. On my way, I texted back.

Turning at the light, I headed toward Christine's. The trees lining the street swayed slightly in the wind, a choreographed dance, their rust-colored leaves falling to the ground like confetti. When Aaron was little he would always point out the colors of the leaves as they fell—orange, red, yellow and brown. Once the trees were bare, we'd head into the front yard to make a pile for him to jump into. Rafael thought I was crazy, doing all the work of raking up the leaves just to allow him to make a mess again. But it was worth it to hear Aaron's stream of laughter as he played in the leaves.

One day Sullivan would be old enough to play in the leaves too.

My thoughts drifted to all of the new furniture that had been delivered. I loved knowing that a part of me was with Sullivan even when I couldn't be there. At least now I wouldn't have to worry about him sleeping on the floor or in that god-awful playpen.

Now he'd have a nice crib to sleep in and a swing to keep him occupied.

Aaron's face emerged in my mind, smiling and laughing as he swung in his baby swing. Lost in my thoughts, I didn't notice the light turning red. I slammed on my brakes, my phone slipping off the passenger seat and falling to the ground.

As I stared down at it, I remembered the time Rafael had forgotten to tighten the bolts when he put together Aaron's baby swing. The whole thing came toppling down after I'd fastened Aaron into it.

Luckily, I'd been standing right there and I cushioned the fall with my hands. Then I'd immediately pulled Aaron out.

Fear prickled up my spine.

Did you know how to put a swing together correctly? Would you remember to tighten the bolts?

You seemed clueless when it came to parenting. I knew you were doing your best. It had to have been hard to raise a child all alone.

That's why I was here.

I wouldn't abandon you, especially not now.

I'd passed your street a while ago, so I flicked on my blinker. After making a hard turn, I headed away from Christine's house and toward yours.

You were more excited than I'd ever seen you.

Not only that but you weren't shocked when I showed up unexpectedly this time. When you opened the door to let me in, you wore a broad smile. Your eyes were sparkling in a way I hadn't seen since we met.

"Thank you again!" you said, pulling me into a tight hug. I melted into you, welcoming the affection. It had been so long since I'd been touched like this. It felt surprisingly good. My gaze slid past your shoulder, landing on the pile of shirts I'd folded. The offending one was still hidden at the bottom of the pile, but I knew it was there. Its existence was a reminder of who you were.

I wanted to ask you about it so badly, I could taste the question lingering on my tongue. But there was a reason you hadn't confessed to me yet. The last thing I wanted to do was scare you or push you away.

I'd learned that when Aaron was in middle school. The art of not saying too much. Of not forcing him to talk but being available when he was ready. It was a skill Rafael had never mastered. He'd coerce and goad Aaron to the point where he stopped talking to his dad at all.

As much as I hated it, I had to be patient. To wait until you were ready. I knew better than to push.

When we separated, I finally got a good glimpse of the room. The swing was set up in the corner. In the kitchen area, the high chair sat. Everything seemed to be set up correctly.

There was only one problem.

I frowned. "Where's Sullivan?"

"That's the best part." Your smile deepened. "He's sleeping. Like really sleeping. For maybe the first time ever. Whenever I put him down in his playpen or on the couch, he would toss and turn and whine. But the minute I laid him down in that crib, he was out." You touched my shoulder. "Thank you so much. I really, really appreciate it. I mean, I know it's been forever since you had a baby, but I'm sure you remember how hard it is when they don't sleep."

I did remember. Sleep deprivation was truly the worst

part of having a baby. Back then, I would've given my right arm for a good night's sleep.

"Yeah, those days were rough." I nodded. "Can I peek in on him? I'm curious what the crib looks like in there."

"Sure." You grabbed my arm and ushered me forward.

You'd never been this touchy-feely before, and my heart lifted in my chest. You were so close to opening up, I could feel it.

"Again, I'm sorry I wasn't here when they dropped everything off," I said.

"Oh, no worries. They found me and got it all set up, no problem." You waved away my apology with a flick of your wrist, similar to what Christine always did.

Oh, crap. Christine. She was probably wondering where I was.

Together, we peeked into the tiny bedroom. My heart seized in my chest, a gasp leaping from my throat. "No." I shook my head sternly. "He's not supposed to sleep on his chest. Babies always…always…sleep on their backs. Don't you know anything?" Your lack of knowledge was appalling.

I mean, come on, hadn't you at least read a parenting book? Or an article online? Even a quick Google search would suffice.

Your lower lip quivered, and you blinked repeatedly.

Way to go, Kel.

God, I was turning into my mom.

"Sorry," I mumbled. "It's just that it's unsafe for a baby to sleep on his stomach. We need to roll him over." As I stepped into the room, your hand grabbed my arm, gripping me a little too tight. I thought of the bruises hidden underneath my shirt, and forcefully yanked my arm out of your grasp.

"Can't we just leave him for now? I won't put him on his stomach ever again." Your forehead gathered together. "It's just that he's sleeping so soundly. I don't want to wake him."

"Do you want him to die of SIDS?" I shot back.

You reeled back, a horrified look on your face. Perhaps I could've been gentler in my delivery, but I had good intentions. I was trying to protect your child.

My phone buzzed in my pocket. Sighing, I pulled it out.

Did you get lost?

I texted Christine back swiftly.

No. Had to make a stop. Be there soon.

"Sorry," I said. "I gotta get outta here, and I can't leave knowing Sullivan is unsafe. Just roll him over onto his back and I'll get out of your hair."

You sighed like a petulant child, and I guess that's kind of what you were. Not quite an adult. Not quite a child. Maybe a better phrase for it would be an "adult child." You clearly weren't equipped to be raising a child of your own. Never was that more apparent than now.

Thank god you'd found me.

Shoulders stooped, you trudged over to the crib.

During Aaron's teen years, I'd seen this behavior a million times. When I'd ask him to clean his room or take out the trash or help with dishes.

The minute your hands scooped under Sullivan's body

his eyes opened, and he started crying. You threw me a look of frustration. I merely shrugged my shoulders.

Welcome to motherhood, I wanted to say.

You rolled him over but by now his hands were balled into fists and he was screaming so loudly his face was all scrunched up and red.

"Thanks a lot," you muttered under your breath.

I wanted to feel bad that you were so upset, but the relief I felt at knowing Sullivan was safe eclipsed everything else.

"Okay, well, I gotta go. Make sure you keep him on his back in that crib." I pointed my index finger at you before turning around. "Oh, and one more thing." I spun back to face you. By now you had Sullivan in your arms and you were rocking him back and forth gently. In this moment, you looked like a mom, the way you held him close, your nose brushing over the top of his head. I smiled. There was hope for you yet. "Make sure you keep him strapped in at all times in the high chair and swing. Aaron was constantly trying to push the tray off the high chair. One time he shoved it off and would've fallen out if I hadn't had him strapped in."

"Okay." You nodded.

Another text came through from Christine.

Hurry up before I have to go pick up the kids.

No, she couldn't leave. It had already been such a tiring day. I needed some time with my best friend.

"I really have to go. Call if you need me." I waved as I headed toward the front door. Once outside, I breathed in the crisp, clean air. I was so grateful to be out of that stuffy space.

I hurried down the path leading out to the curb, Sullivan's cries following me the entire time. As much as I hated leaving him while he was upset, I knew it was only temporary.

Pretty soon everything would be out in the open, and he'd be right where he belonged.

CHAPTER TWELVE

"Where have you been? You were supposed to be here over an hour ago," Christine said, ushering me inside her house. Her hair was pulled up in a tight ponytail and her makeup was flawless, all peachy and dewy.

"Sorry," I said, peeling off my coat. Christine kept her house overly warm.

She was always cold, but didn't like to wear a lot of layers. I handed her my coat and she hung it in the closet near the front door. Then she shuffled into the family room in her bare feet, her maroon nails peeking out from under her yoga pants that skimmed the tops of her feet.

I followed, my tennis shoes thudding against the hardwood floors. It smelled like something was baking, but I knew better. My gaze fell to a cinnamon candle burning nearby.

"Want a snack?" Christine asked. She pointed toward the coffee table where assorted cheese and crackers sat on a wooden board next to two glasses of wine. One had lipstick marks on it, betraying that Christine hadn't waited for me.

Not that I blamed her.

"I meant to be here sooner," I explained. "But I had to stop at Kelly's first." Plopping down on the couch, I reached for a cracker. After spreading on some cheese, I popped it in my mouth. The cheese was rich and buttery, melting on my tongue.

Christine sat across from me, her brows furrowing. "Kelly's, huh?"

"Yeah, her shipment of baby furniture arrived today and I wanted to make sure it all got set up correctly." I washed my cracker down with a sip of wine. "And it's a good thing I did, too. She totally had her son sleeping on his stomach. I swear, she knows nothing about parenting."

"And that's what you're doing?" Christine leaned forward, resting her elbows on her knees and looking at me earnestly. "Helping her become a better parent?"

"I mean, I'm trying," I said, wolfing down another cracker. "Man, this cheese is amazing."

"Oh, yeah, I love that one." Christine eyed it. "Don't ask me what it's called, though. I only know it by the wrapper."

I laughed, snatching up my glass of wine and leaning back on the couch.

"Hey, I'm sorry about how I've been acting lately," I said. She sat up straighter, searching my face. "I know I haven't been a very good friend. You deserve better."

"Yeah, I do," she teased, one side of her lip curving upward.

I laughed again.

Tucking her legs up under her body, she took a sip of wine. "I know I've been kinda hard on you lately, Kel. It's just… I worry, you know." She paused, biting her lip, the lines on her forehead melting together. "I want to be a good friend. I guess I don't always know how. I've never been through what you have." When she swallowed, her slender neck swelled.

"I know," I said. "I get it. I really do." And I did. I would've been the same way had things been reversed.

Smiling at me, she said, "Us girls have to stick together, right?"

"Us girls do have to stick together," I agreed aloud, cementing the words into my brain.

The last six months had been the worst of my entire life. And no one had been there for me like Christine had. Smiling, I sat back on the couch and took another long sip of my wine. The tension in my shoulders drifted away as the wine warmed my body all the way through.

"Because god knows we can't count on the men in our life," I added, swishing the red wine around in my glass.

"Uh-oh. What did Rafael do now?" Christine reached for a cracker.

"Nothing. That's the point. He does absolutely nothing to help me," I said drily. "Even when he was here last weekend, he made it all about him."

"Ooh, that's right. We never talked about the weekend." Christine downed her wine and poured another glass.

I glanced up at the clock. "Don't you have to pick up the kids?"

"No, I thought I did. But then they texted asking if they could go home with friends. Score!" She smiled. "So, tell me about last weekend. Did you end up buying the lingerie?"

I nodded, my skin crawling.

"Did he like it?" Her lips lifted at the corners.

"Too much." I winced.

She frowned. "What do you mean?"

I gulped down my wine, enjoying the spiciness of the heat as it slid down my throat. "I don't know. At first it was nice, I guess. He was like the old Raf, sweet and tender." Smile deepening, Christine nodded, encouraging me to continue. "But then over dinner he was kinda being an ass, and then we never recovered from that the rest of the weekend." I wanted to tell Christine everything. The way he made me feel. How he left bruises on my body.

I wanted to spill everything, including the truth about you.

But I didn't even know where to begin.

"Oh, yeah. Been there. Done that." Christine rolled her eyes. "Why do they always have to ruin everything? Joel was totally like that the other night. The kids were both at friends', and I was dropping hints like mad, being seductive, kissing his neck and thrusting out my chest. But he was all, 'I got laid off today, so you might need to go back to work.'"

"What?" I sat forward. She swallowed hard, her eyes drooping a little. For a second the tough-girl act slipped away and she looked almost scared. I felt bad that I'd been avoiding her this week when she clearly needed me. "Chris..."

She recovered quickly, offering up a nonchalant laugh. "It's fine. We'll figure it out."

"Do you really have to get a job?"

She waved away the suggestion, her eyes narrowing. "No. Of course not. The kids need me. Besides, who would hire me? It's been years since I worked."

I knew firsthand how hard it was to find a job.

"I'm so sorry, Christine," I said earnestly.

"Oh, don't be sorry. Joel has a ton of skills. He's already been networking. I'm sure he'll find another job in no time."

"If not, couldn't you go back to working as a dental hygienist?"

She finished off her second glass of wine. Or at least, her second since I'd been here. "I don't know." Her tone was more somber now. "So much has changed. I'd probably have to go back and take more classes or something." She bit her lip, her gaze downcast.

"I bet you'd catch on really quick." I reached out to touch her hand. Truth is, I'd always been envious that Christine had experience in a trade. I had my bachelor's degree in English, but that didn't seem to help when I was searching for work last year. My lack of recent experience was what hurt me. I would've given anything to have a hirable skill like she did. "It wouldn't be so bad, would it? I thought you liked your job."

"I did. I liked it a lot," she said. "It's just that I was raised in day care, and I never wanted that for the kids. When I quit to be a stay-at-home mom, Joel promised me I wouldn't have to go back until after they graduated high school." Her eyes darkened. "He promised."

I promise to love you in sickness and in health. As long as we both shall live.

Yeah, I knew all about broken promises.

CHAPTER THIRTEEN

A text from Rafael came early Friday morning. He wasn't coming home this weekend. His excuse? He had too many papers to grade. Too many commitments on campus.

Yeah, right.

I wasn't surprised. I wasn't even upset. There was a time when we lived for the weekends, but that was forever ago.

A lifetime, it seemed.

After texting him back, I sat down at the kitchen table with a mug of steaming tea and stared out at the front yard. The grass was wet with dew, a slight dusting of ice covering the cars parked along the street.

I had a vision of Aaron outside at his car, scraping ice off his windshield before school. Rafael had seen him pour water on it once and chastised him, so he was careful never to do it again. Probably thought his dad would praise him for listening. But that never happened. Rafael was always good at criticizing. Not so much at praising.

When Aaron was younger, I'd always hoped he'd end up at UC Fallbrook with his dad. He'd been an independent kid, always wanting to do things on his own. I figured he'd go away to school. But at least if he went to Fallbrook, he'd be near his dad. And he'd only be two hours away from me. That was nothing. I could visit them both, stay at Raf's apartment, get regular lunches with my son. Perhaps my hopes were a touch naive, but I figure I wouldn't have lost him completely.

By the time Aaron went into high school I knew he wouldn't follow his dad. They could hardly stand to be in the same room together. Rafael nagged him constantly. Always putting him down. Nitpicking. Stomping on his ideas and dreams.

It was because of him our son chose Hoffman University, a school that took almost ten hours to drive to.

It was because of him I was alone.

I gripped my tea so tightly, my knuckles ached. Taking a deep breath, I released my hold. The lady across the street was back. The one with the kids. She happily paraded them up the walkway to the front door. *Show-off.* I stood, turning my back on the window, and carried my empty mug to the sink.

After rinsing it, I headed upstairs. Walking down the empty hallway, I shivered. When I passed Aaron's room, a thumping sound from inside stopped me. My heart arrested. When I heard it again, I deliberately stepped forward. The door wasn't closed all the way, so I quietly placed my palm on it and pressed it open. The hinge creaked. My shoulders tensed. I held my breath as I peered inside.

Aaron sat hunched over on the edge of the bed. His hair was scraggly, jagged edges framing his face. Normally, he wore it gelled and styled like Rafael's. His eyes were red, ringed in a blue hue. My breath rushed out of my mouth. Carefully, I walked up to him.

"Aaron?"

He lifted his head, our eyes locking.

My son. He's home.

Reaching out, I went to touch his face. But he jerked back, shaking his head.

"Aaron? What's wrong?" This wasn't like him.

Continuing to shake his head, his eyes widened. Was he scared of me? My stomach rolled. I opened my mouth to tell him he had nothing to be afraid of, but he wasn't looking at me. His gaze was fixed over my shoulder. I whipped my head around. Rafael stood in the doorway, mouth pressed in a hard line, his forehead pinched together.

When did he get home?

What was going on?

My head spun.

"What were you thinking, Aaron?" Rafael's voice boomed, loud and angry.

My body clenched.

"It was a mistake, Dad." Aaron scooted backward on his bed, wiping his hand down his face. "Chill."

My pulse quickened at the last word.

"Excuse me?" Rafael's eyes flashed. He walked farther into the room.

Instinctively, I stood between them. A buffer. Protector. It's what I'd always been.

"I will not 'chill.'" Rafael used air quotes and a mimicking tone on the last word. "You hit a parked car, Aaron. I mean, how stupid does that make you?"

Aaron's face reddened. "I didn't hit it. I scraped it. I just misjudged the turn."

"And now our insurance is gonna go through the roof. You get that, right?"

"I'm sorry." Aaron hung his head. "I'll pay for it."

"No, you know what? Don't worry about it. You don't have to pay for the insurance, because you're no longer allowed to drive."

"What?" Aaron's head jerked upward.

I opened my mouth to protest, but then clamped it shut. My defense of Aaron always backfired. Rafael didn't like when it was two to one.

"But I worked so hard to get my license." There was a slight quiver to Aaron's voice, like he might start crying. I prayed he wouldn't. That would only end in teasing from Rafael. *Real men don't cry*, he'd say.

"Clearly, not hard enough."

"Seriously, Dad, you act like you've never made a mistake before."

"Not like this," Rafael snapped.

Aaron rolled his eyes. "Yeah, right," he muttered under his breath.

Rafael stepped closer to him. I moved my body, keeping it between them. My heart pounded in my chest. "Watch it."

"Okay, that's enough," I said nervously. "Let's just go downstairs and have breakfast. You both are upset. Let's talk about this when everyone calms down."

No one responded. It was like I was invisible.

"It wasn't even that big a deal," Aaron said sullenly, picking at his cuticles.

Rafael shook his head. "See, that's where you're wrong. It *is* a big deal. And this is exactly why you keep making the same damn mistakes over and over again. You're not smart enough to learn the first time. And that's exactly why you're not old enough to drive."

Aaron's face fell. My heart sagged.

"That's not true. You're really smart, honey." I attempted

to erase the damage his father's words had inflicted, but I knew it was futile. Aaron already knew I thought the world of him. But it wasn't my approval he wanted.

Angry, I stormed toward Rafael. I was done sitting idly by while he pushed our son further away. He called me a pushover, said that kids needed discipline. But that was the thing. I believed in discipline. It was the belittling and the character assassinations that I couldn't handle.

"Okay, that's enough." I shot my arms out firmly, but they never planted on his chest. They never touched anything at all.

I blinked.

Rafael was gone. I spun in a circle. Aaron was no longer on his bed. My gaze darted around the room. It was empty.

I walked to the bed, touched the comforter. It was pulled tight. No dents or creases. Sitting down, I breathed in. It smelled stale. Not a trace of Aaron's scent—hair gel mixed with too much deodorant. I used to tease him about how much he put on.

He hadn't been here.

I squeezed my eyes shut, a headache emerging. When I opened them again, I was still alone. It had seemed so real.

I guess it's because it was real. It had really happened that way.

Just not today.

Exhaling, I stood. On shaky legs, I headed out of Aaron's room. Once in the hallway, I firmly closed Aaron's door. Hugging myself, I hurried down the hall toward my room. I gently closed the door and leaned against the wall, taking deep, steadying breaths.

The silence was getting to me. That's all this was. I'd been alone too long. Besides, it wasn't a hallucination. Simply a memory. I was sure everyone experienced things like this.

Desperate for a distraction, I reached for the alarm clock and flicked on the radio. It wasn't my child. My husband. It wasn't even another body in the house. But at least it was noise. At least it filled the hollow space.

On the nightstand in front of my alarm clock sat my grocery list. I'd scribbled down all the ingredients to make stir-fry tonight. That's where I'd planned to go this morning before getting Rafael's text. I snatched it up with the intention of throwing it away. There was no need to make so much food now that I'd be alone. Instead, I rolled the paper between my fingers, Christine's words from yesterday floating through my mind.

Us girls need to stick together.

Still holding the grocery list, I picked up my phone and sent you a text.

My husband won't be home tonight. Making stir fry. Want to come over for dinner?

I waited a few minutes, but you didn't respond. Chewing on my lip, I waited for the little dots to show up on the screen, but they never did. Frustrated, I tossed my phone on the bed and went into the bathroom to take a shower.

As the hot water beat down on my back and steam circled my face, my thoughts drifted to you. When I first realized who you were, I have to be honest, I was a little hurt. Confused too. Why now? Why after all this time?

What did you want from me?

It was the first time you were in my home. Your eyes were wide as you took it all in. I tried to imagine what you were thinking. Your gaze was darting around my living room like you were staking out the place.

Wait. Were you?

I still didn't fully know your intentions. I wanted to believe they were pure, but your secrecy raised suspicions.

Clutching Sullivan tightly, I watched you carefully. Your lips pursed as you peered over at the kitchen table in the breakfast nook. I knew that you were reacting to the brass candlesticks that sat in the center, right past my laptop. They didn't match the modern theme I'd created throughout the house. Even Rafael had scoffed when I first put them out. But they were a gift from Carmen. She'd kept them in the same spot on her kitchen table. Hours she and I spent sitting around that table, chatting and sipping tea, the old-fashioned candlesticks between us. Rafael hated them. Said they looked like something from a garage sale or thrift store. But I refused to move them. I liked having a piece of Carmen in here.

"Is this your husband?" You were staring at a picture of Rafael and me that was propped up on one of the end tables. Your tone was innocent, your expression giving nothing away.

"Yes. That's Rafael."

"You're cute together," you said.

"Thanks," I murmured, the image of Rafael towering over Aaron, calling him stupid, filling my mind. I shook away the memory.

"Where is he tonight?"

"He works in the Bay Area."

"And he doesn't come home on the weekends?"

"Usually he does. He just had stuff to take care of this

weekend." A thought struck me. "But he'll be home next weekend. Maybe you could come over and meet him."

"Yeah, maybe," you said, but it didn't sound convincing.

Sullivan whimpered, so I jostled him in my arms. You'd only been over for a few minutes before you'd easily handed him over to me without qualms or hesitation.

Just, here you go.

And there he was, happily placed in my waiting arms.

I loved that you trusted me with him so easily. I had the hardest time giving Aaron to anyone when he was a baby, even other family members.

When you moved over to a picture of Aaron, unease settled into my chest like a virus. Your mouth started to open, causing panic to surface. I could do a lot of things.

Play with your child.

Smile. Laugh with you.

Cook you dinner.

Pour your wine.

Be your friend.

But I wouldn't talk to you about Aaron.

Not yet. Not now.

Not until I knew I could trust you.

Since the moment you walked in, the words *I know who you are* had been burning a hole in my tongue. It physically hurt to keep the words inside, like they were clawing and fighting their way out. It took all my willpower to keep them quiet. Hidden. Under wraps.

"You want something to drink?" I asked with forced cheeriness.

Nodding, you turned away from the picture. My chest expanded with relief. "Sure."

"Wine?"

I didn't drink wine when Aaron was a baby, but that's because I breastfed. Since you weren't breastfeeding, I assumed there was no issue with offering you alcohol.

"Sounds good," you responded.

I was right.

"There's a bottle open on the counter," I explained. "Do you mind pouring a couple of glasses, since I've got Sullivan?" I could've handed him back to you, but I wasn't ready. Besides, we both knew you weren't eager to take him.

By the way you poured the wine, I'd say you were eager to have a drink, though.

"Wow. That's a generous pour," I mused when you handed me a glass.

You lowered one corner of your mouth, making an embarrassed expression. "Oh. I'm sorry."

"No, it's great. I'm gonna have you do the pouring from now on." I laughed, setting my glass down on the end table and then scooting back into a comfortable position on the couch. You still wore that sad puppy-dog look and it made me feel bad for what I said. For seeming so tough, you were pretty sensitive.

You sat on the other end of the couch, taking a swig of your wine. I moved Sullivan off my shoulder and sat him in my lap, facing forward. He batted at something imaginary and let out a little coo.

Noticing, you sat forward, reaching for the diaper bag near your feet. You fished out a toy and thrust it in Sullivan's direction. "Here ya go, buddy."

His chubby fingers folded around it. Then he shook it up and down, and it rattled with the motion.

When you sat back up, you tipped your wine over and a little dribbled on the ivory fabric of the couch.

"Shit," you cursed under your breath, swiftly lowering your hand to wipe it up.

"No." I stopped you.

Your hand flew back as if the couch was on fire, the sudden motion causing you to spill again. "Oh, my god, I'm so sorry."

"It's okay," I assured you, wishing I hadn't snapped before. "Just leave it. I'll grab a rag. You'll cause more of a stain if you rub it in. Here. Take Sullivan." After you set your wine down, I plopped him into your arms.

As I hurried into the kitchen, I thought about how much I sounded like my own mom. Growing up, I wasn't allowed to eat or drink on the couches in our living room. Being a staunch rule follower, I never did. Until one Christmas Eve when my mom let me have my hot chocolate on the couch, while staring up at the large sparkling Christmas tree. Of course, I'd spilled. And I'd done exactly what you'd tried to do. I wiped it with my hand, hoping Mom wouldn't notice. She did.

I was never allowed on those couches again.

When I had Aaron, I swore I wouldn't be like her. I'd be fun and carefree. I'd let my kid eat and drink wherever he pleased. For the most part, I'd kept my promise to myself. While Aaron was growing up, I'd been the type of mom I wished I'd had.

Except for one thing.

One way I'd failed my son miserably.

Clearing my throat and blinking rapidly, I bent down under the sink and found a couple of towels. After wetting one, I made my way back to the couches. You sat in the recliner now, cradling Sullivan in your arms. His large eyes followed me as I entered the room.

The pattern of the spill resembled blood splatters. My knees creaked as I lowered myself down to wipe it up.

"I can clean it up," you offered.

"I got it." With the damp rag, I rubbed the couch with firm, fast motions until the stain disappeared.

"Wow. You got it all out." You peered over my shoulder.

"Yep. Just takes patience and arm strength." Oh, god. I definitely remember my mom saying that. Man, what was it about you that turned me into her?

After putting away the rag, I rejoined you in the family room. You were almost done with your glass of wine, so I took a few sips of mine to catch up.

"Your house is amazing," you said. Sullivan hit himself in the leg repeatedly with his toy, but he was smiling and cooing, so I guess it didn't hurt.

"Thanks." I glanced around, trying to see it through your eyes. Folsom's an affluent community. Our house was nice, but nothing compared to a lot of other houses in our neighborhood. It was rare that someone acted as enamored with it as you were.

"Have you lived here a long time?" you asked.

"Yeah. Over ten years."

"It must have been awesome for your son to grow up here. Did he love it?"

I can't wait to get outta here. Aaron's words rattled around in my head.

I swallowed hard. "Um…yeah, I think so." It wasn't completely a lie, was it? I pictured him running around in the backyard laughing and smiling, his little fingers gripping mine. I remembered how happy he seemed to be when he was playing with toys or watching TV in the family room.

I could still hear the sound of his laughter as it filled the house.

But that was when he was younger.

"I bet." You glanced up at the vaulted ceiling. "I would've given anything to grow up in a place like this."

"Yeah?" I wasn't sure anymore if what you were saying to me was true or concocted, but still I was curious about your upbringing. "Where'd you grow up?" I slowly brought my wineglass to my lips, attempting to remain nonchalant, as if we were two friends chatting. And I wasn't desperately fishing for information.

"Just a small little house." You shrugged, then took another sip of your wine. "My mom couldn't afford much."

"Your dad was never in the picture?"

You shook your head.

"What about Sullivan's dad? Is he involved with his son at all?" It took all my willpower to stay casually seated, one arm draped over the side of the couch, instead of pitching forward with rapt attention.

Your eyes flashed. My words had hit a nerve. "No," you said so softly I could barely make out the word.

"Is it because he doesn't know about him?"

You laughed bitterly. "Oh, he knows about him all right."

A funny, fluttery feeling filled my gut. "He's met him?"

Frowning, your head swiveled back and forth. "No. The last time I saw him I was pregnant, and he told me to have an abortion."

Your statement was like a kick to the gut. "Oh, my god. That's awful."

"Whatever. I'm over it."

But I could tell you weren't.

I wasn't sure what to do. A part of me wanted to hug you,

to tell you it was all okay. But my arms wouldn't move. It was like I was so horrified, I'd been paralyzed with shock.

You set your wineglass down on the coffee table and stood abruptly. "Sullivan needs a diaper change." Bending down, you retrieved the diaper bag. "Where should I do it?"

"Uh…" I blinked, still stunned by your admission. "You can use the guest room. It's just down that hall to the right." I pointed.

As I watched you saunter down the hallway, I bit my lower lip.

"So, you said you were making new friends. Are any of these friends of the female persuasion?" I waggled my eyebrows at Aaron. He was home for Christmas break. It was the middle of the night and we were sitting on the couch talking near the lit Christmas tree. His guard was down, and he'd been more open with me than he had been in a long time. I decided to capitalize on it.

Leaning back on the couch, his eyes lit up. "Maybe."

Squealing, I gently hit his knee. "Tell me."

"Nothin' really to tell. I just met this girl."

"And you're dating…or seeing each other or whatever."

"Not yet. But I like her. She's cool."

When I found the Hoffman University shirt at your house, I'd thought maybe you were the girl he told me about. I thought maybe he was Sullivan's dad.

I couldn't voice my suspicion, though. Not until I had all the facts.

But your story had thrown me. My son would never say those things. He'd never tell you to get rid of your child. I'd raised him better than that.

He was better than that. So, why would you say he wasn't? Why make up lies about him?

What are you up to, Kelly?

CHAPTER
FOURTEEN

You drank too much and fell asleep on the couch a couple of hours after dinner. It was no surprise based on how many you slammed back. I hoped this wasn't a regular occurrence for you. It wasn't very classy.

And, also, what would have happened if I hadn't been here? Poor Sullivan would have had to fend for himself. And we all know babies are incapable of that.

Earlier, around the time you'd poured your third glass, you'd mentioned that you could call an Uber to get you home if need be. But that was nonsense. There was no reason to do that. You and Sullivan were more than welcome here. I had guest rooms, clean sheets and towels. I had everything you needed. I may have been confused about who you were, but that didn't change my need to help you and Sullivan.

I was generous and helpful, the same things I'd taught my son to be. And there was no way I would turn away a single mom and a baby in a time of need, even if that mom was clearly hiding something.

Glancing down at Sullivan lying on a blanket in the

middle of the family room, I realized there was one thing I didn't have. A crib.

Biting my lip, I searched my memory bank trying to remember what I did with Aaron in these types of situations when he was a baby. It didn't take long for me to come to the conclusion that I hadn't been in this particular predicament.

I didn't get drunk at people's houses when Aaron was a baby. Unlike you, I took being a mother very seriously.

Another reason to keep you close.

You needed me, Kelly whoever-you-really-were.

My heart seized as an idea sprang to my mind. Giddy, I put on my slippers and headed into the backyard. It was freezing. The icy air skated across my skin as I hurried across the back lawn. I ran my hands up and down my bare arms to create friction. It had been warm in the house with the heater on, so I wasn't wearing long sleeves.

My teeth were chattering by the time I reached the shed.

Unlocking it, I stepped inside. It was even colder in here. It was also dark. I pulled out my phone and used it as a flashlight. Scattered on the ground were a couple of Aaron's old toys. A pile of rocks. He used to sometimes play in here. Liked to pretend it was an army bunker or something.

Stepping forward, I reached out and pried open a box marked "BABY." I was expecting to be assaulted by blue blankets and onesies, maybe some of Aaron's baby toys. Instead, a fuzzy pale pink blanket sat on top.

My breath caught in the back of my throat. With shaky hands, I reached out and touched the fabric. It was soft, feathery. Closing my fingers around it, I lifted it out of the box. Bringing it to my face, I inhaled. It smelled damp and stale.

My heart sank.

Eyes welling, I peered back into the box. More pink.

Onesies, dresses, shoes. None of it used. Chest tightening, I dropped the blanket and stepped back from the box as if it were an infectious disease. My throat burned, and I gulped in air. But it wasn't refreshing. It was dusty and dirty in here. I wanted out.

My gaze shot to the door, blowing in the wind.

Then I saw it.

What I came in here for.

My chest expanded as I weaved through boxes to get to it. When my hand lighted on it, I smiled. Rafael wanted me to get rid of all this stuff. Some of it he'd even thrown away. That's how it ended up in here. The shed was originally meant for yard-work supplies. I'm the one who put the boxes and old furniture in here, thinking that one day I might need it.

And it was a good thing I did.

Wait until you see this, Kelly.

"Kelly! Sullivan!"

I rolled over in bed, stretching my body over Rafael's empty side. Even though I kept my eyelids closed there was an orange glow behind them that told me it was light out. I've always been a night owl. Rafael's the morning person. When we first got married, he'd head out for coffee and pastries while I slept in on Saturdays. I'd awake to a hot vanilla latte and a warm scone.

I couldn't remember the last time he did that for me.

Shutting out my thoughts, I pressed my face into my pillow, determined to fall back asleep.

"Sullivan! Kelly!"

I froze. My eyelids flipped open. I'd forgotten you were here.

Footsteps clattered up the stairs.

"In here," I called, but my voice was hoarse.

"Kelly?" Your voice was muffled through my bedroom door.

"Come in." Sitting up, I ran my fingers through my tangled hair.

The door flung open and you stood in my doorway, your eyes wide as if you'd seen a ghost. "Where is Sullivan?"

I was a little irked at your tone. As if I would ever do anything to hurt him.

"Relax." I scooted forward. "He's right here."

Pursing your lips, you stepped farther into the room. Your hair stuck out all over your head in a curly mess. Black eye makeup dotted your under eyes and cheeks, and dark lipstick and wine stained the skin around your mouth. You definitely looked like someone nursing a hangover. Coming around the bed, your eyebrows shot up.

Why did you look frightened?

Sullivan was fine. He was sleeping soundly in the bassinet next to my bed. I'd been watching over him all night. He was safe and content.

"Where did you get that?" you asked, pointing.

"The bassinet? It was Aaron's."

If I thought you seemed scared before, you really looked terrified now. *But why?*

"And you still have it? In here?" Seriously? How strange did you think I was?

"No. Of course not," I said. "It was in the shed in the backyard."

"That came out of a shed?"

"Don't worry. It was stored in a box and I cleaned it up before putting Sullivan in it," I assured you. "It's perfectly safe. And, look, he likes it."

Last night I'd rocked Sullivan to sleep in my arms. I let him stay there for a while, enjoying the feel of his body against mine. By the time I laid him in the bassinet, he was sleeping so soundly he never stirred all night. I watched him for a while, his skin illuminated by the glow of the moon shining in from the window. He looked exactly like Aaron. Same dark skin and hair, same slope in his nose, heart-shaped lips and almond-shaped eyes. You had pale skin, more like mine, your lips were fuller, your nose small with a button-like tip, and your eyes were wide and round.

Deep down, I still felt like this was my grandson.

But if that were true, why had Aaron kept it from me? And why were you lying about what he'd said to you?

"Is that a new blanket?" you asked, your words pulling me from my internal questions. Your face was all scrunched up with worry.

Honestly, you were getting on my nerves. Your behavior was puzzling. You were the one who'd passed out drunk on my couch the night before. I'm the one who took care of your son. You'd think you'd be a little more appreciative.

"Yeah." I smiled, taking in the pink fuzzy blanket wrapped around Sullivan's body. It killed me when I had to pack that away, knowing it had never been used.

Now it finally had.

It felt right. Poetic. Like we'd come full circle.

"Oookay." You dragged out the word. "Well, um, thanks for having us over and letting us stay, but we've imposed enough. We should probably head out."

"Nonsense." Tossing off my covers, I shook my head. There was no way I could let you leave. Not with all these unanswered questions swirling in my mind. "Sullivan is still sleeping and you haven't had breakfast." Sliding off the bed, I stood. "Come on. I'll make us some."

You hesitated, your gaze flickering to Sullivan. My stomach clenched. I bit back the words that were right on my tongue.

"Um…that's super nice and stuff, but you've already done enough. We should get going."

"What kind of host would I be if I let you leave without breakfast?" I teased, grabbing your arm. "After all that wine you drank last night you need some food in your belly." Walking forward, I tugged you behind me. When we reached the doorway, you halted, looking back. "He's fine. We'll hear him if he wakes up."

You didn't appear convinced, but slowly nodded your head and then allowed me to guide you downstairs. I made us a pot of coffee, some eggs and potatoes. It wasn't lattes and scones, but it would have to do.

"Does Sullivan always sleep so well?" I asked as we sat down at the table in the breakfast nook, even though I already knew the answer. I'd listened to you complain on multiple occasions about his inconsistent sleeping patterns, and yet, he seemed to have no problems last night.

"No, actually. He's usually up several times a night and then up for good by six." You take a sip of your coffee.

"He must feel comfortable here, then." I let the implication linger.

If you noticed it you didn't let on. You simply speared a potato on your fork and took a bite. You liked your eggs doused in hot sauce, the same way I liked mine. Aaron always smothered his in ketchup and I thought it was so gross I couldn't watch him eat it.

Rafael also liked his with hot sauce. He's actually the one who got me to start eating mine that way.

"This is really good," you said, your mouth still full. "You're a great cook."

"Thanks. I enjoy cooking," I said, seizing control of the conversation. "What about you? What kinds of things do you enjoy?"

You shrugged, looking past me and out the window. "I don't know. I like being with Sullivan. I like watching TV."

Oh, jeez.

"No, I mean, what are your hobbies? Interests? Things you might want to do as a job someday?" I wanted to add a few other questions. Why didn't you currently have a job? How did you even pay for your place? And what exactly brought you to Folsom? But I had to take it slow. Act flippant. Avoid coming on too strong.

When you didn't readily answer, I started us off. "Before getting pregnant with Aaron, I'd dreamed of being a journalist. I majored in English at Rafael's suggestion because he thought it gave me more options. I could teach or work at a company, but I minored in journalism because that's what I wanted to do."

"Like on TV? Like a newscaster or something?"

"No, like write for a magazine or newspaper."

"God, do people still read those?"

Irritation bubbled up inside of me like champagne before it's uncorked. "Yes, people still read them."

"Oh. Right. Like on their phones and stuff. Gotcha."

I shook my head, and blew out a breath. "Anyway, what about you? Were you in school or anything before getting pregnant with Sullivan?"

"Yeah, I was, but I didn't really know what I wanted to do or anything. So it wasn't a big deal to drop out for me."

Deciding to give it another shot, I asked, "What school were you at?"

"Oh." You shook your head. "A small junior college. You wouldn't even recognize the name probably."

Disappointed, I frowned. *I was getting nowhere.*

"Well, hopefully you'll get to go back someday."

"Yeah. Maybe." You took the last bite of your eggs. A baby's cry filled the air.

Aaron.

My heart leaped.

"Oh. Sullivan's up." You pushed back from the table.

Oh. Right. Sullivan. Of course. I knew that.

As you went upstairs, I cleared the table and cleaned up the breakfast dishes. When you came back down you had Sullivan in your arms and the diaper bag secured on your shoulder. I couldn't help but notice the look of relief on your face.

"Thanks for everything."

"You're leaving?"

"Yeah, we gotta get home."

"You sure? You're welcome to stay longer. Raf's gone for the weekend and I have this big house all to myself. Honestly, you can stay as long as you like…even after the weekend." If there was even the slightest chance that baby was related to me, I wanted him here.

You nodded, backing away from me. "Yeah. Sorry."

It was strange. The night before you'd kept going on and on about how awesome it must've been to live in this house. But this morning you seemed so anxious to leave.

Was I missing something?

When you raced out of the house with Sullivan in your arms as if you couldn't wait to get out of here, I wondered if I'd gotten it all wrong. Were you nothing more than a stranger with my same name? Was this all a coincidence?

You need to see a therapist. You're talking crazy.

Rafael's voice flew through my mind, followed by Dr. Hillerman's words.

You're seeing things that aren't there, Kelly.

CHAPTER
FIFTEEN

Isabella Grace Medina.

That was my daughter's name. She was born almost two years after Aaron. When we brought her home from the hospital it felt like a dream. Like it was too good to be true. I'd been an only child growing up, and I'd always wished for a big family. It seemed like I was getting my wish. Rafael and I already had our boy and now we had our girl.

And she was perfect. She had the same thick black hair as Aaron. The same olive skin, the same heart-shaped lips. In the weeks after her birth, I couldn't get enough of her. Aaron was surprisingly great with her too. I mean, he dealt with the occasional jealousy when I held her too long or had to choose her over him. But for the most part, it was clear he was falling in love with her the same way I was. He'd pat her head and sing her silly songs. He'd kiss her cheek and sit in front of her making funny faces. He had a hard time understanding why she couldn't interact or play with him.

I kept assuring him she would one day.

That may have been the first time I lied to my son.

Rafael was sweet with Isabella. He helped change her diaper and he took care of her in the early mornings so I could get some sleep. But he didn't bond with her the way I did. I wasn't too worried about it, though, because he'd been the same way with Aaron.

When I was concerned about it back then, Carmen explained to me that some men struggled with the baby stage. And I understood that. With Aaron I'd had mild postpartum depression. Perhaps men went through something similar.

Now I wasn't so sure.

Rafael's distance from Aaron never seemed to resolve. It didn't magically change after Aaron stopped being an infant. To be honest, Rafael always seemed to be a little jealous of his son. I'd often blame myself. I knew I overindulged him. I was a little overbearing. I liked to keep Aaron close.

I sometimes wonder now if I still would've been that way had Isabella survived. But I guess I'll never know.

Isabella died when she was two months old.

I wasn't even home. I was out with a few friends that night. It was the first time I'd left her. And it wasn't like she was with a stranger or a sitter. Rafael and Aaron were home. That's why I hadn't been worried. Rafael had assured me they'd be fine. He even said it would be the perfect time for him to bond with his kids.

I'd even convinced myself that it was best if I left. That I was helping.

So while I was laughing and chatting and throwing back glasses of wine, my daughter was dying in her crib.

SIDS.

I wanted an explanation. A reason. But I never got it.

I never got to hold my baby girl again either.

* * *

"Do you blame Rafael for what happened to your daughter?" Dr. Hillerman asked, tenting his fingers the way he always did.

"No," I lied. "I blame myself."

"Why is that?" His brows furrowed.

I forced my gaze away from them. I swear they'd grown bushier since the last time I was here.

"Because I should've been home."

"But you know that's not rational, right? I mean, there's nothing you can do to prevent SIDS."

That's what I'd been told. But I knew better. If I'd been home I could've made sure she was lying on her back, and that there weren't any blankets or toys in her crib. Rafael never paid attention to stuff like that. And whenever I tried to remind him, he'd say I was nagging and that he knew what he was doing.

Clearly, he'd ignored my instructions because she was facedown when I found her.

"I guess I'll never know," I said.

"But it's something you still think about a lot, huh?"

I shook my head. "Not a lot. Actually, for a while I didn't think about her at all."

"What changed?"

You, Kelly. You changed things. I cleared my throat. "My friend Kelly—remember the one I told you about?"

Dr. Hillerman glanced down at the pad of paper in his lap. He tapped the end of his pen against it. "The one with your same name and the new baby?"

I nodded. "Well, she spent the night on Friday and I had to find something for her baby to sleep in. I went in the shed and found Aaron's old bassinet. But while I was in there I also found a box of Isabella's stuff."

"That must've been hard for you."

"It was." I stared past Dr. Hillerman to gaze out the small window behind his back. It didn't overlook anything except for the wall of the building next door. It was dreary and gray, dust coating it. "I found this blanket. It was fuzzy and pink..." My words trailed off for a second as I pictured it. Closing my eyes, I conjured up the soft feel of it between my fingertips, the powder-like scent it held the morning after Sullivan used it. "I'd bought it for Isabella as a Christmas gift, but she died before ever using it." My throat tightened. I swallowed hard against the lump rising in it. Blinking, I stared at the gray wall again. "But Kelly's son only had this flimsy, thin blanket with him on Friday night. So I wrapped him up in Isabella's. He slept with it all night." I smiled. "In Aaron's bassinet right next to my bed." Warmth spread through me at the memory.

"You had your friend's baby in your bedroom?" Dr. Hillerman narrowed his eyes and pursed his lips. Why was he acting so strange about this?

"Yeah." I shrugged. "She was passed out on the couch. I figured he'd be more comfortable in my room. Aaron always liked sleeping next to my bed."

"Isabella hadn't used the bassinet?"

I shook my head.

"I see." Dr. Hillerman wrote something on his pad of paper. My shoulders tensed. "And is that part of the reason you blame yourself?"

"That wasn't my fault." I snorted bitterly. "That was all Rafael's decision."

"She's not sleeping in here," Rafael said firmly.

"But she has to. She's a baby."

Rafael sighed with exasperation. "Lots of babies sleep in cribs, Kel. That's why they make cribs. For babies to sleep in."

"Yes. Babies. Not newborns."

"Same difference."

"It's really not."

"We just got one baby out of our room. We're not bringing in another one."

"It'll just be for a few months," I insisted.

"That's what you said with Aaron and he was in here for two years."

Desperation bloomed in my chest when I pictured my sweet baby girl a whole room away. What if she needed me?

As if reading my mind, Rafael came closer. He snatched up my hands. "We'll have the baby monitor in here. She'll be fine." He kissed my fingers then, his lips soft and warm. "Our bedroom should be a place where you and I can connect...without the kids." Rafael winked then and my knees softened. I knew I wouldn't argue anymore.

"So, you do blame Rafael, then?"

I always did this. Said too much. Didn't guard my words. "I mean, maybe a little."

"You blame him for Aaron being gone too. Do you think this contributes to the problems between you two?"

Sweat beaded along my forehead and across my shoulder blades. Blowing out a breath, I wiped it with the back of my hand. "It doesn't matter anyway," I muttered, desperate to talk about something else. "I can't change the past. I can only move forward, right?"

"And that's what you're trying to do, right? With your friend? The one you're helping with the baby?"

"Yeah." I exhaled with relief, grateful to be on the subject of you rather than me. Sitting up, I felt a little more in control. "Exactly. I guess helping her is kind of like a form of redemption."

"I see." He was writing again.

Shit. What had I said wrong this time? "Or maybe not redemption. I don't know. I mean, I'm just doing what's right. Like I said before, she needs a lot of help. She has no idea what she's doing, and she has no one."

"Kind of like you when you had Aaron."

I bristled. "I had a lot of people. My parents. Raf's parents. Friends. Raf."

"Hmm." Wearing a pensive expression, he tapped his pen to his chin. "I know you've always been close to your in-laws, particularly your mother-in-law. But from what you've told me, I didn't think you had a good relationship with your own parents."

I had forgotten how honest I'd been with Dr. Hillerman. "Yeah, I mean, I guess we're not that close. But they were around at least."

"Do you still talk to them now?"

"Well, Carmen passed away," I said, emotion thick in my throat. I often wondered if things would be different if she was still alive. She always made things better for me. Dr. Hillerman leaned forward, eyeing me. I cleared my throat. Sat taller. "And Rafael's dad lives in a retirement community in the Bay Area. Rafael visits him once a week, I think."

Probably spends more time with him than me.

"And your parents?"

"They're dead."

"But they're not, are they?"

"To me they are."

CHAPTER SIXTEEN

The house was deafeningly quiet. I cleaned up, and then took a shower. After getting dressed, I glanced down at the bassinet, the pink blanket bunched into a ball. I picked it up and held it up to my face. Sullivan's fresh scent drifted from it.

My heart ached.

The silence strangled me.

Why had you been so quick to leave? Didn't you like it at my house? I knew Sullivan did. He was happy here. Content. Safe. It was selfish of you to take him back to that dingy backyard apartment.

I'd offered you a home. A nice one at that. Safety. A helper. Why hadn't you taken me up on it? Honestly, it made no sense.

It was almost winter. That place you lived in was a dump. I think it had been a garage before. Who knew if it even had proper heating?

Babies needed warmth.

There was clearly no way to convince you to stay here. You were desperate to leave.

Damn you, Kelly.

Why were you making this so difficult?

Biting my lip, I dropped the blanket back into the bassinet. I couldn't sit around all day in this big, empty house. I needed to do everything in my power to make sure Sullivan was safe.

Before leaving my room, I glanced back one last time at the bassinet. There was no reason to put it away. It would be needed again.

Very soon, if I had my way.

Bolt cutters.

Black gloves.

Black beanie.

Dark clothing.

Check, check, check and check.

Even with my checklist and all my Google searching, I still had no idea what I was doing. My friends always said you could find anything on Google. Christine was always watching YouTube videos on stuff from how to fix her hair to how to organize her closet or make a garden in a backyard. One time she even DIYed her way to new cabinets in her kitchen.

But I'd been on Google for hours and I still didn't know how to successfully shut off your electricity. Standing in your yard in the middle of the night staring down at your electrical panel wasn't helping.

I mean, sure, I could've simply turned the switch off. But that'd be too easy a fix. I thought for sure there'd be a cord or something I could cut, hence the bolt cutters lying near my feet.

Cool air kissed my cheeks. I shivered. If Raf was here

with me, he'd be wearing shorts and a thin shirt, and probably wouldn't even be that cold. But I was a California girl through and through. Anything below sixty degrees was freezing to me.

A twig broke. Something moved in a nearby bush. I squealed, and then hurriedly clamped my mouth shut.

Calm down, Kel. It was probably an animal or something.

It was pitch-black out here. The moon was nothing but a sliver in the sky and the stars were all covered up by clouds. Your backyard didn't have any lights shining in it. Instead, it was shrouded in trees and darkness. I'd been using my phone as a flashlight.

A real flashlight was probably something I should've added to my checklist.

Sighing, I walked quietly around the side of the house, looking for another electrical panel. Even after walking the perimeter, I didn't find one. Was this really the only one on the property? Was your electricity tied to the main house?

When Rafael's mom died, we'd talked about taking his dad in. We'd looked into building in-law quarters. Something similar to what you're living in. Thinking back, I did remember that the guesthouse would pull from our electricity.

I bit my lip. So, even if I figured out a way to cut off the electricity, I wouldn't simply be affecting you. I'd be affecting that sweet old woman you rented from. I pictured her freezing cold inside her house, all frail and thin-skinned.

Old people and babies. Those were the people who couldn't handle the cold. Well, them and me.

I imagined Sullivan inside your guesthouse, kicking off his blanket like he always did, revealing bare legs since you rarely put him in pants. Moisture filled my mouth and I gagged.

What was I doing out here?

Had I really stooped this low?

I'd spent my day trying to figure out how to turn off someone's electricity in order to force them to move in with me? Aaron's face emerged in my mind. What would he think if he could see me right now? And if that was his son in there? He'd never forgive me for putting Sullivan in danger. Then again, how much danger would you have been in? It's not like it's freezing here. No one would've died if the electricity went out. You would have merely been cold, and uncomfortable. And that's when I planned to call you and subtly slip into the conversation the fact that I was sitting next to a warm fire sipping a delicious glass of red wine. No doubt, you'd see the error of your ways and take me up on my offer to stay at my house.

No harm. No foul. And everyone would be safe.

Stepping away from the electrical panel, I shook my head. What was wrong with me? I was seriously trying to justify this?

This wasn't me. I'd never done anything like this in my life.

Well, I mean, except that one time…

But that was different. Completely different. Besides, I hadn't been in my right mind then. I couldn't use that same excuse tonight.

I glanced down at my gloves, the bolt cutters. My heart seized. I was pretty sure this was a crime. A car sounded in the distance, my breath hitching in my throat. Swallowing hard, I bent down and picked up the bolt cutters.

There had to be another way to get you and Sullivan to stay at my house. A way that didn't end with me in jail.

This was all your fault, Kelly. Look what you'd driven me to. Why were you insisting on staying here alone, when I could help keep Sullivan safe?

Holding the bolt cutters low at my side, I crept toward the guesthouse. It was dark, all the blinds closed.

You still hadn't fixed the little kink in the front blinds. Squinting, I bent down and strained to see inside. Were you both asleep or had Sullivan woken up for his midnight feeding? It was too dark to make anything out. If I didn't know better I'd say this place was empty. Uninhabited. A vacant building in the backyard of an old woman's home.

A noise from behind caught my attention. Hairs prickling on my arms, I spun around. Inside the main house, a light flicked on. When the back door started to open, I leaped to the ground, crawling toward a nearby tree. Hiding behind it, I froze, holding my breath.

A cat meowed.

I didn't move.

The door closed, the sound of the lock clicking back in place reverberating through the silence of the night. I waited a few minutes before moving, though. When I saw the cat racing past me, I finally stood.

It wasn't until I was safely in my car before I saw the blood on my hands.

In my haste to hide, I'd nicked my finger with the bolt cutters.

Yeah, I seriously was not cut out for a life of crime.

After finding a Kleenex in my purse, I pressed it to the cut to stop the bleeding. The cut wasn't very deep. It only needed some Neosporin and a Band-Aid, both of which I had, so I turned on the engine and headed home.

As I drove down the darkened streets, I thought about how this was something Rafael and I would've laughed about when we were dating. He was always pulling crazy stunts—stealing alcohol and cigarettes, crashing parties he wasn't invited to. I was the good one. The rule follower. Afraid to join in his adventures.

But I guess this was way different than that. And there was no way I was ever telling him about it.

When I was first choosing a major in college, I toyed with the idea of law school. Justice is something I believe in. Good winning out over evil. The righteous prevailing. Debate and speech classes were always my favorite, along with English. I'd once taken a criminal justice class and loved it. A professor of mine had even encouraged me to think about becoming a lawyer.

It was Rafael who'd talked me out of it, encouraging me to pursue writing since being a journalist was what I'd always talked about when we first met. And, according to him, writing was what I was good at.

So, I majored in English, and eventually became a stay-at-home mom.

But I still remembered some of the things I'd learned in my criminal justice class. Or maybe I only remembered the stuff I'd learned from all the crime dramas I watched on TV and the legal thrillers I liked to read.

Either way, when I got home from my disastrous midnight trip to your house, I decided to take a safer, legal approach to getting Sullivan into my home.

It was time to think like an adult. A professional. A responsible citizen.

After pouring myself a glass of wine (necessary to calm my nerves), I went and found the journal I'd bought on impulse the last time Christine and I went shopping. Now I finally had a reason to use it. Sitting on the couch, I spread the empty journal over my lap. I thought for a moment before drawing a line in the center of the clean page.

Whether or not Sullivan was related to me (and I still felt like he was), he wasn't safe with you. You'd made that clear when you raced out of here the other morning. My house was clearly the right choice for the two of you, and yet you selfishly took your son back to that mold-infested, thin-walled guesthouse. A mom puts her child's needs ahead of her own, and you rarely did that.

Pen poised over the paper, I tried to recall dates, times, incidents.

Then I started writing them down, carefully, methodically, with as much detail as possible. If I couldn't get what I wanted by playing dirty, I'd do it by keeping my nose clean.

By gathering evidence. Proving my case.

It might take longer, but in the end it would be worth it.

CHAPTER SEVENTEEN

I learned a lot about you.

You weren't a health nut like Christine. You liked your chips and dip, your candy and soda. Must've been nice to have that young woman metabolism. After living in a world of gluten and peanut allergies, no red dyes and organic foods only, it was weird how shamelessly you walked around your house holding a bag of Doritos in one hand, a soda can in the other.

You spent way too much time watching mindless reality TV, and when you weren't doing that you were glued to your phone. Often even when you held Sullivan you stared at your phone over his head.

It was sad, actually. The way technology had taken over our lives. When Aaron was a baby, we read books all the time. I'd read to him and then I'd stick him in my lap while I read my novel and he'd flip through his own books.

I'd never seen you read a book.

Were you a reader at all, Kelly? Had you ever been?

It would be a shame not to instill a love of reading in Sullivan. Just one more thing I was going to have to do for you.

You wore your hair different throughout the day. One minute it would be long and straight, and the next it would be up in a bun. By evening, you might have it in a ponytail or little braids.

How you had time to mess with your hair so often while tending to a baby was beyond me.

My hair was in a perpetual ponytail when I had babies.

I had to be careful when watching you. It's not like I could park on the curb and watch from my car. You knew what I drove. So did your landlord. That's why I parked down the street and walked down to your place. I always wore workout clothes, a hat and sunglasses. There were so many joggers down here, I easily blended in.

Since you lived in the older part of Folsom, there were plenty of trees and bushes. The newer subdivisions like ours had hardly any trees.

What I'm trying to say is that it wasn't difficult to find spots to hide out while watching you. It was easiest at night, though. You always left your blinds open, almost like you wanted to be watched. You also left every light on, as if you craved the spotlight.

Tonight, you put Sullivan to bed and then immediately started watching reality TV.

Your life made me sad, Kelly.

You needed friends. Connections.

And maybe a better understanding of nutrition. It's not like you were going to stay thin forever. Trust me.

My phone buzzed in my pocket, causing my pulse to jump-start. You had your phone pressed against your ear. Were you calling me? You'd been avoiding me all week. I'd texted you multiple times, asking if you wanted to hang out. But you always said you were busy. Funny, you never looked busy. Often, when I texted I was standing right outside your window. Your excuses never matched your reality.

I didn't want to stand out here in the cold like some weirdo stalker. But you gave me no choice. I had to keep an eye on Sullivan. I'd wanted it to be at my house. I'd invited you to stay there. In a warm, big house where you'd have your own room and someone to help with your baby.

But you said no.

You chose this—this dump where neither you nor your child was safe, and where you spent all your time on your phone or watching reality TV.

Shaking my head, I sighed, and yanked out my phone.

It was Rafael. I stepped away from the tree and made my way down the street.

"Hi, Raf," I greeted him, walking briskly.

"Where are you? You sound out of breath?"

I still hadn't told him about you or my suspicions. No need to give him any more ammunition against our son. He was the reason for Aaron's silence, for his disappearance from our lives. If Raf knew what I was thinking, he'd make everything worse. "Oh, I'm just taking a walk."

"Is it nice there? It's pretty cold here."

It was always colder in the Bay Area. That's why I didn't enjoy it there. "It's a little chilly. I mean, colder than it normally is in October, but it's not bad. It feels good to be out in it," I said. "And you know how much I love to exercise."

A pause. "I know how much you used to love exercise. You know, before…"

My chest tightened. I sucked in a breath. "Well, now I do again."

"That's great."

"Yeah." I nodded, even though he couldn't see me. A

car drove past. They'd have no reason to notice me. Still, I turned slightly from the street, only the back of my hood visible to onlookers.

You could never be too careful. *Right, Kelly?*

"What else have you been up to today?" he asked.

I shook my head, weary of our conversation already. When had our marriage turned into this? Conversations that sounded more like a job interview or first date than years of togetherness. We used to talk about deep stuff. Profound stuff that mattered. Like our values. Beliefs. Ideas. Hopes. Dreams.

Then again, maybe it was safer this way.

Did I really want to know Rafael's hopes and dreams? Did he want to know mine? Would they match up at all? I doubted it.

"Oh, nothing exciting," I responded. "Errands, cleaning the house…" *Spying on the other Kelly.* "What about you? How was your day?"

"Good. I have some really promising students this year, so that's cool. There's this one kid. Trevor. He's taken a real interest in my class. He reminds me so much of myself when I was younger."

I rolled my eyes. Yeah, I knew how much he liked his students. He'd always taken a lot more interest in them than in his own son.

He's nothing like me, Rafael used to say about Aaron as if that was a bad thing. An unforgivable thing.

Maybe to him it was.

After hanging up with Rafael, I hurried back toward your house. A young man made his way to your front door. My heart stopped. Was this a friend? Boyfriend?

Was this who you were talking to on the phone? You'd

never mentioned anyone else to me, so I had no idea if you had other friends in the area. I'd felt sorry for you, thinking you were all alone in the world. But maybe you weren't.

Inching closer, I hid behind a large tree trunk and watched. The hairs on the back of my neck stood on end. A rough breeze skated along my skin as a car drove by.

You opened the door slightly and reached your hand out. That's when I noticed the bag in the young man's hand.

My heart sank. It was a delivery person.

Frustrated, I sighed.

Ella appeared in the kitchen window, peeking out. I shivered as her gaze fell to the tree I was standing behind. She held her gaze for a beat too long. *Could she see me?* Her eyes narrowed.

This was a waste of time anyway. I needed to get out of here.

Spinning around, I walked swiftly down the street toward my car.

I woke to a baby crying.

It was loud. Insistent. Near.

I tossed my covers off and leaped out of bed. The hardwood floor was cold on the soles of my feet. Goose bumps slithered up my calves. I shivered. Hugging myself, I hurried toward the bassinet next to my bed. Dropping to my knees on the floor, I landed with a thud. I bit my tongue. A copper taste filled my mouth. I gagged.

"Aaron?" I reached inside.

My stomach plummeted, my body going cold. The bassinet was empty.

"Aaron?" I screamed, my hands frantically searching

the bassinet. I snatched out the blanket, bringing it to my face. It smelled fresh and clean, like a baby.

Isabella?

No. I shook my head.

She was gone.

It was Aaron's.

Where was he?

My heart pounded in my chest.

I couldn't lose another one. Where was he? Gripping the blanket so tight my knuckles hurt, I raced out of the bedroom. The crying continued, but it was farther away. I stopped running, honed in on the sound. It was coming from downstairs.

I tore down them, almost slipping a couple of times. When I got to the bottom, the crying stopped. I froze, my heart arresting.

"Aaron?" I called out, inspecting the room.

A picture stared back at me. A teenager with braces and tousled hair. My breathing was shallow. I walked forward, slowly, with trepidation. My heartbeat matched my footsteps as it slowed down. I picked up the picture.

"Aaron," I breathed out, tracing his face.

Blinking, I glanced down at my other hand—the one that held the blanket.

Whose baby was crying?

Who was in the bassinet?

Setting down the picture, I heard it again. The wailing. But it was in the distance. Outside? I padded across the floor, quickly reaching the window. I pulled back the curtain. A woman stood on my front lawn, hair whipping in the breeze, a baby in her arms.

I screamed and stepped back.

She looked just like me.

With shaky hands, I pulled the curtain back again. The lawn was empty. No one was there. I blinked a few times. Had I been seeing things?

I stepped closer to the glass, pressing my face against it. The coolness seeped into my skin. It actually felt good. Made me feel alive.

The street was empty, the houses all dark and closed up. It was eerily quiet. No baby crying. No noise at all.

But I swore I heard it. It was loud. Clear.

And the woman on the front lawn seemed real. But she also looked exactly like me. So it couldn't have been real, could it?

Was I dreaming? I pinched the skin on my forearm. I squeezed my eyes closed and then opened them again. Nope. Nothing changed. Still here. Still standing in my family room, staring out at my empty front lawn.

CHAPTER EIGHTEEN

As a kid I was terrified at night. Darkness breathed life into my imagination. Innocuous items like laundry hanging over a chair or toys in the corner morphed into monsters, evil creatures. A cold sweat would coat my body as I lay in bed, covers up to my chin. I also had horrible nightmares. As the sun went down every evening, my neck would prickle, my chest tightening as I anticipated what was to come. Anxiety would grip me tightly, holding me in place. All night I was rigid, tense, scared.

But then the sun would come out in the morning and my body would relax and my chest would expand. I could breathe easily, the terrors of the night disappearing with the darkness.

I wish it was that way now. But morning no longer brought me relief. The darkness followed me around, a perpetual black cloud hanging over my head.

This morning as I stood in my front window drinking mint tea, I stared out at the street. The lady was back with her kids, running around the front yard. A man left for work. A woman jogged down the sidewalk. It was less ominous than when it was pitch-black and quiet, yet fear and dread lingered in my stomach, rattled around in my chest like a lung infection.

Something wasn't right.

It hadn't been for a long time.

Breathing in the minty aroma, I spotted the pink baby blanket on the floor in the family room.

I pictured myself running down the stairs and pressing my face to the window. There were smudge marks on the glass which resembled my nose and cheeks.

Great.

After I finished my tea, I cleaned the glass and left the kitchen. When I reached the top of the stairs, something shiny caught my eye. Bending over, I picked it up. An earring. A tiny star earring. I turned it over in my palm, inspecting it. Costume jewelry. Silver in color only. Rusted in spots. Reaching up with my free hand, I touched my small gold hoops. I rarely wore silver. Even when I wore my costume jewelry, I preferred gold.

This wasn't mine.

As I stared at the earring nestled in my palm, it hit me where I'd seen it before. Not this exact earring, but something like it. A matching star ring. You'd worn one the day we'd gotten our nails done. In fact, you always wore cheap rings. You lined your fingers with them. Come to think of it, you always wore earrings like this too. Little studs. Nothing flashy. Nothing expensive.

It had to have been yours.

But how did it get here?

I'd cleaned the stairs the day after you and Sullivan had spent the night, so it couldn't have been here long.

Closing my fist around it, I spun around and raced down the stairs. Tearing out the front door, I ran across the front lawn. When I reached the spot where I thought I saw someone standing in the middle of the night, my breath hitched in my throat.

Two footprints.

I knew it. I wasn't crazy.

You'd been here. At my house. In the middle of the night. But why?

Friday morning I texted to see if you wanted to go to breakfast.

A few minutes later you replied that Sullivan had gone to bed late and was now napping. It was a lie. I'd been at your house until late. Sullivan went to bed early. In fact, I remembered thinking it was too early when you put him down.

But I placated you, replying with, I understand. Maybe next week.

Then I drove to your house, irritated that you were forcing me to stalk you. It was annoying. I wanted to hang out with you in a noncreepy way, but you weren't allowing it.

So, really, this was your fault.

I parked down the street, got out of my car, pulled my hood over my head and hurried down the sidewalk. Your car was gone. Your house was all closed up.

Huh.

Biting my lip, I glanced around, wondering where you'd gone. From watching you over the past few days, I'd learned that you rarely left the house.

I figured you must've been at the store or something and would be back soon. Needing to hit the store myself, I left.

Rafael and I had been invited to Christine and Joel's for dinner, so I only had to get food for Saturday and Sunday. I bought stuff Rafael liked: bagels, cream cheese, chicken, vegetables and his favorite chocolate ice cream.

It was like I believed I could summon him home with food.

When I told him about the invite from Christine he acted like he'd planned to come home this weekend, but I wasn't holding my breath.

As I shopped, I kept my eyes peeled for you. This was the closest grocery store to your house, so I assumed this was where you shopped. Maybe not.

Or maybe you were already back home.

After I left the store, I made my way to your place again.

Nope. You still weren't there.

I wanted to wait, but didn't want the chicken to spoil. Reluctantly, I went home and unloaded the groceries.

After everything was put away, I felt restless. Frustrated. I was starting to hate it. This house. This quiet. This emptiness.

I wanted noise again. A family. You'd teased me. Made me believe I could have that again. Or at the very least, a friend and a little baby I could watch over. And now that you'd cruelly ripped that away, I felt more alone than ever.

Sighing, I sent you a quick text asking if you and Sullivan got enough sleep. It's what a good friend would do, right? Check up on you? Maybe if I reminded you of how nice and helpful I was, you'd finally come around and stop avoiding me.

Hadn't you once called me an angel?

You texted back almost immediately.

Still pretty tired, actually. Think we'll just stay in today.

Stay in, huh?
I couldn't help it. I had to press.

So you've been in all day?

Yep, you texted back. Been holed up in here, resting.

It was the words *holed up* that threw me. Your blinds had been closed. No sign of life at your house. But maybe you were inside after all. Maybe this time you hadn't lied.

I glanced over at my bed. It was made, the comforter pulled tight, the pillows fluffed and neatly arranged, exactly the way Rafael liked. Everything clean and in its place. Rafael's biggest complaint had always been the house. It was messy, and he had no patience for it.

Some days I was so exhausted I couldn't stand it. Yet, I cleaned. I picked up. I straightened and organized.

To appease Rafael.

But when he was gone I could breathe easy. I could rest. The bed was left unmade. Dishes were piled in the sink. When Aaron was little, he'd make cities with his Legos all through the house and we'd leave it there for days.

You didn't have a Rafael.

You were free.

You could lie in bed all day with your bed unmade.

You could leave the blinds closed, the house dark. You could hole up in your house, as you said.

Jealousy struck me, hot and fast like a slap to the face. I was also hit with something else—reality.

You'd been avoiding me all week because I'd been like

Rafael. I'd pushed too hard. I'd tried to box you in. To control you.

But I wasn't the same as Rafael. My intentions had been good. I'd only been trying to help Sullivan.

You found me, Kelly. Remember? You could have stayed free, but you chose to find me. You brought this on yourself. If I'd been free, I would've stayed that way. I wouldn't have come here.

But you did.

And now that I knew about you, I couldn't let you go.

I couldn't let Sullivan go.

I'm sorry, Kelly, but that's the way it is.

Grabbing my jacket, I headed downstairs. The last thing I saw before leaving my room was the pink blanket. The one that once belonged to my daughter, but now belonged to Sullivan.

CHAPTER NINETEEN

You lied to me.

You weren't holed up at home all day.

I'd driven down your street multiple times and your car wasn't parked anywhere. Not even around the corner.

When a voice at the back of my mind told me it might be in the shop or something, I investigated further. I stared inside your apartment through the kink in your blinds. Since your place was so small, I could see into every room from my vantage point. It was dark. No movement anywhere.

You weren't home.

So, where were you?

I would've stayed at your house all day, waiting for you to return. Waiting to make sure Sullivan was with you and that he was safe. But I couldn't. Rafael was hopefully coming home, and we had plans with Christine and Joel tonight.

It was late afternoon when I slipped into my favorite black dress. Then I curled my hair and put on some mascara and lip gloss. I thought about you and your edgy hairstyles and dark lipsticks. What would Rafael think if I fixed my hair that way? If I wore a bold lipstick shade? Would it freak him out or would it turn him on the way the lingerie did?

Shuddering, I decided to stick with the nude gloss.

I was putting on my earrings when I heard Raf's ringtone. My chest tightened as I answered.

"My dad fell. He's in the hospital," Rafael said in a rush.

I'd been half expecting it. The phone call. An excuse. But not this one.

"I'm sorry. Is he okay?"

"I'm not sure. I'm headed there now." It was hard to hear Rafael's voice with all the noise behind him. It sounded like he had me on speaker while he was driving. He never did like using Bluetooth. "Please tell Christine and Joel I'm sorry I have to miss dinner. You go without me, though. I'll call you later."

"Okay." I hung up, my head spinning. Reaching down with a shaky hand, I fingered the thin gold strand around my neck, the one Rafael gave me a few birthdays ago.

My phone rang again, but it was my usual ringtone. Not Rafael's.

"Hey, girl." It was Christine.

"Hey."

"Just wanted to see what time you and Raf were coming, so I know when to put in the lasagna."

"You made lasagna?"

"No." Christine laughed. "I picked one up, but it needs reheating."

"Aah, okay. Well, Raf just called. His dad's in the hospital, so he won't make it."

Christine's gasp floated through the line. "Is he okay?"

"I don't know." Looking up, I stared at my reflection, at the wrinkles gathering around my eyes and across my forehead. They'd become more pronounced the last year or so. I thought about your unwrinkled skin, and the familiar jealousy wrapped around my heart.

I'd been jealous of people before. I'd sometimes coveted Christine's life. Her money. Wealth. Pretty clothes. When I was in high school, I was jealous of the cheerleaders and popular crowd. But this was different.

I didn't want to be you.

I'd *been* you.

I wanted to be where you were.

Time was fleeting. It went by too fast.

I guess what I really wanted was the last twenty years back.

"Kelly?" Christine's voice startled me.

I blinked. "Sorry. What were you saying?"

"Are you on your way, then?"

"Um…" I bit my lip, wondering if you were home yet. Since Rafael wasn't coming home, I thought about going back to your place and checking on you. But at Christine's there'd be food and wine. It would be comfortable and fun. That sounded so much more appealing than standing outside your house hiding behind a tree. "Yeah. I'll leave in a minute."

"Cool. See ya soon."

I thought about changing out of the black dress, but I hadn't been wearing it for Rafael anyway. Christine would be dressed nice. She always was when having people over for dinner. I did change out of my flats and into boots, though, since they were more comfortable.

I headed out the front door and before I knew it I was sitting in Christine's living room, already through half a glass of red wine. Christine sat next to me, her legs propped up on the coffee table. Joel sat across from us in the recliner. I tucked my feet up under my body and held the wine in my lap.

"Too bad Rafael couldn't make it," Joel said after taking a swig of his craft beer. He always drank his beer from a frosted mug rather than in a bottle or can. When he held his large beer mug, foam fizzing out the top, I thought he looked like he was on a commercial. He had that moviestar vibe already with his perfectly gelled dark hair, contrasting light blue eyes and supertanned skin. All the other women we hung out with thought Joel was the most handsome of all our husbands. I never thought so. Don't get me wrong. He was good-looking, but also sort of fake looking. He didn't have the natural charm that Raf had.

"I know," I said with the right amount of disappointment. Truth is, I was relieved. I was much more at ease without him here.

"I hope his dad is all right," Christine added, sticking out her bottom lip in a sympathetic pout.

"Me too." I glanced down at my phone, surprised he hadn't called or texted yet. Surely, he'd made it to the hospital by now.

"I wanted to tell him the good news," Joel said. "But I guess you'll have to tell him for me."

"What good news?" I raised my brows, sitting up a little taller.

"The lead Rafael sent me panned out. I had an interview yesterday." Joel smiled, his impossibly white teeth gleaming as the yellow glow from the nearby lamp reflected off of them.

"That's great." Curious, I shifted in my seat. "I didn't realize Rafael had sent you a lead on a job." Or that he would even have a lead for Joel. It's not like they worked in the same field. "I didn't even know he had any connections to financial planners."

"Well, it was indirectly," he explained. "A family member of a lady he knows."

My eyes caught Christine's. She quickly shook her head. "I think it was just a woman he works with at the university. Isn't that right, Joel?"

I forced a smile and nodded, even though my stomach soured. "How did the interview go? Did you feel good about it?" I'd learned over the years that interviews didn't always mean anything. For a little while, Rafael had been trying to find a job closer to home. He'd been on several interviews and they never amounted to anything.

Joel's smile grew. His gaze landed on Christine and she grinned back. When was the last time Raf and I looked at each other like that?

"They offered me the job today," Joel said.

"Congratulations," I said.

"Thanks." He lifted his mug to his lips.

"Wow. That happened so fast," I added. Must've been some recommendation by Rafael.

"I know. He was only out of a job for like a week or something. And it literally couldn't have come at a better time," Christine interjected. "Before he got the job, I was totally stressing out. Our dishwasher went out this week and Maddie has to buy a bunch of stuff for cheerleading tryouts, and then yesterday the brakes on my car started squeaking. When it rains, it pours, am I right?"

When it rains, it pours.

Swallowing hard, I nodded.

Red-and-blue lights flashing in our driveway. Opening the door, two cops standing on our front porch.

"Give me back my son!" The baby being ripped from my arms, leaving them cold and empty.

Rafael driving away, not looking back. Not once.

"Kelly?" Christine's voice yanked me back. "You okay?"

"Yeah." Lifting my wineglass, I took a careful sip. "I'm really happy for you guys."

Her head cocked to the side slightly, her gaze catching her husband's. "Hey, Joel, you wanna take the lasagna out of the oven?"

"Sure."

When he left the room, Christine sat up, scooting to the edge of her chair. "You sure you're okay? You seem kinda distracted tonight. Is it about Raf?"

"Um…yeah, I guess, I'm kinda worried about him." *Liar.* Her hand touched my knee. "He'll be fine."

"Yeah, I know. You're right."

She paused, studying me. "It's more than that, though, huh?"

At her concerned tone, I crumbled. "I'm just feeling sorta lonely lately, that's all. The silence and that big house…it's all getting to me."

"Yeah, I get that," Christine said softly. Then she suddenly smiled. "Hey, I know. You can stay here this weekend if you want. The kids are with their grandparents all weekend."

It was tempting, but I shook my head. "Thanks for the offer, though."

"You sure?"

"I don't want to impose on your alone time with Joel."

I could tell she wanted to protest because that's what

kind of friend she is, but instead she smiled. "Yeah, it's actually been forever."

"What's been forever?" Joel stood in the doorway of the living room.

Christine shot up. "Since I ate. Is dinner ready?"

"Yep."

"Awesome." Standing, she smiled at me. "You want more wine?"

I drained the rest of my glass and then nodded. Rafael's ringtone sounded from where my phone sat on the coffee table. I flinched, my pulse jump-starting.

Laughing, Christine took my glass. "You answer. We'll be in the dining room."

Turning my back on her, I pressed the phone to my ear. "Raf?"

"Hey." He sounded tired, far away.

"How's it going?"

"I don't know much, but it's not looking good."

"How did he fall?"

"Not sure. He's not making much sense. He does keep talking about you, though."

"Really? What's he saying about me?"

"He thinks you've been here. That you've visited recently."

"What?" Guilt racked me. It had been way too long since I had gone to see him.

"Honestly, he's saying a lot of odd things. He's pretty delusional." Noises broke into our conversation. "Um… Sorry, Kel, I gotta go."

"Oh. Okay."

"I'll call later?"

I opened my mouth to respond, but a deadly click sounded in my ear.

I stared down at the phone in my hand, a sick feeling descending into my gut.

"Everything okay?" Christine appeared in the doorway.

I swallowed hard. "Um…yeah, I think so. Raf didn't really know much."

"Is he coming home tonight?"

"It didn't sound like it."

"Well, remember, my offer still stands."

"Thanks, but I'll be fine." After telling my best friend yet another lie, I followed her into the dining room.

CHAPTER TWENTY

Early Sunday morning, I sat at the kitchen table eating cereal and drinking tea. I listened to the house settle, the clock tick, dogs bark in the distance. This was what my life had become. Quiet and empty. Leaning back, I yawned. I hadn't slept well. Thoughts of you and Sullivan crowded my mind, making sleep impossible.

Glancing over at the chair Aaron always sat in when he lived here, I imagined him bent over a plate of cookies. I used to bake all the time when he was growing up. He loved milk and cookies after school, even when he was a teenager. Raf thought I should feed him something more nutritious, but it's not like he ate it every single day. Besides, he was a growing boy. A cookie every once in a while wasn't going to kill him.

"Who was that girl you were talking to after school today?" I asked him as he took a generous bite of his chocolate-chip cookie.

After swallowing it down and wiping sticky chocolate from the side of his mouth, he glanced up. His hair was tousled, messy across his forehead. "Oh, that's Tessa. The girl Ben was dating."

I nodded. "You haven't brought Ben around much lately."

"Yeah." He shrugged. "We're kinda not hangin' out as much."

Interesting. I raised a brow. "Is this because of Tessa?"

"I mean, kinda, I guess."

"Do you like her?"

"Tessa?" His voice heightened. "She's cool, but I'm not like into her or anything."

"Is it because of Ben? Like you'd be breaking the guy code?" I asked, proud of myself for sounding so hip and in the know.

Until Aaron's face scrunched up and he kind of laughed. "No, Mom. Not because of a guy code. Ben wouldn't care if I dated her. He doesn't really care about girls at all. Just uses 'em."

"Oh." My gut dipped. Sometimes I forgot how old these boys were now. I remembered when Aaron was a little boy and I'd take him and Ben to the park. It was hard to imagine that same boy was using girls for sex now. I swallowed hard. "But... I mean, you don't... I mean, well, you're not having..."

Aaron shook his head vehemently. "No, Mom."

Nodding, I exhaled with relief.

When Aaron was living at home, we talked all the time. He shared a lot with me. More than most boys did with their mothers. Things had changed when he moved out. It was like his need to distance himself from Rafael had extended to me. It hurt, but I tried to understand it.

Still, I didn't think he'd keep you from me, Kelly. If

Aaron knew about his son, he would've told me. So there's only one explanation—he didn't know.

You're lying, Kelly.

Aaron would never tell you to get an abortion. And he would never stay out of Sullivan's life. No one knew the pain of rejection by his own father better than my son. I was certain he wouldn't inflict that on his own.

I was done with all your games.

Heart pounding in my chest, I picked up my phone. With quivering fingers, I typed a message to Aaron, telling him everything about you. Drawing in a long, steadying breath I held it momentarily. Then I pushed Send and released it.

The minute the bubble landed securely in our text thread, my phone started singing, "I know you want me..." I jumped, my shoulders tensing.

Breathing deeply, I answered. "Hey, how's it going?"

"Okay. Dad's got some broken bones, but other than that the doctors think he's fine," Rafael explained.

"Oh, good," I said, relieved.

"They're releasing him this morning," he continued. "But I don't want him by himself, so I might stay with him a few days."

"That's probably a good idea."

"I'm sorry I didn't make it home again this weekend," he said, his tone apologetic. I wanted to believe it, but wasn't sure I did. "I promise I'll make it up to you."

I didn't know what to say, how to answer. There was so much he needed to make up for. And I wasn't sure how he'd be able to.

All of the pain and secrets. They'd added up.

At this point it felt like it was too little, too late.

After hanging up, I made more tea. I was glad I'd given

up coffee years ago. I didn't need anything to make me more anxious than I already was.

As I finished it, I got a text from Christine.

Guess what? Joel got tickets to take the kids to a play tonight. So I'm free. Want to go out?

The thought of going out exhausted me. But I did want to hang out with Christine. Yesterday had been unbearably long and silent. I'd kicked myself for not taking Christine up on her offer to stay at her house.

Why don't you come over? We can have a girls' night in.

After shooting off the text, I headed up the stairs. When I reached my bedroom, her response came.

Sounds good. I'll bring wine.

Yesterday, I'd only gone by your house once. You weren't home.

As I made my bed, a panicked thought struck me. What if you'd taken off? What if you'd run off with Sullivan and I never saw either of you again?

The fitted sheet had come loose on one side. I stretched it tight, fastening it over the edge. My bare toes brushed over something furry and soft. Bending down, I found a little stuffed monkey hiding under my bed.

How did it get under here?

As I stood up, my gaze landed on the bassinet nearby. I remembered Sullivan waking up in the middle of the night and crying. I'd flung half my body off my bed, and dragged the diaper bag across the floor to find a pacifier inside. I'd knocked quite a few things out before finding what I was looking for.

I thought I'd cleaned everything up, but clearly I hadn't. As I tossed the pacifier into the bassinet, something else caught my attention. Something shiny was stuck in the fur of the monkey. Pieces of synthetic fur obscured most of it, as if it had been tangled there awhile. But as I picked up the monkey to get a closer look, a shudder ran down my spine.

I recognized it immediately.

"I want you to have these, son." Rafael held out his hand. A giant balloon with the words Happy 13th birthday *bobbed behind his head.*

"Really?"

My eyes dampened as I stared at the cuff links bearing the Medina family crest.

When Aaron's gaze shot to me, shock written on his face, I smiled and shrugged. I was as stunned as he was. Rafael hadn't told me he was going to do this. It was the nicest thing he'd ever done for his son, and in that moment I loved him fiercely.

"But they're yours," Aaron added, still afraid to fully accept the gift.

"And before that, they were my dad's. One day you'll pass them on to your son."

I pried the cuff link off the monkey and stared at it in disbelief.

Why did you have this?

Had you stolen it?

You were back home, thank god.

Relief flooded me. You hadn't taken off.

Your blinds were all the way open, giving me a straight

shot into your house. Sullivan rocked back and forth in his swing, his eyes bright, his mouth stretched wide. The rhythmic motion momentarily hypnotized me. The television played. I couldn't see you, but I guessed you were lying on the couch, probably with your hand elbow-deep in a bag of Doritos.

The jagged edge of your earring pierced the flesh of my palm as I watched from behind a tree. The cuff link burned like a flame in my pocket. I wanted to march right up to your front door and shove the cuff link in your face. Ask where you got it, and why you had it.

But I knew that wasn't the right way to play this. Maybe there was a logical explanation for why you had it. Maybe Aaron gave it to you. If so, I didn't want to make things worse.

I thought back over our conversations about Sullivan's dad. It seemed like the last interaction you'd had with him was when you were pregnant. According to you, he didn't know Sullivan. Hadn't met him.

And here you were. In my town.

There had to be a reason for that. Even though you were avoiding me, that still gave me hope.

A car sped down the street. Biting my lip, I shrank back. A breeze blew at my back, rustling my hair. When I saw a couple making their way down the street, I leaned against the tree, pulled out my cell phone and pressed it to my ear.

"Yeah…okay," I spoke into it, ducking my head and staring at the ground.

Once they passed, I put my phone down and turned toward your house again. I gasped. You were standing up, looking in this direction. I dropped to the ground, my heart hammering in my ears. My knees crashed into the mud hard and my teeth knocked together, causing a jolt of pain through my entire face. I cringed.

A door opened and closed. Footsteps neared me. My gaze shot around as I tried to come up with an escape route. But I knew there wasn't one. The minute I tried to move, you'd spot me again.

"Kelly?" Your voice rang out, your footsteps clattering. *Shit. Shit. Shit.*

I'd been careless.

"Kelly?" You came around the tree, your forehead gathered together, your lips cast downward.

"Um…hey." *Smooth. Real smooth.*

"What are you doing here?"

My throat was scratchy and dry. I swallowed. "Well… you haven't returned any of my texts or anything."

"So, you're spying on me?" Well, at least you didn't look scared of me anymore. Now you looked pissed.

"No." I pushed up off the ground and stood. The knees of my jeans were caked in mud. I wiped them to no avail. "I, um…came to see if you were okay. Then I dropped something on my way up to your door." I glanced down. It wasn't a lie. I did drop your earring when I fell. But I didn't see it now.

"What did you drop?" You spoke slowly, with suspicion. Your eyes were narrowed, your mouth pursed.

"An earring," I answered truthfully, hoping it would spark something.

Your face remained unchanged, your gaze shooting between my two ears. "But you're wearing both earrings."

"Oh." Reaching up, I fingered both ears and laughed in an embarrassed way. "Oh, jeez. I thought I was missing one. Okay, well, maybe I didn't drop anything." Thank god I never went into acting. This was a train wreck.

"Oookay." You dragged out the word in a way that told me you weren't buying any of this. "Well, Sullivan and I are fine. I'm sorry I haven't returned your texts. We've just been kinda having a rough week. And actually, I need to get back to him." You turned toward the guesthouse.

"Wait," I called after you, desperation blooming in my chest. "The monkey!"

"Huh?" You turned to me.

"That's why I came by… You left something at my house." I allowed the statement to linger, watching for a reaction.

Your expression didn't change. I studied your hardened face, lips taut, eyes narrowed. You were pretty, but hard-edged, jaded. Not at all like the girls my son usually dated. Doubt surfaced in my mind again.

I closed my eyes and blew out a breath.

A headache emerged, poking at my temples.

"Do you have it?" you asked, holding out your hand.

I thought of the earring on the ground and the cuff link in my pocket. "Have what?"

"The monkey." You spoke slowly, your eyebrows rising more with each word.

"Oh. Right. Nope. I forgot it."

"You came over to give it to me and you forgot it?"

"Yep." I laughed and shook my head. "Total space cadet right here."

You took a step back from me, your eyes watching me like I was a mental patient. I didn't blame you. "Okay, well,

I have to get inside. Sullivan's not feeling well. I'll call you when he's better."

I kept my mouth shut as you raced back to the guest-house. I'd already screwed up enough today.

CHAPTER
TWENTY-ONE

"Dad's back home. I'm helping him get settled," Rafael said.

"That's good," I answered, absently staring out the front window, a mug of tea on the table in front of me.

"I'm gonna spend the rest of the day organizing his stuff. This place is a disaster. You wouldn't believe it, Kel. He still has stuff from years ago cluttering up his counters. Old mail, grocery lists. It's a wonder he can find anything."

His words irked me, but instead of giving in to the irritation, I chuckled. "Listen to you. You're turning into a regular Suzy Homemaker."

He laughed lightly back. "I wouldn't go that far. It's a onetime thing."

"Figured," I muttered under my breath. It's not like he'd ever lifted a finger around here.

"What?"

"Nothing," I answered swiftly. Reaching out, I ran my fingertips along the edge of the mug. It was still too hot to drink. Plumes of steam rose and circled the air above it. "How is he doing mentally, though? Has he still been saying delusional stuff?" About seeing me, I wanted to add, but didn't want to sound like I was fishing. Or being a complete narcissist.

"He's actually been talking about Aaron a lot."

My body went hot, my mouth drying out. "What's he saying?"

"He's asking for him."

I sat forward, my fingers gripping the edge of the table tightly. "Has he... I mean, does he think Aaron's been visiting him too?" *Had he seen my son?*

"No," Rafael said softly. "He doesn't think he's seen Aaron. He *wants* to see him."

"Oh." I blew out a shaky breath and slumped back in my seat. It creaked beneath me.

"Kelly?"

"Yeah, I'm here." Reaching out, I snagged the laptop sitting on the edge of the table and yanked it over to me. Then I opened it and logged on.

"You okay?"

"Fine," I said, pulling up Facebook. "Are you taking tomorrow off work?"

"Not planning on it. Dad'll be okay. I can stay the night and then check on him again after classes. Plus, they take pretty good care of him here."

"Hmm." I was on Aaron's page now, scrolling through his news feed. There hadn't been anything new posted in months. It was all the same pictures. The same posts. The same messages from his friends.

I went into his friends list and clicked on Chase's picture—he'd been Aaron's roommate last year. His page came up, his posts filled with some game he clearly spent too much time playing.

Biting my lip, I went into his photo albums. My fingers were slick, the tips buzzing as I scrolled through them. When I found a bunch of shots that included Aaron, I started clicking on them.

I'd looked through all these pictures before dozens of times. Searching each one didn't bring any new information. Aaron was hardly in any of them anyway. His roommate seemed to love the camera, though, posing anytime it was near.

I was about to click out of one when my heart seized.

It was one I'd passed over before because Aaron wasn't in it. But there was a girl in the background that looked kind of like you.

"Kelly? What are you doing?" Rafael asked.

"Listening to you," I said, leaning over to look more closely.

"You seem distracted," he said, his tone was annoyed, a little impatient.

On the touch screen, I placed my thumb and forefinger on the picture and zoomed in to the girl standing in the background, talking to someone outside of the picture.

"Oh, my god."

"What?" Rafael asked in a concerned tone. "What's going on?"

"It *is* Kelly," I breathed. Your face was a little rounder, your hair darker, but it was you. I'd finally found proof. Aaron may not have been in this picture, but he was definitely at that party. And so were you.

This changed everything.

I was done staying silent. Playing it cool. Waiting for you to come forward when you were ready. *Screw that.*

"Raf, I have proof that Kelly knows Aaron."

"What are you talking about?"

"There's a picture. She's in a picture," I blurted out, my body surging with adrenaline. "It was on his roommate's page...from that night... I'd seen it, but he's not in it...but I mean, he was there. And so was Kelly. I mean, I knew she knew him. I knew all along, but now I have proof. Not just that she knew him, but that she was there that night..." I was rambling now. Talking too fast, but I didn't know how to slow down.

"I'm sorry, Kel. I'm not following. You're not making any sense."

I was shaking. Hysterical. I swallowed. Took a deep breath. I had to calm down so he'd listen. "I'm on Chase's Facebook page looking at his pictures."

"Kel," he said in that pitying tone I hated. "Why now? I thought things were getting better."

"They are. I'm getting better. I was just on here wanting to see if I could find any pictures of him with Kelly."

Silence.

"Raf?" Had I lost him?

"I'm here. I just don't understand. You're looking for pictures of yourself on Chase's page?"

"No. Not me. My friend Kelly. Remember I told you about her? My new friend." How did he not know who I was talking about?

"Oh. Right. The one with the baby that you bought all that stuff for," he said. "Her name is Kelly?"

"Yes!" Did he seriously not listen to me? Or had I really not told him her name? I couldn't be sure. I'd been keeping so many secrets.

"And she knows Aaron?"

"Yes. She's in a picture with him. And she had his cuff link. I found it in my room next to the bassinet, and—"

"The bassinet?" Rafael snapped. "What the hell are you talking about?"

"The bassinet isn't important. Didn't you hear me? Kelly knows our son. In fact, I think her baby may be—"

"Kel, you've got to stop this," he growled.

"What?" Confused, I drew the phone slightly away from my ear.

"God, I thought you were getting better, but now this."

"I am getting better. I just told you that," I insisted, but— "Oh, my god, do you think Kelly had something to do with what happened?"

"I can't do this anymore," Rafael said with a sigh. "You're not the only one who lost him, you know."

"Mrs. Medina? I'm afraid we have some bad news. It's about your son, Aaron."

"...found unresponsive in his dorm room... The paramedics did all they could..."

"Of course I know that."

"You're the reason I can't grieve him. Hell, I can't even talk about him like he's dead because you insist on acting like he's alive. But I'm done placating you. It's not helping. It's making you worse." His voice wavered. "You won't even let me turn off his phone. And I know you still call it."

"I like to hear his voice." A tear slid down my face.

"He's gone, Kel. You need to let him go."

I wiped the tear with the back of my hand and sniffed. "You think I don't know that? You think I don't feel his absence every single day of my life? I miss him. That's why I call and text. A boy needs his mom."

"He's dead. He doesn't need you anymore."

His words were like a hard punch to the gut. Holding my middle, I winced. "I need him, okay! I'm not crazy, Raf. I know Aaron is gone."

"You talk about him like he's alive and away at college."

"Yeah. So what? It makes it easier for me to pretend. Who is that hurting?"

"Me," Raf said. "It's hurting me."

Like a deflated toy, I slumped over. I'd made a mess of everything. Again.

"I know how much you loved him. I loved him too," Rafael continued.

"You had a shitty way of showing it," I muttered.

"What did you say?"

I folded in on myself under the intensity of his venomous tone. But he was too far away to hurt me, so I continued, "It was your crazy-high expectations that killed our son."

"He was partying, Kel. He drank too much, mixed pills. How is that my fault?"

"Seriously? Don't you remember what you said to him in your last conversation? You told him you were going to stop paying his college tuition if he didn't get his grades up."

"He was partying because he was a college kid and that's what they do. It had nothing to do with me or our conversation. If what I said had mattered to him at all he would've been studying, not partying."

I shook my head, anger simmering. "You always did choose to think the worst about him."

"And you always thought he was perfect."

"You sound like my mom."

Maybe if you hadn't indulged him so much he'd still be around. Kids need discipline, Kelly. You were always enabling him. The last words my mom ever spoke to me floated through my mind. If only Carmen had been alive when Aaron died. She would've said the right thing. She would've helped me. When I went to my mom, I had hoped that for once she'd be there for me. But she proved to be predictable. Dad too. He backed Mom. It's what he'd always done.

I don't know why I'd held on to the hope that this time would be any different.

"She was just trying to get you to move on," Rafael said in an exasperated tone.

"I can't do that," I confessed. "Aaron was my whole life. He meant everything to me."

There was a pause and then finally in a soft voice, Raf said, "Trust me, I know." Without another word, the phone clicked in my ear.

I dropped it on the table and drew in a ragged breath. I should've felt bad about what I'd said to Rafael, but I didn't. Oddly enough, I felt liberated. Lighter. I'd been holding all of that in for a long time.

Getting up from the table, I carried my mug to the sink. On my way, I glanced over at the couch we were sitting on when you told me blatant lies about my son.

He told me to get an abortion.

Lie. He would never do that. And now I had proof. You'd been with him after Sullivan was born.

Hands trembling, I dropped my mug into the sink. Only I dropped it a little too hard and it shattered.

My heart pounded in my chest so loud I could hear it in my ears. It caused my head to spin. The walls closed in around me as the events of the last couple of hours finally hit me. Taking a deep breath, I reached in to grab the cracked ceramic pieces. They were cold. Jagged. The largest pieces dug into my palms. I welcomed the pain of it, though. It gave me something tangible to hold on to. I felt like I was drowning. Having an out-of-body experience. Closing my fist around the broken pieces grounded me. After tossing the pieces into the trash, I wiped my palms on my pants, leaving a red trail in my wake.

What?

I held up my palms. One of them was coated in blood.

Thanks a lot, Kelly.

Blowing out a frustrated breath, I stormed down the hallway into the bathroom. It stung when I ran cold water over the broken skin. Once the blood mixed with the water and ran off my hand, I could see multiple cuts sprinkling my palm. None of them were very deep, though. With my free hand, I reached into the medicine cabinet and grabbed a couple of Band-Aids.

A funny feeling brushed over the back of my neck. I froze. Goose bumps rose over my flesh. A creak. A footfall. Turning off the faucet, I stood still and listened. Silence spun around me. After a few seconds, I exhaled. My hand was bleeding again.

I turned the faucet back on, chastising myself for being so jumpy. It was you, Kelly. You were messing with my mind. Had been since you'd gotten here. I knew it wasn't a coincidence. I knew from the beginning that you'd come here for a reason. That you'd sought me out. Chosen to find me.

After washing off my hand, I put Band-Aids over all the cuts. Before leaving the bathroom, I caught a glimpse of my reflection.

Good lord. I looked terrible.

Blue ringed my eyes as if I hadn't slept in weeks. My

face was pale, drawn. There was no bounce in my hair; it hung limply around my sallow cheeks.

In the weeks after Aaron's death, I resembled a corpse. Skeleton. Ghost. Dead woman walking.

I never fully recovered, but eventually I made myself eat, work out, go through the motions; I regained color in my face, put on some weight. But seeing you in that picture with Aaron yanked me back. Now I felt like I'd lost him all over again. Like he'd been brought back to life only to be cruelly snatched from me a second time.

It was like with that other baby. The one I took. The one I thought was Aaron.

But it wasn't.

He wasn't mine at all.

Swallowing the lump in my throat, I turned away from the mirror.

Away from the woman with sad eyes and a gaunt face. As I stepped out of the bathroom, the hairs on my neck prickled. I stiffened, my ears perked. This time I was sure I'd heard a noise.

"Hello?" I called out, walking slowly down the hallway.

"Hello," a voice responded, and I let out a little yelp.

I came around the corner and there you were, standing in the middle of my living room.

"Kelly?" My heart lodged in my throat.

"Sorry. You left your door open." You glanced back at my front door. "I called your name several times."

I narrowed my eyes. Had I really left the door unlocked and opened? It seemed unlikely, but how else would you have gotten in? Where was Sullivan? I spotted the carrier against the wall in the family room. A blanket smothered it, but I assumed he was underneath sleeping.

When I was a kid, we had a bird and when we wanted him to shut up we put a sheet over his cage. That's what it reminded me of when you put the blanket over Sullivan's carrier. You were treating him like my mom treated her bird.

"Are you okay?" You stepped closer to me.

Flinching, I stepped back. "Fine. What are you doing here?"

"Sullivan's feeling a little better so we thought we'd stop by. Maybe pick up that monkey." Your gaze flickered to the computer on the dining table. It was still zoomed in to the picture of you. Of you at the same party as my son.

"I know why you're here," I said, adrenaline surging.

"Yeah, I just told you." You spoke slowly like a preschool teacher to a child who isn't getting it.

This only fueled my anger. Stoked the fire. "No, I mean I know why you're here in Folsom." I glanced over at the carrier. The bird's cage. The white-and-blue blanket. "Sullivan's my grandson, isn't he?"

"What?" Your forehead pulled together so fiercely it was like an invisible pin had been inserted into the center of it. "No."

Your vehement denial emboldened me. I took a step forward. "He looks like Aaron. Same dark hair, same olive skin."

"You've just described a lot of people." Your feet shuffled backward a couple of steps, your eyes shifting back and forth, your face a mess of confusion.

"I found a Hoffman University shirt when I was cleaning up at your house."

"Yeah. So?"

"So, you never told me you went there."

"I didn't. I got that at a consignment shop."

I laughed bitterly, shaking my head. "You can cut the shit, Kelly. I know you were with my son."

Your eyes widened. "That's crazy. I don't even know Aaron."

"Then why did you have one of his cuff links? Did he give it to you or did you steal it from his dorm room?" I was taking a gamble, but I knew my son. Even though his relationship with Rafael was estranged, I was certain he'd taken the cuff links with him when he left. He and his grandpa had been close, and they were a family heirloom. I shoved my fingers down into the pocket of my jeans, but it was empty. Where had it gone?

"Look, I don't know what you're talking about." You threw up your hands, your palms showing as if this was an old-fashioned stickup. "I've never even met your son, and I don't even know what a cuff link is."

Sucking in a breath, my gaze found the computer. I marched over to the screen and pointed at the screen. "That's you. At a party my son was at."

"Kelly, that's not me. I mean, she looks kinda like me. But that's not me."

Red-hot rage rose up in my belly, like a fire burning out of control, obliterating everything in its path. "It is you. You were with my son the night he died. Why are you lying to me?"

"Died? I thought your son was away at college."

"No, he's not away at college." I mimicked the stupid tone of your voice as you spewed lies. "He's dead, but you already knew that, huh? You've been playing me this whole time."

"I'm sorry, Kelly. I had no idea about your son." Pity

filled your eyes, painting your expression. "You seem pretty upset. Is there someone I should call or...?"

No, I wouldn't let you twist everything around again. I knew what I saw. Jabbing the computer screen with my finger, I shouted, "This is you! Why do you keep lying to me?"

You flinched, and for a second, I saw it. The recognition. The knowing. Oh, yeah, you were playing me all right.

"Kelly, calm down." You took two steps toward me, holding your arms out in front of you.

"You knew my son," I repeated. "You were with him." It was the closest I'd come to answers, and I was desperate for them.

You were nervous. Scared. You knew I had you. A tiny whimper came from Sullivan's carrier, but you didn't even turn. Your eyes stayed fixed on me. As always, you were thinking of yourself before your son.

"You don't deserve him," I said. "Sullivan. You don't know the first thing about being a mom."

"That's not true," you said defiantly, lifting your chin.

"It is true. He's my grandson. He belongs with me."

Something flashed in your eyes. I was getting to you now. Gone was the confused, innocent look. *Finally.*

"He's not your grandson, and he's never going to belong to you." You came closer. I backed up, my tailbone hitting the table. Your eyes darkened. A chill ran up my spine. "I'm sure it was hard losing your son, Kelly." Your voice was different now, methodical. It reminded me of the way Rafael and Dr. Hillerman talked when they were trying to calm me down. I bristled, turning my head slightly. "I can see that you're going through a lot. But you're not making any sense."

"I am making sense and you know it."

"No." You shook your head, using that stupid, condescending tone again. "Honestly, Kelly, you sound kinda crazy. Should I call your therapist or something?"

Biting my lip, I shook my head back and forth. I wasn't crazy. And how did you know I had a therapist? You were the one not making sense. Everyone had been telling me I was imagining things for months, but I wasn't. I knew my son didn't kill himself. I'd talked to him earlier that day. He wasn't suicidal. And it wasn't accidental either. He wasn't a huge partier. He was a good kid.

Someone hurt him.

You hurt him, Kelly.

And now you were trying to hurt me.

And my grandbaby.

I couldn't let you.

Reaching out, I grappled with the table behind me. When my fingers lighted on one of Carmen's brass candleholders, I picked it up. "Tell me what you know about my son right now," I demanded, lifting my arm.

You took in the candleholder, your eyes getting bigger. "Kelly, put that down. I don't know anything. You've got this all wrong."

"No, I don't. And you're gonna tell me what you know. You're going to tell me everything." Thoughts of Aaron lying dead in his dorm room filled my mind. I saw the red-and-blue lights flashing in my front window. The two officers standing on my front porch. Their somber faces as they revealed the news. My body falling. Crumbling. My heart breaking.

You were responsible, Kelly.

And you were going to pay.

I lifted my arm higher.

"No!" Your lips formed an O shape and you reached up your arms, your messy hair falling over your face.

And that's when it hit me.

Where I'd seen you before.

Naked. Posing. Lips parted. Head back. Arms up.

As I brought the candleholder down, I uttered one word. "Keith."

When our gazes locked, I saw the word register. Understanding passed over your eyes.

Gotcha.

PART TWO

CHAPTER TWENTY-TWO

Your blood stained my hands, dark red pooling under my fingernails and gathering in the grooves of my palms. Standing under the spray of the shower, I watched the crimson slide off my flesh and swirl down the drain. Reaching for the pungent soap, I scrubbed my skin until it was raw, attempting to wash off all traces of you. Until I was pale, white and clean.

But there was no way to get you out of my head. The image of you on the ground whimpering played on a loop in my mind.

It made me feel sick. Like I was on the verge of hurling at any moment. The warmth of the shower only made it worse.

But it had happened. There's nothing I could do to change that now. It was over. Done.

Time to focus on what was best for Sullivan.

He's what's important. His safety. Security.

Once I was satisfied that I'd gotten all the blood off, I stepped out of the shower onto the plush bath mat, my toes sinking into the warmth of it. Wrapping myself in a towel, I walked toward the mirror. It was fogged up, so I wiped it with my hand until my blurry reflection emerged. It was only visible for a second before fogging up again.

I opened the bathroom door to let cool air in. Goose bumps arose on my arms and I shivered.

Pulling open the top drawer, I fumbled around until I found a brush. Then I combed my wet hair carefully, parting it to the side. It was soft and smelled like coconut shampoo. I imagined how I'd fix it in soft waves and put on neutral makeup. I'd wear a pair of jeans, an oversize sweater and minimal jewelry. Dressed like a typical suburban housewife. As if nothing out of the ordinary happened tonight at all. Seeing it all in my mind, I smiled to myself, feeling every muscle in my body relax.

Yes, I was certain I'd pull this off. Soon it would all be behind me. You'd be nothing more than a distant memory. Like a dream that felt so surreal I wasn't sure if you really existed or not.

Sullivan's faint cry reached my ears, and my heart stopped. I'd momentarily forgotten about him.

Feeling stupid and neglectful, I hurried into the bedroom where he was lying in the bassinet, the fuzzy pink blanket wrapped around his tiny body. He squirmed, his hands fisting in the air.

"It's okay. Everything's going to be okay, I promise," I cooed. "I'm gonna be right here, okay?" Standing, I hummed a tune while searching for something to wear.

I didn't stop humming until I was fully dressed. Sullivan was still whining a little, but his big eyes followed me around the room. I was careful to keep eye contact with him, all the while smiling broadly. My insides were jelly. A part of me felt like I might unravel, becoming nothing more than a scattered mess on the floor.

The reality of what I'd done repeatedly slammed into me, almost stealing my breath. But Sullivan grounded me. He was what mattered.

I'd done this for him.

Aaron's face swam in my mind. His trusting eyes. His innocent smile. A knot formed in my throat, but I swallowed it down.

No, I couldn't think about him right now. I had to stay focused on Sullivan. On our future. No sense dwelling on the past. It's not like I could reverse time.

What's done is done.

After drying my hair and fixing my makeup, I finally scooped Sullivan up. I situated him up against my shoulder and lightly bounced him in my arms. He cooed, and my stomach settled a little.

"Yes, baby, it's all going to be okay. You're safe now," I whispered to him as I headed out of the bedroom and down the hall. My nose brushed over his head and my pulse quickened. He smelled like you. I drew my face back and held my breath.

When I reached Aaron's room, I stopped. With a shaky palm, I pressed open the door and peeked inside. My stomach rolled so intensely I thought it was finally going to happen. I was going to puke. But I breathed deeply, reining it in. My gaze swept the room—the posters, the desk, the made bed. It was like he was expected back at any minute.

Moisture pricked at the backs of my eyes, and I blinked rapidly.

What was I even doing in here? It was only depressing me.

After closing Aaron's door, I made it down the stairs, Sullivan quiet and content in my arms.

Then I went into the kitchen and made myself some tea, hoping it would calm my nerves.

Swaying Sullivan back and forth, I sipped my tea and stared out the big front windows. The sky was getting dark, the sun slipping behind the clouds. I always liked this time of day. The transitioning.

My chest expanded.

Sullivan rubbed his face into my shoulder and started fussing. When his mouth clamped onto my shirt and he started sucking, it hit me that he was probably hungry. When I entered the family room, the scent of bleach wafted under my nose.

Another thing that was your fault. If you hadn't bled all over the damn place, I wouldn't have had to use so much bleach to clean it up.

Thank god for the hardwood floors. I never would've gotten it out of the carpet.

"Shut up!" he hollered, his fist colliding with my mom's face. Her head flew backward, her neck snapping. Holding in a gasp, I pressed my hand to my mouth. He couldn't know I was hiding back here behind the couch.

Squeezing my eyes shut, I heard her cries. Cocooning me, they were all I could hear. He tore out of the room, slamming the door so hard the walls rattled. Opening my eyes, I hurried to my mom. After cleaning up her face and getting her an ice pack, I went to work on the floors.

For hours, I scrubbed the carpet, but I couldn't get all the blood. It stuck to the fibers, stubborn and unyielding.

Years later, I could still see remnants of it staining the carpet.

Sullivan's soft whimpers brought me back to the present. Swallowing hard, I hurried toward the diaper bag by the front door.

"Don't worry, my love." I spoke soothingly, rubbing his back. "I've got your bottle right here." Bending down, my knees cracked. Wincing, I unzipped the diaper bag and dipped my hand inside.

That's when I saw it.

Blood spattered on the floor. A bloody handprint on the strap of the diaper bag.

Anger burned through me, hot and sudden. *God, you really couldn't let me be, could you?*

I felt you in the room then, your breath at the back of my neck, your eyes following my every move. I forced out a shaky breath. A panicky feeling rose in my chest and planted itself there.

None of this had gone as I planned. It all happened so fast. So sudden. It was your fault. You forced my hand. And now I'd made mistakes. Big ones.

Was there more blood that I missed?

It was all so much messier than I anticipated when I first came to town. The plan had seemed so simple.

Slip into your life.

Become your friend.

Get you to trust me.

And then when the time was right and I had all my plans secured, I'd get rid of you—in a quiet and humane way, obviously. I'm no monster. Then I'd take off to a tropical paradise with my new little family.

End scene.

How hard could it be?

But I didn't anticipate you figuring out who I was. I guess part of that was my fault. It was that damn cuff link.

"What is it?" I asked, pointing to the pattern etched in the gold. We were sitting in Aaron's dorm room, side by side on the floor, our backs to the wall.

"The Medina family crest." A smile played on Aaron's lips.

But my son had a right to it. It was his family crest as well.

I suppose the biggest mistake I made was leaving it in the diaper bag, especially with how handsy you were with all of Sullivan's stuff. But it was small and I was always afraid of losing it, so I kept it in the diaper bag where I knew it would be safe.

Big mistake.

You'd been so aggressive with me since I'd met you, it probably should have come as no surprise that you would force me to move faster than I had wanted. Faster than I was ready to.

Also, it really is your fault it got so messy. My plan hadn't involved blood or pain. But you attacked me first. So, I guess you "get what you get" as my mom used to say.

It did complicate things, though.

Sullivan's cries grew louder. Reaching up with both arms, I cradled my head in my hands.

My mind spun like I was on a ride at the fair. I felt sick. Nauseous. Confused, my head jumbled and chaotic.

Inhaling sharply, my gaze flew to the front door and the walls. I heaved a sigh of relief that I hadn't left traces of you there too.

The splatters on the floor would be easy enough to get rid of. *Yes, that's what I had to do.* Just use more bleach and clean it the same way I'd cleaned the rest of the floor. The panicky feeling didn't subside, but it shrunk back a little.

I just had to keep going. Pushing through. Moving forward.

By the time anyone came looking for you, I'd be long gone.

Living it up in another country. But I still had to dispose of all the evidence. Couldn't have any of it pointing back to me.

Once I got everything I ever wanted, I didn't want to spend the rest of my life looking over my shoulder. I wouldn't let you taint my happily-ever-after.

After locating a blanket, I set it on the ground and lay Sullivan on top of it. He fisted his hands into little balls and screamed bloody murder. The ear-piercing sound caused my heart rate to spike.

"Shh…shh…" I repeated desperately over and over, but he didn't quiet.

Sullivan was kicking now, fast and manic, in time with his loud wailing.

I hurried into the kitchen. The bleach was under the sink. After opening the cabinet, I lowered my body and reached inside. I put on a pair of gloves and grabbed a sponge and some bleach. The sponge was tinged red. I blew out a breath. I'd dispose of it once I was certain every trace of you was gone.

When I stood up, I was facing the back window. My gaze landed on the shed. A reminder that you weren't truly gone yet. It was getting darker. Sullivan's screams amped up.

It was all too much.

My body shook.

"Shut up!" I screamed at Sullivan, and then instantly regretted it.

This wasn't his fault. He was innocent. He was my reason.

I couldn't forget that.

"So sorry, buddy." I knelt beside him, touching his face. It was warm, and sticky with tears. I could tell even through the kitchen gloves.

Pull it together, Kelly. Stop panicking.

He shoved a fist into his mouth and sucked.

Hungry. He was hungry.

First things first. I yanked off the gloves, set the bleach down and made him a bottle. Once it was in his mouth, he drank greedily.

I exhaled, savoring the silence for a moment.

Sweat had formed on my upper lip and I wiped it with my free hand. Lights shone out the front window, the sound of people talking outside. As I sat on the couch feeding him, I glanced outside through the shiny glass. It wasn't smudged like the windows at home. Clearly, you were more meticulous than me. Two kids were running around on the front lawn directly across the street. A man and woman stood on the front porch, watching. I smiled, my gaze traveling back to Sullivan, who still sucked hungrily on his bottle.

Pretty soon, it would all be okay.

I was giving my son a new life. A better life. A family. Something I had never had.

There was no reason to panic over the blood now. It was only Sunday night. I had plenty of time to clean it.

Almost an entire week. I just had to be ready by Friday.

For now, I needed to relax. It had been a long, stressful day. Time to take a load off. I glanced around the vast family room.

This was all foreign to me. When I was growing up we lived in run-down apartments. The nicest home I'd lived in was my grandma's, but even it didn't compare to this.

Sullivan was getting heavy in my arms. His sucking had ceased. I peered down. He'd fallen asleep. Not wanting to wake him, I decided against carrying him upstairs to the bassinet. Chances were all the movement would wake him.

As carefully as possible I stood and laid him down on his blanket, which was sprawled out on the floor near the couch.

Holding my breath, I took a step back from him. He stirred momentarily, but then eased back into a deep sleep. I exhaled.

What did rich, suburban housewives do in the evenings?

Glancing up at the vaulted ceilings, I trailed my fingertips along the edge of the couch. My bare feet were cold against the hardwood floors as I walked into the kitchen. I flicked on the wall switch and bright yellow light flooded the room, illuminating the clean, slick, bare countertops. Not a dirty dish or empty carton in sight. No wonder you were always so uncomfortable at my house. Yours was clean. Too clean. Seriously, you might have had a problem, Kelly. OCD or something like that. I mean, houses should at least look lived in.

In the corner sat a wine rack filled with bottles. I headed over to it, pulling out a couple. I knew nothing about wine. But I knew it was your drink of choice. And not just from the times we hung out.

Before we ever met, I'd researched you. It wasn't hard. You posted pretty much everything online. For an older woman, you really knew your way around social media. You had an Instagram and a Facebook account. I've never understood people's need to post their lives on the internet. Why would I want the world to know everything about me?

I guess I'd always been kind of a private person.

But you weren't. For months before moving here, I'd stalked your pages. Watched your life unfold. Found out your hobbies. Your likes and dislikes. I mean, there wasn't anything I couldn't find out about you.

Every week, you checked in at your gym a couple of times. Even tagged your friend. Not only was it super narcissistic to think anyone cared how often you went to the gym, it was also dangerous. I mean, your accounts were public, so anyone in the world could find you, track you down. Join your same gym.

You even followed your son's former pediatrician on Facebook. One time you shared his post, something about the importance of flu vaccines. I remember several of your crunchy anti-vaxxer friends taking issue with that particular post.

After locating a wineglass (dude, you had a lot of them), I popped open a bottle of wine. Then I poured the bright red liquid into the glass. I filled it to the brim, even though I knew that wasn't proper. See, that was the difference between me and you. I didn't do things for show.

I did what I wanted.

To hell with society and their rules.

I shuffled back into the family room. Standing over Sullivan, I watched him sleep for a minute. God, he was perfect. He deserved the best life had to offer. And I was going to give him that.

Wine in hand, I plunked down on the couch, propping my feet up on the coffee table. Your TV was the biggest one I'd seen. It practically took up the entire wall. Using the nearby remote, I clicked it on and went to Netflix. There were three accounts listed—you, Rafael and Aaron. My gaze lingered on Aaron's name, my gut twisting.

I thought about how lost and sad you looked when you told me about Aaron's death. I couldn't imagine losing my son.

I thought about Aaron's kind smile and naive idealism. I'd never met anyone like him.

Shaking my head, I forced away the memories. This was no time for regrets. Taking another sip of my wine, I clicked on Aaron's account. Scrolling through, I found *The Office* and clicked on it. When it started, I sank further into the couch and took a long sip of my wine.

Ah, man, this was the life.

I got about fifteen minutes into the show when a sound from outside startled me. The hairs on the back of my neck prickled. Slowly, I turned my head. Lights shone outside the front window, tires rolling up over the curb and into the driveway. Was someone here?

My shoulders tightened at the sound of a car door slamming, followed by footsteps on the pavement. Knocking on the front door caused my entire body to clench. I sat completely still, afraid to move a muscle. Without turning my head, my gaze shifted toward Sullivan. He stirred slightly.

Please don't wake him up.

There was a moment of silence before the knocking started again. Who could it be? An image of you standing outside the door, blood dripping down your face, came to mind. But there was no way. You weren't coming back. Not now. Not ever.

I was sure of it.

Maybe it was a Jehovah's Witness or a delivery person. Then again, it was kind of late for that, wasn't it?

"Kelly?" a woman's voice called out while the knocking resumed.

Sullivan stirred again, his little hands coming up and balling into fists.

Oh, god, no.

With deliberate motions, I set the wine down on the coffee table and then dropped to the floor. Crawling on my belly, I dragged myself across the room. Your purse sat in the entryway. I fished through it until I found your phone.

Lying on the floor, I turned it on.

It was locked.

Funny how you blasted every detail of your life on social media, but you kept your phone locked. As if you actually cared about your privacy.

The password was five letters long.

I smiled. Could it really be that simple?

After typing in AARON the phone unlocked.

Yep. You were too predictable, Kelly.

You had several unread texts. One was from Christine. On my way, it read.

With my thumb, I slid up the thread. *Shit*. You'd made plans for a girls' night in with Christine.

You also had an appointment reminder from your nail salon. That would have to wait. First, I had to get rid of your friend, who clearly couldn't take a hint.

As she continued knocking and calling out your name, I shot a text back to her.

So sorry. Not feeling well. I need to cancel.

The knocking stopped. I breathed out.

Little dots appeared on the screen. I clutched the phone tighter, waiting for the words to appear.

What? You were fine this morning.

I shook my head and typed back. It came on suddenly.

Whatever. I'm already here. Can't you hear me knocking? Open up.

Man, your friend was really pushy.

Sorry. Already in bed, I texted back.

Holding my breath, I pressed my back into the wall and waited for her to leave. My heart hammered so violently I could feel it pulsing through every muscle in my body. Sullivan was still asleep on the floor, but barely. He was stirring, his legs kicking a little, his fingers opening and closing. Music played in my palm, startling me. *Shit.* Hurriedly, I shut the volume off. Was she really calling you? What kind of people were you friends with?

Another text came through: Just let me in. Wine will kick whatever illness you have.

I stared down at the screen, dumbfounded. Was she for real?

When I didn't answer right away another text followed: I'm not leaving until I know you're okay.

Rolling my eyes, I groaned. Oh, great. How was I going to get rid of her, then?

"Kelly?" I flinched, startled. "What's going on? Are you okay?" Her voice was no longer coming from the front door. When her face appeared in the window, I shoved my back farther into the wall, wishing I could melt into it, become one with the paint. I stared up at the ceiling, holding my body completely still.

Oh, no. Sullivan.

He was visible from the window.

What if she saw him?

The TV was on too.

Why the hell had I left the blinds open?

I groaned, hitting my head on the wall. No way was I letting your nosy friend ruin everything. I was so freaking close to getting everything I ever wanted. Adrenaline spiking, my gaze landed on the diaper bag. There was a gun inside. It would only take a minute for me to get it.

But then what?

No. The gun wasn't the answer. It was the last resort. I wouldn't use it unless absolutely necessary.

I hadn't even used it on you.

Once I shot it and the blast rang out, it would be over for me here. It would draw too much attention. I'd have to leave. And I couldn't yet.

I had to stay put until Friday. Even though everything else had changed, that hadn't.

I may have had to improvise in getting rid of you, but I still managed to do it in a silent way.

I'd have to be smart in getting rid of your friend too.

But, honestly, I didn't want to hurt her. It had already been a super exhausting day. All I'd wanted was to drink wine and watch mindless TV. Frustration burned through me. How was I going to make your stupid-ass friend leave?

With trembling fingers I scrolled up through your conversation, hoping for something to use. Smiling, I found it.

Biting my lip, I typed: You def don't want me to open the door. I think it's the flu, and you can't miss Maddie's recital on Thursday.

Stiffening, I listened intently. The yelling and knocking ceased. When I dared to glance up, her face was no longer in the window.

The phone buzzed in my palm.

She'd responded: Ew. The flu? Yeah, I can't get that.

Then she added: Ok. Feel better. I'll call tomorrow.

Slumping against the wall, I exhaled with relief.

Thanks, Christine. TTYL, I typed back.

Her footsteps click-clacked over the pavement. A car door opened and closed. The engine rumbled, tires buzzing along the asphalt. The muscles in my body slowly unclenched. Just when I'd finally gotten relaxed, an ear-piercing scream filled the air.

Sullivan had woken up.

Awesome. There went my relaxing evening.

CHAPTER
TWENTY-THREE

You would've made a good detective, Kelly.

You were right about Keith.

"What are you doing?" Rafael leaned over my shoulder, that leather smell of his wafting under my nose.

"Putting my number into your phone," I said as I typed my name into his contacts. K-E—

"No," he said. "You can't put your name in my phone."

"Afraid your wife will see it?" I lifted my fingers so they hovered over his phone, and I raised a brow.

"Yeah, actually."

I bit my lip, an idea springing to mind. "What about this?" I-T-H.

"Keith?"

"Yep. As far as your wife's concerned, he's your new work colleague." I winked. "And he's going to be texting you a lot."

"Is he now?" He tugged me forward, his lips covering mine.

If you knew I was Keith, then you had to have seen the naked pictures I'd sent.

How weird that you'd known all this time that your husband was cheating, and you hadn't done anything about it. I guess we differed in that area. I didn't like sharing.

Not even with you.

Not even knowing that he was your husband first.

I knew about you from the beginning. He mentioned you in our very first conversation.

I'd heard of Professor Medina before I ever set foot in his class. Every girl on campus knew about him. He was hot, that's what everyone always said. All the professors I'd had were old or plain looking. I couldn't even wrap my brain around a hot professor.

Until I saw him.

The first day of class, he stood at the doorway, shook each of our hands as we walked in, and introduced himself. I remember he'd teased me about my hand being so cold. But it wasn't in a flirty way. More of a friendly comment. That's how he was. He treated us like we were his friends. Equals.

He'd made me feel comfortable when we'd first met.

For a week I sat in his class, drooling over him. And then it happened. He talked to me. I lingered after class one day, making sure I was the last student to leave. When I did, I tossed out a shy goodbye. I assumed he would just say goodbye back, but instead, he stepped toward me.

"Kelly, right?"

I nodded, my face heating up.

His eyes were a dark chocolate brown, his hair tousled, falling in a perfect wave over his tanned forehead. I felt like I finally understood all those romance novels my grandma used to read, and I sometimes sneaked into my room.

His smoldering, piercing eyes.

His musky scent.
His wavy, windblown hair.
Tall, dark and handsome.

I used to laugh, thinking guys like that weren't real. They lived exclusively in the pages of a book.

But when I met Rafael I knew that wasn't true. There were guys like that in real life. There was one standing right in front of me.

"I remembered because my wife's name is Kelly," he said.

My stomach dropped, the romance-novel vibes weakening a little. Being compared to someone's wife wasn't sexy. He was already making me aware that he wasn't available. That he belonged to you. I almost walked away then. Gave up.

But then he added, "You look a lot like she used to." His lips curled upward slightly. "We met in college, you know."

"No, I didn't know that." I smiled, running a hand through my hair in a flirtatious way.

He stepped even closer, his eyebrows rising slightly. "How would you? We don't know anything about each other."

Yet, I thought to myself with a smile.

It wasn't the only time he talked about you. Every once in a while, you came up in our conversations.

"You're not going home this weekend?" It was Friday night and we were in his apartment, cuddled up on the couch watching the latest season of Stranger Things.

He shook his head.

"Why not? Isn't your wife expecting you?"

"I think she prefers when I'm not home." There was a sadness in his eyes that melted me. I knew what it felt like

to be rejected and unwanted. I'd felt like that most of my life, and it sucked.

What was your problem anyway? I would give anything to be in your shoes. To be married to Rafael Medina. Why would you take him for granted? Did you have any idea how rare a guy like Rafael was? There were plenty of losers out there. Trust me, I knew. My mom and I had both dated our share.

Rafael was nothing like the losers we'd been with.

If he was mine, I'd never let him go.

Turning away from the TV, I straddled Rafael, framing his face with my hands. "Well, I prefer it when you're here, so I guess it works out for me."

"Really? I'm not cramping your style?"

I laughed. "What does that even mean?"

"You wouldn't rather be doing something else? Partying with friends or something?"

"There is absolutely no other place I'd rather be." I pressed my lips to his.

His hands traveled up my back and he kissed me hard. I wrapped my legs around his middle and he picked me up, carrying me to the bedroom. After throwing me on the bed, he tore off my clothes. I pulled his shirt off and pushed down his pants. Then he jumped on top of me.

"I brought some toys," I whispered in his ear. "They're in my purse." Men liked kinky and adventurous. They didn't like boring. With Rafael, I was always upping my game, terrified he'd lose interest in me. I couldn't let that happen.

"Let's try something different tonight." He kissed me again.

When his palm slid around my neck, I knew what he

planned to do. An ex had done this to me before. I braced myself.

"Is this okay?" Rafael asked, his hand barely squeezing.

I'd never been asked that before. My feelings had never mattered to other guys. Even my virginity had been taken. Stolen from an asshole my mom brought over who apparently hadn't been taught what the word no *meant. Not that any of it surprised me. I'd learned from watching my mom's relationships that women were nothing more than pawns for men to use as they pleased.*

But Rafael didn't treat me like that.

"Just tap on my hand when you want me to stop," he said before applying pressure.

When we finished, he thanked me for letting him do it. Said you had lost your shit when he tried it with you. That's why I lied when he asked me if I liked it. I told him it felt good, like a high. Euphoric. Exciting. An adrenaline rush.

And I guess it wasn't a total lie. The choking part sucked. But the rest of it was amazing. That's what I chose to focus on. Nothing was perfect, after all. But what I had with Rafael was pretty damn close.

Rafael was bored with you. That's why he turned to me.

Don't get me wrong, though. Our relationship wasn't all about the sex. He took care of me.

Once when I was sick, he stayed with me all weekend, forcing liquids and soup down my throat. He nursed me back to health. I kept asking him if he needed to get back home, but he said I was more important.

Me.

Imagine that.

I'd never been chosen like that before. And most definitely not by a man. Hell, I hadn't even been taken care of by my own dad. He took off when my mom was pregnant with me and never looked back.

But Rafael took care of me. Sometimes even choosing me over his own wife and kid. I'd always dreamed of being that important to someone.

With Sullivan in my arms, I shuffled into the kitchen and stared out the back window. Clouds rolled in overhead. The sky was dark even though it was daytime. Wind raked over the glass, carrying debris and leaves in its wake. My gaze landed on the shed in the back corner. The lock was securely fastened, the doors unmoving despite the heavy winds. My stomach tightened.

I really was sorry it had come to this, Kelly. A part of me thought you were pretty cool.

It wasn't personal.

Sullivan made little sucky noises. I leaned down, my lips lingering over his soft, warm skin. My son deserved a better life than I had. He deserved to be with both parents.

This was about him. Not you.

You understand, don't you?

The smell of pee wafted under my nose. I felt Sullivan's diaper. It was warm, heavy. I turned away from the window. You'd have to wait.

Hurrying into the living room, I found the diaper bag. The bloody handprints on the handles taunted me. Shivering, I fished inside for a diaper. I only had two left. Last night, I'd acted recklessly.

I hadn't been fully prepared, and now it was catching up to me.

After changing Sullivan's diaper, I went through my wallet. I was running out of money. It was hard to believe I'd already blown through most of what I'd inherited from my grandma. Sixty thousand dollars seemed like a lot when I got it. But I guess it wasn't so much after a year of college and the highway robbery of the delivery room.

Oh, well. Soon enough, Rafael would be home and all would be okay again. He'd keep taking care of me the way a man should.

The way my dad never did.

I just needed to get through the rest of the week.

My stomach twisted as I looked through the items I'd hurriedly shoved into the diaper bag before heading over here. Not only did Sullivan need more diapers, but he needed more clothes. I did too. Last night it was kind of fun to pretend I was you for a minute, wearing your clothes and prancing around your house like a typical suburban housewife. But, let's face it, your clothes were boring and ugly. I missed mine. I was going to have to go back to the guesthouse and get some of our stuff.

This was not how it was supposed to go down.

Man, I felt like a dumbass.

I drew in a breath and then slowly released it. Then I held my chin up, resolving to calm down. To stop worrying over what I couldn't control. No sense crying over spilled milk. Wasn't that how the saying went, Kelly?

Picking Sullivan back up, I headed upstairs. Laying him down in the bassinet, I went to your dresser and picked out an outfit, reminding myself that soon I could take it off and put on something of mine. I was barely out of Sullivan's line of sight when he started crying. I swear that kid couldn't stand being alone for two seconds. As I sifted through your dull sweater collection, I rolled my tense shoulders. Maybe having Rafael around would help Sullivan chill out. My mom once told me that I cried all the time as a baby. Perhaps it was a single-parent thing.

I forced on a pair of your jeans and a gray sweater. The pants were a little baggy, but I cinched them with a belt, and I had to roll the sleeves on the sweater a couple of times. But I made it work.

I glanced at my reflection in a nearby mirror and laughed.

I was you. Well, the new and improved you anyway.

Kelly Medina, 2.0.

Sullivan's cries intensified, so I raced over and snatched him out of the bassinet. This would all be so much easier once I had help. Sullivan kicked and flailed while I changed him out of his dirty diaper and into a fresh onesie and clean socks.

"Stop it," I hissed, holding his leg in place. He fussed, his leg turning slightly red from where I gripped him. "Sorry." I released my fingers, feeling guilty for grabbing him so hard. Thank god you weren't here to see it, Kelly. You would've shaken your head. Maybe offered up some advice on how to be gentler next time.

As if you were an authority on parenting.

Your son was dead. You hadn't done everything in your power to protect him.

Not like I was doing for Sullivan.

Who was the better mom now, huh?

Heart hammering, I carried Sullivan into the family room and snatched up the diaper bag.

Ella went to her knitting club on Monday mornings. She was usually gone from nine to noon. That gave me enough time to get what I needed and get back here safely. Last night, I'd already transferred Sullivan's car seat into your car and hid my van. The storm had made that little chore a thousand times harder. But it was easier than dragging your body outside had been.

I was so grossed out at the memory that I involuntarily trembled.

Sullivan had no idea the things I'd already done for him in his short life. The things I'd sacrificed. The people I'd hurt.

Your wide eyes filled my mind, blood spilling from your head.

I hoped it would all be worth it.

I strapped Sullivan securely into the car seat, then threw his diaper bag onto the floor. After closing his door, I put on a hat and a pair of sunglasses. Then I hopped into the driver's seat. My van had smelled like chips and sweat. Your car smelled like leather, and faintly like designer perfume. It was also way cleaner than my car, which had been littered with trash, baby toys, soda cans and tissues.

Luckily, you had tinted windows in the back, so to anyone driving past it would look like you were out running errands alone. I pulled out of the garage and drove slowly down the street, careful to stay within the speed limit. The last thing I needed was to get pulled over.

We'd only been in the car a few minutes when Sullivan started fussing again. My shoulders tensed. He'd always been a fussy baby, but he was crying even more lately. Maybe he was teething or something. It was the kind of thing I would've asked you about last week. A pang of regret stabbed me. I shifted in my seat, breathing deeply.

You'd gotten under my skin. There were traces of you embedded in me. Your words were in my head, your voice too familiar.

When this plan had first started to take shape, you weren't real to me. You were on a computer screen, in pictures, in my imagination.

But now I knew you, and it made this all so much harder. More challenging than I thought it would be.

Slowing down, I neared the house I'd been staying in. I remembered the first time you came over. How disgusted you seemed with my lifestyle. I had to bite down so hard on my tongue I tasted blood to keep myself from blurting out the truth. The guesthouse was only temporary. It had always been merely a place to stay until I left town with my new little family.

Ella's driveway was empty, and the curtains were closed. When she was home, they were always open. Day and night. She clearly wasn't fearful, even though she lived alone. I guess it was because she was so trusting.

She'd let me move in without even doing a background check or asking for referrals. I met with her one time after reading her ad on the computer at the public library. I sat on her plush couch that smelled like old lady perfume, turned my charm up full blast, let her hold Sullivan and then I had her—hook, line and sinker. The next day I was moving in.

Good thing too, because prior to that I'd been sleeping in my van.

I pulled up to the curb and cut the engine. Sullivan was still fussing when I went around the back to him. All of his wiggling and crying made it hard to get him out.

"Do you want out or not?" I snapped.

He cried harder.

"Sorry. Sorry," I mumbled, feeling like I'd been saying that to him a lot lately.

"Kelly, just shut the hell up!" Mom snapped, holding

her head in her hands. On the ground near her feet sat an empty vodka bottle. Her eyes were puffy and red.

The air smelled sweet, but not in a good way. In an overripe mushy-banana kind of way. The curtains were closed and it was dark inside even though it was early afternoon. Shuddering, I thought about how it was always nighttime in here.

"Sorry," I mumbled, feeling bad. Mom was going through a tough time. She'd asked me to leave her alone. Why hadn't I listened?

Scrambling over to her, I picked up the vodka bottle and threw it in the trash. I didn't want her to have to see it when she woke up.

While rinsing off the dirty dishes, I stared out the window. The sun was high, beaming down over the blue sky. A man walked down the sidewalk, his daughter's hand tucked into his. My insides twisted. Swallowing hard, I told myself the familiar lies, repeating them over and over in my head like a mantra.

My dad is in the CIA. He stays hidden for my protection.

My dad died while my mom was pregnant. But his dying wish was to meet me. To hold me. To tell me he loved me.

But no matter how many times I told myself these things, I always knew they were nothing but lies. My dad stayed away because he didn't care. He didn't want to know me.

Skimming my lips over Sullivan's forehead, I rained down promises to never make him feel like no one cared. Pressing my lips down firmly against his sweet little cheek, I sealed the promises with a kiss.

Pretty soon this would all be over.

Pretty soon we'd be a family and then things would be good for us. No, not just good. Perfect.

Smiling, I clutched Sullivan tighter and made my way toward the guesthouse. A cool breeze kicked up, rustling through my hair and causing a chill to snake up my back. My teeth involuntarily chattered. God, why had it been so stormy this year? It was annoying. I was so ready for tropical living.

It was even colder in the guesthouse and my entire body trembled after a few minutes inside. My nose turned to ice, my teeth continuing to chatter. Sullivan shivered and I held him closer. He nestled his face into my chest as I hurriedly packed up a few of his things. It was difficult to do with him in my arms, but I didn't want to put him down. The shame I felt for all my earlier outbursts kept me from releasing him.

In the bedroom, my gaze landed on Sullivan's crib. I remembered how angry you got at me for laying him on his stomach. You acted as if I was trying to hurt my son.

In that moment I realized you didn't know me at all.

Everything I did was for him.

Once I'd stuffed Sullivan's diaper bag as full as I could, I sighed, my gaze scouring the room. I hated the idea of leaving all of his furniture here. I had to hand it to you, Kelly. You'd bought him some nice stuff. He loved his swing, and so did I. It gave me some time to myself. But there was no way I could lug that thing all the way out to the car.

Maybe once Rafael was home, he'd bring me back here to get the rest of my stuff. Ah, who was I kidding? I wouldn't need it then. He could buy me new stuff.

Better stuff.

I smiled. See, I didn't need you anymore.

Breathing out, I flung the diaper bag over my shoulder and backed out of the guesthouse. When I came around the corner, my breath hitched in my throat. "Ella." Her name burst out of my mouth like a gasp. "I, um… I thought you had knitting group or something this morning."

"I did. I just left early." She stared at me intently with her watery eyes. It took all my willpower to hold her gaze. "Was feeling a little tired, I guess."

Her wrinkled skin was almost gray out here. She did look a little sick. Involuntarily, I stepped backward, shielding Sullivan from her. The last thing I needed was for him to get whatever she had. It could derail all my plans.

"I'm sorry," I mumbled.

"I didn't see your car out front," she said, her eyes narrowing.

The hairs on the back of my neck stood at attention. But I offered an easy smile. "Oh, yeah, it's, um…in the shop. A friend is picking me up."

"Oh, dear. I hope everything is okay."

I nodded. "Just routine maintenance."

"Good." She patted my arm distractedly, then touched her head. "I really need to get inside."

"Of course. Feel better." Relief flooded me when she turned around and headed into her house.

Heart hammering, I hurried to the car. After throwing the diaper bag in the back seat, I strapped Sullivan in. It took several tries, since my hands were shaking so badly. I finally got him all situated and then hopped in the front. Blowing out a breath, I locked all the doors and leaned my head against the seat. I couldn't afford any more close calls.

Once I got back to your house I'd have to stay there until Rafael came home. No more errands. No more leaving.

I sent Rafael a text and then turned on the car.

My jitters dissipated the closer I got to your house. Pretty soon we'd be long gone. Somewhere no one could find us.

And then all would be right with the world again.

I laughed, thinking about how much I sounded like my mom lately.

My mom was the queen of inspirational quotes. She used to get those daily calendars filled with them. Then she'd tack them on the fridge and throughout the house. It wasn't uncommon to walk into the bathroom to get ready for school and find a piece of paper taped to the mirror, reading, "Shine on, you crazy diamond." Or to go pour a cup of coffee and find a Post-it stuck to it, my mom's handwriting scrawled on it: "Don't quit your daydream."

When I was old enough to work, I used to buy my mom those calendars for Christmas. One year, I had a hard time finding one so instead I made her one. It wasn't a daily calendar (that would have taken forever). Instead, I did one quote per month. I made most of them up, and some I stole from online.

They were probably more silly than inspirational. I wrote things like "Don't be a dud, be a dandelion." And "Your day job may suck, but that's why they made alcohol." My mom didn't laugh as hard at that one. In fact, she gave me a little lecture on the side effects of drinking. As if I needed that particular talk. I'd seen firsthand what drinking did to people.

Or at least, what it had done to her.

I thought she might be upset that I didn't get her the real calendar, but she wasn't. She still stuck those stupid quotes all over our house like they were actually inspiring to her.

She even had my grandma crochet one on a pillow. It

was one I'd stolen, not made up, and it read: "Be a unicorn in a field of horses."

In the guesthouse I had a box of my grandma's and my mom's stuff. But there were only two things I wanted from it.

That pillow, and a picture of my grandma and me.

Those two items were literally the only things I had in your house that belonged to me.

When I got home from my trip to the guesthouse, I displayed the pillow on your bed. And I set the picture on your nightstand, so my grandma's face would greet me every morning when I woke up and it would be the last thing I saw when I went to bed.

It ensured that they would both be with me.

I knew you probably thought I was a monster, but I wasn't. I was a woman in love, and that meant I had to fight to keep that love in my life, right?

More than that, I was a mom doing whatever it took to give her son the best life she could.

You understood that, didn't you?

CHAPTER TWENTY-FOUR

No wonder your husband cheated on you, Kelly. You didn't own one sexy piece of lingerie. Your underwear drawer was a sea of beige granny panties and giant bras with wide straps. You couldn't even splurge and get something with lace? It was all cotton, no embellishments or patterns.

Some were even shredded or had holes or tears.

There were times when I'd felt bad, even guilty, about sleeping with Rafael, knowing he was married. But not now that I'd seen this. You practically handed him to me on a silver platter. It was like you wanted me to have him.

While Sullivan napped, I slipped out of my clothes and drew myself a bath. You had one of those deep tubs that you had to step down into. Around it were clear jars filled with colorful bath salts and bath bombs. I pulled out a pink one that smelled like bubble gum. I threw it in the bath that was now almost half-filled. It dissolved, turning the water a color that resembled cotton candy.

Dipping my toe in, a shiver worked its way up my calf. It was a little too hot, so I sat on the edge of the tub and waited for it to cool. Steam rose in front of my face, dampening the edges of my hair.

Once the water had cooled, I sank into the warm, pastel-colored bath and let out a contented sigh. Apparently, bathing was a lot more fun when I was you. In my former life, bathing was a necessity. A box to check. Quick. Efficient. Part of my daily routine. Not entertainment or a way to unwind.

As I leaned my head back, I wished I'd had the forethought to pour myself a glass of wine. That's probably what you did when you took a bath, huh? You and your friend seemed to drink a lot of wine. If your text thread was to be trusted.

By the way, your friend was still bugging the hell out of me. She texted incessantly. If I didn't know better I'd think you two had a thing going on. You definitely texted her more than you texted your own husband.

Did you swing that way, Kelly?

Swirling my arms in the water, I thought about how overbearing you were. How you practically forced our friendship. How you texted me all the time, constantly inviting me over and paying for things. Were you into me? Ha. Seemed like all the Medinas were.

I sank lower into the tub until the water was up to my chin. The pink liquid clung to my skin, painting it a candy hue. My toes peeked out on the other side. The polish was chipped. I made a mental note to search for more when I got out of the bath. I was sure you had a nice stash somewhere, and I needed to make sure to look my best by the time Rafael came home.

Maybe I'd paint them something bright, like yellow or hot pink. Usually in the winter I'd go for dark purples or blues, but where we were going, tropical colors seemed like a good option.

Closing my eyes, I nestled into the warm water and daydreamed that I was on the beach, an icy drink in my hand.

Sullivan's screaming cut into my fantasy. Every muscle in my body seized. A second ago I'd been relaxed, my muscles loose, my head a million miles away. After blowing out a breath, I lowered myself all the way to the bottom of the tub. Once the water went over my head, it was silent again. The warm water cocooned around me. If I could live without breathing, I would've stayed down there forever. But eventually my lungs screamed at me, and I popped up. The minute my head broke the surface, Sullivan's cries filled my ears once again.

Groaning, I hoisted myself out of the tub, dried off and then wrapped the towel around my body before hurrying to the bassinet. Sullivan's face was bright red, his fists thrusts upward like he was cursing god.

"It's okay. Shh," I murmured as I picked him up. He continued to cry even after I held him close. "You hungry?"

He kept crying, and I decided to take that as a yes. I couldn't wait until he was old enough to formulate a response.

After feeding him a bottle, he was still pretty cranky.

"What's going on, bud?" I asked, bouncing him in my lap. Sometimes I felt silly, asking him questions he couldn't answer. Reaching out, I brushed back his dark patch of hair. "You look just like your daddy," I told him, my insides warming.

It was a phrase I'd never heard about myself. My mom didn't talk about my dad, no matter how many times I'd pressed. As a child, I often asked her about him. Sometimes she tactfully changed the subject; other times she got angry. But I never got answers.

One year, we worked on a family tree in school. When the teacher handed out the worksheets with the outline of a tree, empty boxes on each branch, I thought that finally my mom would have to open up. She'd have to tell me everything. It was homework, after all. And she was always up my butt about doing homework. But even that hadn't worked.

I'll never forget the disappointment I felt when I handed in that paper, one side of the tree completely blank.

Throughout my childhood, I held on to the hope that maybe my grandma knew something and one day I'd get her to spill everything. But even after Mom died she swore she knew nothing.

So both of them went to their graves without ever telling me about my dad.

My mom and I didn't look a lot alike. She was blond, fair. I had pale skin but with more of a yellow undertone, and darker hair. I figured I probably favored my dad, but I'd never know for sure.

I loved that my son would know.

The rain beating down on the roof got so loud it startled me. Standing up, I went to the window. The sky was almost black even though it was only afternoon. Rain poured from the clouds like giant sheets. Wind whipped branches and leaves into the air like a whirlpool. I was still only wearing a towel, and goose bumps rose on my skin, causing me to shiver.

Sullivan whimpered again. I lowered my mouth down to his forehead. His skin was hot against my lips. Too hot. I paused, brushing them over his flesh again. Yep, still warm.

My pulse skittered. Did he have a fever?

I touched his forehead with the back of my hand the way my mom used to do to me. He was hot, all right. But I couldn't tell if it was truly a fever or not.

Oh, man, what happened if he was too sick to travel?

I drew in a breath. Surely, he wouldn't still be sick on Friday. It was only Tuesday.

My gaze dropped to the shed, my stomach bottoming out. I bet you would know what to do. You'd been a mom for years. And I could tell you were one of those know-it-all moms. The moms who read all the parenting books and took classes and shit.

But it was too late.

You were gone. I couldn't ask you now.

And it's not like I could take him to the doctor. He didn't have one. Yes, I know you thought he did. But that doctor's appointment was never about Sullivan. It was always about you.

My mom used to say that we all had our own kryptonite. A weakness. An obsession. Something that had the potential to destroy us.

I'd read online about the incident at the grocery store, so I figured babies were your kryptonite.

After seeing you share the pediatrician's Facebook post, the idea came to me.

When I called to book the appointment, I'd given them two numbers. One was yours. I'd lifted it from Rafael's phone almost a year ago, just in case I ever needed it. And this seemed like a good reason to finally use it.

You played so well into my hands, even showing up for the appointment before I did. Talk about eager.

It's not like I needed to know you. I could've simply

broken into your house and gotten rid of you. But I wanted it to seem like an accident. Like you'd gone crazy. Taken meds or drank too much.

It was the only way to ensure things worked out for my future with Rafael.

Once I got to know you, I realized you played right into the crazy thing so well.

The problem was that you also made my life easier. After staying the night at your house, I started to have second thoughts. I was actually kind of starting to like you. And I was hoping to come up with a different way. One that didn't involve you being dead.

But you really jacked that up, didn't you?

Sighing, I felt Sullivan's head again. He was getting hotter. I kind of wished the pediatrician thing hadn't been a ruse. Problem was, I didn't have insurance.

I'd have to figure this out on my own.

Panic threatened to overtake me, but then it hit me. I wasn't really alone. I mean, you weren't here to answer my questions, but that didn't mean you still couldn't help.

"Hang in there, sweetie. Mama's got you," I said in the best soothing voice I could muster. *Man, I really was turning into you.*

I tried your bathroom cabinet first, but it was filled with hair and bath products. Seriously, what you lacked in the lingerie drawer you made up for in beauty products. Such a shame because your hair never really looked that great.

As I headed down the hallway, Sullivan whimpered in my arms. His face was scarlet, his skin on fire.

"It's gonna be okay, sweet boy," I assured him, silently praying that I was right.

Across from Aaron's room was another bathroom, so

I tried that next. Leaning down, I opened the cabinet underneath the sink, but found only cleaning supplies and a dusty half-empty bottle of men's shaving cream. Straightening, I yanked open the top drawer to the left of the cabinet. It was filled with framed pictures. They were caked in dust and a couple had broken frames, almost like they'd been thrown in here.

I picked one up. It was of you and Aaron. If I had to guess I'd say he was around seven or eight. Your cheeks were pressed together, and both of you wore large smiles. His fleshy hand curved around the other side of your face as if he was pulling you as close as humanly possible. I inhaled deeply and then blew out. Swallowing hard, I tossed the picture back in the drawer and then slammed it shut.

"Do you have any kids?" I propped myself up on my elbows and kicked my legs up in the air behind me.

Rafael rolled over in the bed, the hotel sheets rustling beneath him. Staring up at the ceiling, he frowned. "A son."

"How old?"

He was quiet a minute, his lips pressed tightly together.

I reached out and dragged my fingertips up his bare chest. Growling, he caught my hand in his and gently bit it. I giggled. Drawing me on top of him, he kissed me long and hard.

"Nuh-uh." I pulled back, shaking my head. "Not this time. You always do this when I ask you questions."

"This is so much more fun than talking." Winking, he wrapped his arms around me and pulled me to his chest. His lips pressed firmly against mine, his palms sliding up my back. My body went slack, melting into him. It would be so easy.

But... "No." I tore away from him.

"What's the deal?" His eyes flashed, his arms falling to his sides. My body went cold. I'd never seen him angry before. It almost made me cave. But we'd been sleeping together for almost a month and he hadn't shared anything about his life. I'd never even been to his apartment. I knew he had a kid. I'd found you on Facebook. You were constantly sharing pictures of your boy and posting about how proud you were of him. God, it was nauseating.

But it also made me jealous that you shared something with Rafael that I didn't. That you and he talked about stuff. Real stuff. And all Rafael and I did was hook up in this hotel. Sure, the sex was amazing, but I thought I might be falling in love with him. And I wanted more.

I'd told him about my family. It was time he told me about his.

A son was a big deal. And I knew we'd never connect if he kept such a huge thing from me. I wanted him to be able to talk about his kid if he wanted to.

"I just..." I bit my lip, trying to come up with the right thing to say. I'd never been great with words. "It's just that... I want you to know you can talk to me about anything."

His eyes softened as he peered up at me. "I know I can."

"Then why won't you tell me about your son?"

He sighed. "Because I'm afraid, okay?"

"Afraid?" This was surprising. I lowered myself onto the bed next to him. "Afraid of what?"

For a minute he didn't say anything. He simply stared at me, his eyes narrowing as if he was trying to read something that had been written on my face. Then he reached out and touched my cheek. "Afraid of this all ending, I guess."

"Why would it end?"

"My son is actually...around your age," he said in a sad tone, and then he shrugged as if to say, "Your move."

"That's cool," I answered. "I bet you guys are super close, huh?"

"Uh, not really."

"What? You're kidding." I jokingly punched his arm. "I'd give anything to have a dad as cool as you."

He laughed. "I really don't think his opinion of me is as high as yours."

"I guess that's normal," I told him. "We're not supposed to really like our parents at this age, right?"

Rafael nodded, brushing a strand of hair off my face. "Thanks."

"For what?"

"For not freaking out over this."

"Why would I freak out? It's not like I didn't already know how old you were."

"Did you just call me old?"

"Hey, if the shoe fits," I teased.

"Get over here and I'll show you how young I am." He winked, and I happily obeyed.

In the downstairs bathroom I finally found a first-aid kit. I sighed with relief as I opened it, but my relief quickly turned to horror. Dumbfounded, I picked up the baby thermometer still in the package and turned it over in my hands. Below it was baby Tylenol, baby cough syrup, baby syringes, all unopened. The expiration dates were years away. This was all new. Most likely bought in the last month.

Why had you bought a baby first-aid kit?

I thought of all my furniture at home. All the stuff you'd bought me. Maybe this was going to be my next gift.

But then why was it in your bathroom?

Sullivan rubbed his nose on my shoulder and fussed. I felt his head. He was getting hotter. I didn't have time to speculate about the kit anymore.

I put Sullivan down for a few seconds so I could open the packaging on the thermometer. It was one of those fancy forehead ones, so it only took a second to swipe it over his forehead and get a reading.

103.

Well, I guess it could have been worse.

And he *had* been teething. Hadn't I read somewhere that teething caused fevers? I wasn't sure. Again, it was something you probably could've answered.

Regardless, I swiftly opened the Tylenol and gave him the recommended dosage. Within a half an hour, his fever started to go down. The cooler his body got, the calmer I got.

See, I was nailing this parenting thing. I didn't even need you.

Before long, Sullivan was asleep. My arms were like rubber. I shook them out as I went into the kitchen to pour a glass of wine. As I left the kitchen, I noticed a leather-bound journal sitting near your laptop. The same laptop you'd been looking at when I came in on Sunday. How had I missed the journal then?

Snatching it up with my free hand, I went into the family room and sank down onto the couch. While sipping my wine, I flipped to the first page.

There were two columns. On one side you'd written a date. On the other was short, choppy sentences. Your penmanship was seriously the worst, so it took a lot of squinting and guessing before I could make out any of it.

The first sentence I deciphered was: *She put baby on stomach in crib. Was mad when I told her to flip him.*

My mouth dried out. I sat forward, tried to figure out the next line.

Diaper was full and heavy. She hadn't changed him for hours.

The milk in his bottle was spoiled.

Sullivan had a scratch and bruise on his upper thigh.

How dare you? Sometimes Sullivan scratched himself. His nails were sharp. He'd scratched me too.

What was the point of this list? Were you trying to prove I was an unfit mother? With a trembling hand, I set my wine down on your glass coffee table. Who were you going to show this to?

Anger rose up inside me, whipping around my insides like a tornado.

I thought about the first-aid kit and the bassinet up in your room. You were going to try to take Sullivan from me, weren't you?

And to think I'd felt kind of bad about what I'd done to you.

But you deserved it.

Discarding the journal, I headed into the kitchen. The wine was making my stomach sour. I needed a snack. What went well with wine?

I opened your fridge and scanned the shelves.

Nothing was super interesting. It was all bland and boring, like your underwear.

I opened the top crisper drawer, expecting to see fruits and vegetables. But it was filled with cheese. And not the wrapper kind my mom always bought. No, these were fancy cheeses. And you had so many of them.

What did you do with all of this cheese?

I picked up a package, reading the label. *Perfect for charcuterie boards.*

What the hell was a charcuterie board? Leaning against the counter, I pulled out your phone. Then I googled "charcuterie boards."

After gathering all the cheeses and a log of salami, I rifled around in your pantry and cupboards. It wasn't hard to find the crackers and a round wooden board that looked kind of like what I saw online. You had everything in labeled bins like someone with a legit case of OCD. *God, you really had a lot of time on your hands, huh, Kelly?*

I assembled the meats and cheeses until it resembled the picture I'd found. Standing back, I assessed my work. *So fancy.*

Maybe I was cut out for this suburban-housewife shit after all.

Carrying my wine in one hand and my cheese board in the other, I made my way up the stairs. I'd been dying to sit out on the balcony outside your room ever since I'd gotten here. It was still stormy, but I figured the awning would keep me dry. I bundled up in one of Rafael's coats, inhaling the familiar scent of him that lingered in the fabric. Then I stepped out onto the deck. Wind whistled around me, like a group of construction workers. Clutching tightly to the wine and cheese board, I sat down on a wicker chair. It squeaked and groaned. I prayed it wouldn't break. It didn't feel sturdy.

Once I got settled, I set the board in my lap and sipped the wine. The warmth of it slid down my throat, coating my insides. Leaves skittered on the ground; the branches on the trees in the distance rocked back and forth as if they were dancing in time to a manic drumbeat. Rain pelted the awning above me, and every once in a while, a spray of mist flew in my direction. But mostly I stayed dry.

I didn't like all of the cheeses. Some were a little stinky. One tasted like feet. And one was more like a dessert than a cheese. I finished off all the salami, though.

Staring down at the yard, I eyed the shed in the corner and thought about your stupid journal. I still couldn't believe what you'd been plotting. And here I thought I was the only one with an ulterior motive.

I mean, yeah, I knew you were into Sullivan. I saw the way you looked at him with your googly, "oh, no, my eggs are all dried up" eyes. And, okay, yeah, I knew all about how you took that lady's baby at the store. But you seemed pretty stable to me. At least, you had until the night we slept over. You were acting like Sullivan was your child, and it scared me.

Still, I never could've imagined what you were plotting.

Leaning back in my chair, I took another sip of the wine. I hadn't drunk much wine prior to hanging out with you. Mostly, I'd stuck to cheap stuff that got me drunk fast. Whiskey, rum, vodka, tequila.

Actually, tequila's what I'd been drinking the night that I first met Aaron. His roommate had posted about a party, and I assumed he'd be there. I didn't realize there would be so many other people at the party, though. I'd gone to get close to Aaron, but kept getting hit on by other guys. Finally, I'd given in and started taking tequila shots with some guy I'd just met.

But it ended up working out, because those tequila shots were the reason I first talked to Aaron.

My head was fuzzy, my eyelids so heavy it took actual effort to keep them open. I reached for the wall to steady myself but missed it and my body toppled forward.

"Whoa." Arms came around me, locking me in place.

I looked up. Aaron stood over me. Staring at his face, I tried to find traces of Rafael, but could barely find any. His face was softer, rounder, where Rafael's was sharper, more angular.

"You okay?" Aaron asked, studying my eyes.

I looked down, bit my lip and nodded. My stomach rolled, moisture filling my mouth. I tried to breathe in through my nose and out my mouth to ward off the nausea, but it was no use. Within seconds, I was doubled over, about to puke all over the ground. My face was hot, and beads of sweat formed along my upper lip.

Awesome.

"Hang on." Aaron guided me down the hallway. "Let's get you in here."

He ushered me into a tiny bathroom that smelled faintly of soap, mostly of BO. I fell to my knees in front of the toilet and threw up, some of it missing the bowl. I heard the door click behind me and assumed Aaron had left. Not that I blamed him. This was pretty gnarly.

Leaning over, I hurled again. My hair started falling in my face, but then I felt hands at my neck, brushing the hair back and gathering it at the nape of my neck. I turned slightly. Aaron was on his knees behind me.

"You don't have to—"

"Don't worry about it," he said, cutting me off.

I was about to protest but ended up throwing up again. God, how much tequila did I consume?

When I sat back up, I breathed deeply. Aaron still held my hair. I wiped sweat from my brow and leaned against him.

"Aren't you grossed out?" I asked.

"Not gonna lie, it's pretty nasty in here."

I laughed. "How are you not throwing up?"

"For starters, I didn't drink an entire bottle of tequila."

So, he'd been watching me. Interesting.

"No, I mean, like, seeing someone else barf makes me barf."

"Aah, yeah, I see. I guess my stomach is made of steel."

"That's your superpower, huh?" I joked.

He laughed, but there was something lingering behind his eyes. A seriousness that wasn't there before. "If I was a superhero, I'd be the one with the lamest power. Yeah, that'd be just my luck." He shook his head and looked at me. "What about you? What superpower would you want?"

Biting my lip, I thought for a minute. "I don't know."

"C'mon, there has to be something. Superhuman strength, invisibility?"

"I already feel pretty strong, and I definitely don't want to be any more invisible than I already am."

"Yeah, I get that." Aaron was quiet a minute. "But you're not invisible. Trust me."

I averted my eyes from his intense gaze, uncomfortable with how nice he was being. When I thought about my plan, my stomach hurt again. If he kept being so nice to me, I worried I wouldn't be able to go through with it. Then again, I was too drunk to do anything tonight, so at least that bought me some time.

A knock on the bathroom door startled us.

"I think I'm done anyway," I told him.

He helped me up and took me back to his room. I thought maybe he was going to try to make a move on me. Instead, he laid me down, covered me with a blanket and left me alone to sleep it off.

So, anyway, yeah. That was the last time I drank tequila.

CHAPTER
TWENTY-FIVE

On Tuesday night, I slept in your bed wearing one of your husband's T-shirts. It was one of the best nights of sleep I'd had in a long time. For the first time in weeks, I felt like things were looking up. I no longer felt guilty.

I still had Sullivan. And you were gone.

The universe had righted itself. The good guys were winning.

When I threw off the blanket, the edge of it skimmed the jagged scar on my right kneecap, sparking a memory.

"How did this happen?" Rafael traced the outside of *my scar with his fingertips. It tickled, but in a good way.*

"Broken beer bottle," I said.

His eyes crinkled at the corners, and he opened his mouth like he was going to make a joke. But when he caught my expression, he clamped his mouth shut.

Over the years, I'd made up lots of stories about how I'd gotten this scar, every one more dramatic than the last. But I'd never actually told anyone the truth. Something about Rafael's concerned expression made me want to open up.

"I was cleaning up after a fight between my mom and

my stepdad. I knelt down to wipe up some blood. There was broken glass in the carpet, but I didn't see it."

"You've never mentioned a stepdad before."

"He wasn't around long."

"And your dad?"

"Never met him." I frowned. "Never knew anything about him, actually."

"I'm sorry." Rafael's hand covered my scar. "You deserved better than that."

Did I? I wasn't sure. But Rafael made me want to believe I did.

Smiling, I peered up at him. "You're a good guy, you know that?"

He frowned, his eyes lowering. "I doubt my wife would agree with you on that one."

"Hey." I tucked my finger under his chin. "She's wrong. Trust me, you're one of the good ones."

Sliding out of bed, I padded over to the bassinet and peered inside. Sullivan was still asleep, even though it was past six a.m. It was a miracle.

See, what did I say?

All was right with the world.

Content, I watched Sullivan's chest rise and fall steadily. His cheeks were their normal pale color. I didn't want to touch his skin for fear I'd wake him, but he didn't look like he had a fever anymore.

A noise in the distance caught my attention. It was familiar, a loud rattling noise followed by beeping. My insides sagged. *The garbage truck.*

It must have been garbage day on your street. When I was growing up, the garbage was always my responsibility. Anytime I forgot, the older gentleman who lived next door would knock on the door and offer to take our garbage cans out to the street. He knew I was raised by a single mom, so he was always helping out. He was maybe the only nice guy I'd ever known growing up. Sometimes I wished my mom could date him, but he was at least seventy years old.

It was the same at Ella's. She had a neighbor who helped with hers.

But no one had reminded me here. There were no knocks on the door last night.

That's because you were probably good about remembering garbage day. You probably wheeled your garbage cans out every Tuesday night like clockwork. Probably never missed a week.

Panic clawed at me. Which was exactly why it would seem suspicious to the neighbors that you'd forgotten today. For all they knew you were home. Why would you forget the garbage cans?

I ran a hand down my face.

Good going, Kelly.

Groaning, I walked slowly toward the window overlooking the backyard. I pressed my palm to the cold glass and stared down at the shed in the corner. It was locked tight. Rain pelted the roof, flooded the backyard.

It had been two days.

After the garbage incident, I couldn't afford any more mistakes.

The neighbors would start to notice the smell. I'd put it off long enough. It was time to take care of business.

I waited until Sullivan's early-afternoon nap before heading outside. Grateful for the break in the rain, I wore my favorite pair of shredded jeans, a long-sleeved shirt and

Chucks on my feet. I'd thrown my hair up in a messy bun. It was a look you probably couldn't pull off.

I checked on Sullivan one last time and was satisfied to see him sleeping soundly. *Suck it, Kelly.* I was a good mom.

Then I made my way over to the diaper bag. Fishing around, my fingertips lit on something cold, slick and metal. I closed my fingers around it and lifted it out. I didn't need to check to see if there were bullets in it. I knew there were.

Swallowing hard, I tucked the gun in my back pocket and hurried down the stairs, my feet thudding loudly with each step. The gun was merely a precaution. I didn't anticipate having to use it.

The key to the shed hung on a hook near the back door. Snatching it up, I slid the key ring around my index finger.

A slight breeze whisked over my face when I stepped outside and swiftly trampled across the back lawn. When I reached the shed, I took a deep breath. Sniffed. Cleared my throat.

All I smelled was damp earth, mud, grass, cool air. I bit my lip, my body shaking slightly, not from cold but from adrenaline. I glanced back at the house, thinking of Sullivan asleep upstairs. Thank god he wasn't old enough to walk to the window and peek out. What would he think of his mom then?

Exhaling, I slid the key ring off my finger. The key dangled from it, swinging in the wind. A breeze circled me, kicking up leaves and twigs. A few strands of hair broke loose from my bun and tickled my face. As I wiped them away, the key dragged across my skin. The metallic scent reminded me of blood. I shuddered.

What would I find when I opened the shed?

Your dead body?

It's what I expected. What I hoped for even.

But now that I was out here, I wasn't so sure.

I thought about your journal. Sullivan. Rafael. Our future.

Come on, Kelly. Buck up. You can do this.

It was like that time in high school when I went to the lake with a group of friends. They were all jumping off this high rock. I was afraid, but I wouldn't admit that. Instead, I forced myself to jump. I was terrified on my walk up, but I had to just go for it.

Using that philosophy, I grabbed the lock and stuck the key in it. After turning it once, the lock disengaged. Reaching out, I grabbed on to one of the shed doors.

"Kelly!"

I froze.

"Kelly? Are you here?"

Rafael? My heart leaped. He's back early. He came for me.

Finally. My chest expanded, air flowing freely. All of the tension and stress I'd felt for days already started to dissipate.

I no longer had to do any of this on my own. He'd take care of me now. He'd take care of all of this.

Releasing the door, I spun around and raced back to the house.

Good riddance, Kelly.

PART THREE

CHAPTER
TWENTY-SIX

I was swimming.

Water hugged my body like two arms wrapping tightly around me. It was warm, the sun shining bright and intense against the blue sky. It was peaceful. The water around me was still like glass. In the distance I spotted Rafael on the beach. He was lying on a brightly colored towel reading a magazine. My chest expanded. I smiled and waved.

He waved back, his teeth gleaming in the sun when he grinned. The air smelled like salt water and sand and I breathed it in, swirling my arms to keep myself upright. Waves gently lapped against my body.

It was the most activity I'd had all day. Earlier, I'd lounged on the beach drinking margaritas and reading a good book.

Lying on top of the water, I spread my arms out wide like an airplane and floated.

Ah, this was the life.

Splashing and kicking nearby caught my attention. I turned my head to the side.

Aaron was a few feet away, kicking his little legs frantically. At first I thought he was fine. Happy. But then his head slipped under the surface and didn't come back up. I popped up, my feet hitting the sand underneath me. Shielding my eyes from the sun, I looked back to the beach, hoping to signal Rafael. But he was gone. Clouds moved in overhead. I shivered. Aaron was still underwater, kicking and flailing so rapidly the water foamed around him like he was taking a bubble bath. Quickly, I reached out to snatch him up. But my fingers wouldn't latch on. They kept opening and closing, never touching his skin. Water slipped through them, elusive and weightless.

Panic strangled me. Sputtering, I pushed through the water with my arms, but didn't gain any traction. Darkness blanketed me, a loud noise penetrating my ears.

"Aaron!" I called out. I could no longer see him.

Where was he? I slipped farther underwater. Losing control. Drowning right along with him.

My eyelids flipped open. I sucked in a breath. My heart was beating wildly. I sat up, my gaze darting around. The room spun. I blinked. Squinted. Held my head. My fingers grazed my temple, touching something hard and crusted. When I pulled my hand back it was red, stained with dried blood. Razor-like cuts lined my palm, a couple of Band-Aids wrinkled and hanging precariously from my skin.

It all came back to me, a reel of snapshots.

Breaking the mug in the sink.

Carrying the pieces outside.

Cleaning my hand in the downstairs bathroom.

You showing up.

Me confronting you.

You and me fighting.

You attacking me.

Hitting me in the head.

Blacking out.

My insides turned to ice. Where was I?

Glancing up, it took me a minute to recognize the space. It was dark. Small. Made of plastic or something.

My heart sank.

Our shed.

I was in the shed in the backyard.

Rain hit the roof. Wind howled. The doors rattled and clanked, but didn't budge, which meant you'd locked me in. I peered up at the walls. There were no windows. When Rafael and I had bought the shed, we'd looked at ones with windows, but couldn't afford them. So we'd ended up buying a used one from some guy on Craigslist.

A headache pricked behind my eyes, smothered my entire head. It was the worst headache I'd ever had.

Was it a concussion?

How long had I been in here?

In the tiny sliver between the doors, I caught a glimpse of light. It wasn't nighttime. But with the storm it was impossible to tell what time of day it was.

Or *what* day it was.

Lying back down so my headache would subside a bit, I fought to remember what day it had been when you and I fought. It only took a minute before I remembered it had been Sunday.

Sunday.

My pulse jump-started.

Christine and I had a wine night planned for Sunday. Surely, she knew something was wrong. Hope sparked like a lit match. She'd rescue me.

Reaching down, I stuck my hands into my jeans' pockets.

Empty.

Of course you didn't put me in here with my phone.

Closing my eyes, I saw the picture in my mind. The one of you at the party. You never answered my questions. Never told me how you knew Aaron.

Instead, you lied. Tried to make me feel crazy. Mistaken.

But I wasn't. I knew what I saw. I knew the truth.

And the fact that I was locked in my shed, bleeding from my head, told me I was spot-on. Why else would you attack me?

My throat was parched; my head pounded. I had to get out of the shed. Why had you put me in here? What were you up to?

It seemed like an odd choice. To keep me close. To leave me in my own backyard.

Unless…

My heart pounded.

Did you think I was dead?

Shifting on the hard ground, I looked down at my jeans. They were caked in mud. The sleeves on my arms were wet and dirty too. You'd dragged me out here. Like someone would a dead body.

Fingers of fear played down my spine.

Reaching up, I touched my head again. The cut was bad. I probably needed stitches. Glancing back at the locked doors, my stomach dropped. I was too light-headed and weak to try to muscle my way out of here. But I couldn't lie here and bleed out either.

Was that what you were banking on? Did you leave me in here to rot? Were you in my house? Living my life?

Or worse. Were you gone?

Frustrated, I stared up at the bowed ceiling. Rain still

pattered against it. Listening to the steady rhythm, I imagined you far from here. Maybe in another country.

I didn't know what was worse. You here or you gone.

Either way it was shitty.

Boxes dug into my side, so I rolled over slightly, but it didn't help. As I struggled to find a comfortable position, a hysterical laugh tumbled from my throat. For several minutes I continued to laugh until my belly ached and my throat burned. If anyone could see me now they'd think I had cracked up.

And maybe I had.

It *was* crazy. Me being locked in my own shed in my own backyard by you. A girl with my same damn name. A girl who had known not only my son, but my husband.

Sure, you'd denied both. But I didn't believe you. Not for one second. I knew what I saw. I knew the truth.

How had this become my life?

The laughter turned into sobs. Racking my body and stealing my breath. I thought back to the morning the doctor's office called me. The morning I'd first learned about you. If only I'd been able to forget it. To let it go. If only I hadn't sought you out. Then maybe none of this would've happened.

But then, dizzy, vision clouding, I remembered the texts to Raf's phone, the picture of you with my son.

It wasn't a coincidence that we met. I'd been right all along. You found me. Not the other way around.

Now, black waters pulling at my mind, the only question was why.

"Mommy! Mommy! Help."

It was pitch-black. I blinked, and squinted, but couldn't see a thing.

"I'm coming, baby. Hang on," I hollered into the darkness and started running blindly.

Crying.

A baby.

My heart pounded.

I ran faster. Harder.

The crying got closer.

"I'm here. Mommy's here."

Finally. A sliver of light. Dim, but visible. There was a room at the end of the hall. The crying was coming from it. I raced inside, and the light brightened.

The bassinet was in the corner. I hurried to it.

Only it wasn't Aaron. It was Sullivan. He was crying so hard his face had turned beet red.

"It's okay. Shh." Reaching inside, I picked him up.

Holding him in my arms, I turned away from the bassinet and gasped. The room had been empty when I got here. But now you were here standing next to Rafael and Aaron, smiling at me.

"Get away from my son," I said, my chest tightening.

"You first." You touched Aaron's shoulder.

Panic choked me. "Don't touch him. Don't hurt him."

You started laughing then. Loudly. Maniacally.

"You can't stop me. Not anymore," you said.

Red-and-blue lights flashed behind you. Sirens rang out. Dread sank into my gut when I caught sight of the officers. The ones who came to my house that night. The ones who told me my son had died.

Not again. No, please. Not again.

Pain woke me. My headache wasn't going away, and I was pretty sure the wound was still bleeding. I had no idea how long I'd been in here. Hours? Days?

Pushing myself up on my elbows, I scoured the small space. It was cramped. Not only had we bought one of the cheaper storage units, but we also bought a small one. The cold seeped through my shirt, and I shivered.

I was surrounded by boxes. Narrowing my eyes, I struggled to read what I'd written on them. When I found the one marked "kitchen," I moved over to it.

My head swam as I pried open the flaps.

Grabbing out several dish towels, I tied them together and then wrapped them around my head wound. I wasn't sure if it would work. I'm not a doctor. But I'd watched a lot of television, and it seemed like something the characters would do on one of those hospital dramas.

If nothing else, it made my head a little warmer.

It was still raining. The pounding on the roof had become like white noise to me now.

In the corner of the shed, I spotted a few of Aaron's action figures. I conjured up the memory of his sound effects when he played. The way he'd make his voice deep when being the characters. I remembered the way he'd scrunch his face up, making himself look stern and tough.

But to me, he was always my sweet little boy.

My heart.

My truest love.

A tear slid down my face.

"The autopsy report said they found drugs and alcohol in Aaron's system," Rafael explained. "He OD'd."

"No." I shook my head, confused. It was morning. Rafael had been getting ready for work when he got the call. I got out of bed, making my way over to him. "That can't be right. Aaron doesn't do drugs."

"Apparently he does... Did."

It was the correction that caused me to slap him in the face. The way he had to cruelly remind me that my son was gone. Dead. As if I wasn't aware. As if I needed it constantly thrown in my face.

His eyes flashed. Shaking his head, he backed away from me. I knew I should apologize. Make things right. But I didn't. When he left the room, he slammed the door so hard the windows rattled. I slid down the wall until my butt hit the floor. Cries spilled from my mouth, unspooling on the ground.

They were wrong. All of them.

It was a mistake. Aaron didn't use drugs. He didn't drink, not recklessly. He was a good boy. I knew him. They didn't.

I sat there against that wall until day turned to night. I never went after Rafael. I never said sorry or begged him to come back to our room. When he left for work that day, I never even said goodbye.

I didn't have it in me. Maybe if I had, things would've been different. Maybe we would've been all right.

But he wasn't the one I was sorry about.

He wasn't the one I wanted back.

I knew I wouldn't last long without food or water. My stomach cramped, ached. I waffled in and out of hunger and nauseousness. My throat was parched and scratchy.

Head spinning, I lay back. Aaron's face swam above me, flickering like a light being turned off and on in rapid succession. I reached up, trying to grasp the apparition, attempting to hold it tight. Keep it here. Believe in it. Closing my eyes, I imagined him here. In the weeks after Aaron's death, sleeping was my favorite. Aaron visited me in my dreams. He sat with me. Talked with me. Held me. It was in the harsh light of day that he disappeared, that I had to live without him.

Keeping his face cemented in my mind, in the place I could control, I softly sang to him the way I did when he was a boy.

"Twinkle, twinkle, little star..."

I was thirsty. So thirsty.

Slumping, I melted into the floor. As the cold permeated me, I imagined myself becoming one with the floor. Of letting myself go.

It would be so easy. I could lie here until my body drifted away.

Then I'd be with Aaron. My baby boy.

Was he waiting for me? Did he want me to leave this life? Did he want me to find him?

Rain gently hit the roof of the shed, steady and fast like a drumbeat. Like a song I vaguely remembered.

Warmth filled me. I dived underwater, sweeping my arms out wide. Water weaved through my fingers. I felt like I was floating. Far, far away. As if I was hovering over my own body. I saw Aaron calling my name, bubbles escaping through his lips. Waving me forward, he sank farther and farther underwater.

Without looking back, I swam to him.

CHAPTER TWENTY-SEVEN

It was a month after Aaron died when I took that little boy from the grocery store. To hear other people tell it, you'd think I kidnapped him at gunpoint or something equally horrifying.

But that wasn't how it happened at all.

I'd hardly left my house in a month. Most days I stayed inside hiding under the covers, willing the day to end. Praying it had all been some horrific nightmare. Or one of those shows where they would pop out and say I'd been punked. But weeks turned into a month and I still hadn't woken up or been told it was all a joke.

Rafael was at work and our fridge was empty.

I'd been taking antidepressants like they were candy, and I was pretty fuzzy-headed. At the store I lazily made my way down the aisles, throwing items absentmindedly into my cart. I do remember glancing in my cart at one point and thinking it didn't look at all like what I normally bought. Almost as if I hadn't been paying attention at all.

It was in the ice cream aisle that it had happened. I was looking for plain chocolate, which I assumed would be easy enough. But it wasn't. There were so many different flavors. When I finally found it, I felt so relieved I almost cried.

Not because I liked chocolate ice cream. I rarely even ate ice cream. But Aaron did. And chocolate was his favorite.

Turning, I dropped the ice cream into the cart and pushed it forward.

"Ice-keme," a little voice said. I peered down, and it was like a miracle. Aaron was back, sitting in the cart.

Finally, it had happened. The thing I'd been waiting for for weeks.

Chest swelling, I scooped him up and pressed his face to mine.

"Mama," he said.

"Yes. Mama," I repeated excitedly, my insides all warm and cozy.

I abandoned the cart then. Not for any sinister reason, but because I didn't care about the food. Not once I'd gotten my child back.

I'd barely reached my car when I heard her.

The child's actual mother, screaming bloody murder. It only took seconds before I was surrounded by men who worked at the store, along with a security guard.

"Ma'am, give back the child."

"No." I shook my head. "He's my son."

"He's not yours. Please, give him back."

"But he'd been in my cart," I mumbled as they pried him from my arms.

I'd spent the rest of the day at the police station, answering questions. Rafael was livid when he showed up later that night. But in the end, the woman didn't press charges. Everyone in town knew about Aaron's death.

Rafael explained that I wasn't trying to steal her son.

I was delusional. That was how they'd described me. The police officers. My therapist. My husband. I hated that word, but I guess I should've been grateful for it because it kept me out of jail. At first, Rafael wanted to have me committed to a mental hospital, but I'd talked him out of it by agreeing to see Dr. Hillerman once a week.

A part of me had hoped the sessions would help both of us find healing. But Raf refused to even take me there, let alone go with me. I thought going to therapy would show him that I was strong, or at the very least trying to be.

But ever since I'd fallen apart after Aaron's death he refused to see me as anything but weak.

Thunder clapped, sharp and fast like a gunshot. I flinched, my eyelids fluttering momentarily. My throat burned, and my tongue was so dry it felt swollen. Swallowing was like knives slicing my throat.

Rain.

That's it.

I shot up, sucking in a breath. My head swirled, but I reached out and steadied myself on a box. You'd been with my son right before he died. You knew something, I was certain of it. And I wasn't leaving this earth until I found out what.

You could attack me. Hit me. Lock me in this shed.

But if you thought that was all it would take to break me, you thought wrong.

You'd grossly underestimated the determination of a mom.

Adrenaline surging, I hoisted myself up and crawled over to a wall of boxes. Scanning them, I found the one I was looking for. I was so weak it took several tries to pry it open. When I did, I had to rifle through almost to the bottom to find what I was looking for. My arms were tired and achy by the time I pulled out one of Aaron's old sippy cups.

I tore the cap off the top and dragged myself over to the double doors. The bottom of them bowed a little. It was something I remembered Rafael complaining about ad nauseam. He kept going on and on about how the guy had hidden the flaw and how he'd tricked us into buying it.

Never thought I'd be grateful for those warped doors.

Holding the cup in my right hand, I attempted to shove my hand through the tiny space between the doors. But my hand wouldn't fit. The space was too small.

My heart sank, my shoulders sagging.

I only let myself sulk for a few minutes. This wasn't the time to give up.

After taking a few deep breaths, I tried again. I gripped the edges of both doors, my knuckles bumping. Using all my strength, I moved my knuckles away from each other in an attempt to pry the doors open.

It didn't budge.

My fingers stiffened, the tips like ice cubes. I pumped my fingers to regain circulation. Then I blew on them to create heat and went back to trying.

Finally, after what felt like forever, I gained a little traction. The opening was wide enough to fit my hand through. Getting the cup out with it was a little more difficult, but even that I could eventually manage.

Sighing with relief, I held my hand out of the opening and listened to the raindrops as they pinged against the inside of the cup. When it became heavy in my palm I pulled my hand back in. It bumped and a little spilled, but there was still water in the cup when I got my arm back inside.

I drank it greedily. It was cold and tasted like earth, but it felt good as it coated my tongue and slid down my throat. The cup was empty in seconds and already I wanted more. But my stomach groaned in protest, so I decided to wait a few minutes.

Staring at the tiny gap, I wondered if I'd ever be able to get it large enough to fit my entire body through. I doubted it, but I knew I had to try.

There was no way I could rot away in here forever.

Leaning my head against the wall, I breathed deeply. A raindrop hit the toe of my shoe. The little opening was allowing rain to seep in. Cool air brushed my face. I shivered.

But it was a small price to pay for something to drink. Without it, I would've surely died.

I guess technically I still would if I couldn't get some food. But the water supply definitely bought me some time.

A familiar sound cut through the raging winds and pelting rain. Voices. I sat up taller. Someone was in the backyard next door. Kids, I think. Probably playing in the rain. Aaron loved doing that. And where there are kids, there are adults, right?

I scrambled to the door and pressed my lips to the opening. "Help!" I shouted. "I'm stuck in the shed. Help!" Pausing, I listened for a response.

Nothing.

Now I didn't even hear the talking.

"Hello?" I called. "Anyone there? Please help! I'm stuck!"

When several more minutes passed without any response, I slammed my palm against the door and groaned in frustration. "Please, somebody help me!" I screamed again and again for what felt like hours but was probably only minutes. I didn't stop until my voice was hoarse and unable to project. Defeated, I slumped back down.

The rain was quieter than before.

I needed to get more water before it stopped raining altogether.

With a trembling hand, I snatched up the cup and shoved my hand out the small opening again. It stung as it scraped my skin.

This time it took a little longer to fill and I was way more careful pulling my arm back inside. I couldn't afford to lose any.

What if it stopped raining and didn't start again at all? It's not like we got a lot of rain around here. We'd been in a drought forever. This had been the rainiest fall we'd had in years. That meant the lake would be lush and full this summer. I prayed I'd be alive to see it.

I slowly sipped the water. Once I'd finished all of it, I filled the cup again and then didn't allow myself to touch it, in case I needed it later. I set it down beside my leg and leaned against the side of the shed again.

The shed was cooling down as the air outside darkened. I rummaged through the baby box until I found a couple of blankets. They were Aaron's when he was an infant, so they weren't very big. I had to use multiple to cover my entire body.

I thought about how proud Aaron would've been if he could see me now. He loved those survival shows on TV. Whenever I watched them with him, he'd comment on how I would never last. I didn't disagree with him at the time. *Outdoorsy* was not a word anyone would use to describe me. I didn't camp or hike or fish or any of that stuff.

But look at me now. I was surviving.

Wrapping the soft, fuzzy blankets tighter around me, I caught a whiff of their scent. Mostly they smelled musty like cardboard. But when I dug deep, I could faintly smell baby. Or maybe I was imagining it. Either way, I inhaled deeply and closed my eyes.

I was still holding on to hope that someone had heard me yell. Perhaps they were on their way right now.

Actually, I was surprised Christine hadn't busted in here yet. Surely, she was worried when I wasn't here for wine night.

How did you play that off when she showed up? Did you just turn off the lights and pretend I wasn't here? Or did you answer? Tell her I was gone or had plans?

My stomach soured.

You probably had intervened.

Yeah, that made sense. Christine wasn't worried because you'd spoken to her. Given her an excuse. And I'd gone on and on about my good friend Kelly. She had no reason not to trust you.

My heart fell. I banged the back of my head against the side of the shed and blew out a defeated breath. Were you my only way out of here?

No way.

This wasn't the way it ended for me.

I wasn't going to let you win.

When I woke up there was a dead bug floating in my water.

In the summertime, sometimes Christine and I would sit on her back patio and drink wine. Inevitably, one of us would end up with a dead fruit fly in our half-drunk glasses. Joel would tell us to fish them out and keep drinking, but we both thought that was disgusting. We'd dump the wine and get a new glass.

I didn't have that luxury today.

With my finger, I scooped out the bug and threw it on the ground. Water splatters coated the ground like one of those modern paintings. Picking up the cup, I took a swig of the water. It wasn't raining, so I didn't finish the entire thing. It took all my willpower, but I left half for later.

Through the crack in the doors, I saw the trace of light.

So, it was no longer night, then.

Had I slept through it?

Did that make this day two? Or three?

My stomach rumbled.

Too long. I needed food.

Every January, Christine went on these fasts. Sometimes it was all fruit juice or "dry" January, where she went without wine. One year, she did some horrible thing where she drank this concoction of lemon juice and cayenne pepper.

I only tried to join her once. It was a disaster. I ended up cheating after one day. She was so upset with me, but I explained that my body wasn't made for fasts. I felt sick if I skipped lunch.

How long could a human live without food? It was something I would've googled if I had my cell.

I fantasized about all my favorite foods. Juicy hamburgers with crunchy French fries, ranch on the side. My mouth watered imagining the saltiness lingering on my tongue. Pizza with pineapple and ham. A guilty pleasure I only ordered when Rafael was gone, since he hated cooked fruit of any kind. Chicken enchiladas with spicy red sauce. Chips and guacamole.

Clutching my stomach, I rolled over, tucking my legs

up to my chest. The position helped a little with the hunger pains, but not entirely.

I couldn't stay in here like a sitting duck. You could come back at any time and finish me off. In the weeks that I'd known you, I never thought you were dangerous. At worst, I thought you were here for money. But in my wildest dreams, I never thought you were capable of this.

You seemed harmless.

A little dumb, yeah.

Naive, certainly.

But not dangerous. Not scary or calculating.

Then again, I still didn't really know who you were.

I knew you had Aaron's cuff link.

I knew you were at the same party as him the night he died.

I knew that Sullivan looked like him.

But I also knew you were Keith, so that definitely changed things.

It was Friday night. Rafael and I were sitting on the couch watching a movie. He'd been quiet tonight. Almost like he was distracted. Not as if that was abnormal. Just bothersome. I'd been trying to snuggle, but he kept checking his phone. When he did, a small smile would pass over his lips.

I tried to remember the last time he smiled at me like that.

"Who keeps texting?" I finally asked.

He looked up from his phone in a daze, as if he'd forgotten I was there. "Oh, Keith. He's a new professor in my department."

Yeah, right. "Why is he texting you so much on a Friday night?"

"Just guy stuff. He's cool. We've become friends."

When another text came through a few minutes later, I discreetly peered at his phone, even though he was strategically facing it away from me. My gaze connected with the word Keith.

My muscles softened. Maybe I was being overly paranoid.

But I couldn't shake my suspicions, so later that night while Rafael slept, I went into his phone. He'd changed his password and I had to try so many that I almost got locked out.

Finally, on a whim, I tried KEITH. It worked.

For a split second, I wondered if my husband was gay. But then I clicked on his text thread with Keith. By the looks of the naked pictures, it was clear Keith was no guy. I wanted to read the messages they'd sent to each other, but Raf started stirring, so I locked his phone and slipped back under the covers.

I'd thought about confronting him a million times. Even thought about leaving him. But I was scared. I'd never been on my own. I didn't even have a job, and wasn't sure I'd ever find one that could support me. But mostly I was afraid Aaron would suffer. That Raf would cut off all financial support from him. Then Aaron died, and my whole world blew apart. Leaving Raf was the last thing on my mind.

Now that I knew you were Keith, I had no idea what you were capable of.

Lying on my stomach, I tried to peek through the crack I'd expanded between the doors. But I couldn't make out anything other than the wet grass.

What were you doing?

It was getting darker. Clearly, the neighbors hadn't heard me. I was all alone. No one was coming to rescue me.

Aaron loved those true-crime documentaries. Once I watched an episode with him. It was about a woman who'd been abducted, and I remember saying how hard I would fight. That I would never allow anyone to take me away, and that if by some miracle they did, I would escape.

Turns out, it's easier to get captured than I'd thought.

All this time I'd wrongfully assumed I was the one with the upper hand. Turns out, you were.

Downing the last of my water, I held it in my mouth a minute, savoring it. After swallowing it down, I went to work.

Getting up on my knees, I grabbed the edges of both doors like I'd done earlier. In my mind I saw Aaron give me a smile and nod. Grunting, I used all my strength to pry the doors open. I swore they'd moved, but when I stuck my arm through, the gap didn't seem any larger.

I should've taken my workouts with Christine more seriously. She could probably tear this shed apart. If I ever got out of here, I'd work out more. Lift weights. Maybe take a self-defense class or two. No way would I ever be a victim again.

But first, I had to get the hell out of here.

I kept pushing on the doors, struggling to manipulate the opening. The sky outside turned pitch-black. Wind howled like a wolf. Rain played on the roof.

The storm had returned.

My arms burned and my eyelids felt weighed down.

Giving up for the night, I collected more rainwater, took a few sips and then slid back down onto the floor. Once I was wrapped in Aaron's old baby blankets, I closed my eyes. My fingers wound around the soft fabric as I drifted off to sleep.

CHAPTER TWENTY-EIGHT

I awoke to the sound of the garbage truck.

Any other week, I wouldn't have noticed it. But today it mattered. I finally had a benchmark. It was garbage day. Wednesday. You'd put me in here on Sunday, so that meant I'd been in here for two days and three nights.

Mulling this over, I sipped what was left of my water.

It was quiet. The storm had died down. It was bright through the crack in the door, and warmer in here than it had been. A sweet scent slipped inside that reminded me of flowers and wet grass. There was probably a rainbow in the sky. A promise. I wished I could see it. I wasn't raised religious, but I'd been to church occasionally. And when Aaron was young, I'd taken him a few times, thinking that was what a good parent did.

I knew many Bible stories, Noah and his ark being one of them. So I understood the significance of the rainbow, and they always gave me peace.

I needed some of that peace now. I needed to believe in that promise.

Setting down my empty cup, I dropped my head. I shouldn't

have drank it all, but I was so thirsty. It probably wouldn't rain again, which meant I had no choice. I had to get myself out of here today.

A headache raged behind my eyes. Every muscle in my body ached. Even my skin hurt. Last night the storm had given me strength, but it was gone now. I imagined my strength being unleashed by the wind and rain in another town.

Deflated, I leaned my head back and silently pleaded with you to come back.

With daylight came harsh reality. It felt impossible.

My head snapped up at the sound of a car door slamming in the distance. A dog barked. Tires buzzed.

My flesh prickled. Maybe the storm leaving was a blessing in disguise. People were no longer holed up in their homes.

"Help!" I screamed at the top of my lungs. Well, I tried to anyway. My throat was so dry and scratchy it came out more like a gentle croak. Like I'd turned into a reptile or something equally small. I tried again. "Help! It's Kelly Medina! I'm stuck in my shed. Please." Oh, god. It was no use. I could barely hear myself.

I'd only succeeded in making my headache worse.

Lowering my head into my hands, I massaged my forehead with my fingers, trying to assuage the pain. My vision was blurry, soft at the edges. Slipping back down to the floor, I closed my eyes for a minute.

"Hey, Mom."

My pulse jump-started. Smothering the half-wrapped gift with my hands, I looked up. He'd only been home for Christmas break a few days. I still wasn't used to having him here. "What are you doing up?"

"It's not that late." Aaron lowered himself down on the couch. The room was dark, only lit by the Christmas tree.

I hurriedly pulled the wrapping paper over the bottom side of the box, tore off a piece of tape and crudely pressed it down over the seam. "It's midnight."

He smiled. "Like I said, not that late."

Sometimes I forgot how old Aaron was. To me, he'd always be my baby boy. But he was practically a grown-up now. I discreetly shoved the messily wrapped present under the tree. "Well, I thought you were sleeping. That's why I was down here wrapping presents."

"I didn't see a thing." He raised his hands, palms showing. "Promise." His gaze swept over the boxes under the tree, all wrapped in bright reds and greens. "Does that one say, 'from Santa'?"

I chuckled. "Yeah."

"I stopped believing in Santa years ago."

"I know that," I said, maybe a little too defensively. "It was the year you turned eight. I remember it like it was yesterday."

He flashed me an amused smile. "Yeah, you were pretty upset with me when I wouldn't go to the mall with you to see Santa."

"Well, it was weird. Two days before you had been begging me to take you. Then the day we're supposed to go you told me you don't believe in him." I looked up at my son's face, now chiseled and manly, all traces of the little boy hidden. Some days it seemed unfathomable that I'd never hear his toddler voice or his baby laugh again. There are so many parenting books, but none of them prepared me for all the little losses. No one warned me that I'd spend Aaron's entire life mourning who he used to be, how he *talked and acted. "You never did tell me what happened. How did you figure out Santa wasn't real?"*

He sat back, weaving his fingers together and putting them behind his head. "Dad told me."

"What?" Hot betrayal leaped to my skin.

"It was right before we were supposed to go. I was making a list of the things I wanted to ask Santa for. He asked me what I was doing and when I told him he laughed at me. Told me I was too old to believe in that nonsense. Said I needed to grow up."

"He never told me that." My gaze flickered to the ceiling over my head. Rafael was asleep in the bedroom right above where we sat. My heart pinched. "I'm sorry that happened."

Aaron shrugged. "He wasn't wrong. I was too old."

"No, you weren't."

"Mom, I think if it was up to you, I'd stay a little kid forever."

"Would that be the worst thing?" I threw him a teasing wink.

His smile slipped a little. "I guess not."

I paused, shifting my position on the floor. "Are you happy, Aaron?"

"Yeah, I'm good."

"No, I mean, are you happy? Do you like your life?"

He was quiet a minute, his eyes narrowing. He lowered his hands into his lap. The clock on the wall ticked. I caught a whiff of the tree. "Yeah, I really am."

"So, you like school? And you're making friends and stuff?"

"Yeah." He nodded. "It's cool."

I was surprised at how happy his comment made me.

Ever since he'd left, I secretly hoped he'd get homesick and come back. But as he sat on the couch in front of me, looking like a grown man, I realized I didn't want that for him. I wanted him to have a full, happy life away from here. A life that was all his own.

"I'm so glad. That's all I want for you, you know? To be happy." Moisture pricked at my eyes, and I blinked swiftly, turning toward the tree. I didn't want to freak Aaron out. This was the most we'd talked in months. Since he'd come home on Christmas break, he'd mostly spent time with friends, or locked in his room playing video games or watching YouTube. Even when he was down here he was usually distracted by his phone. Tonight I had his full attention. I wouldn't go and ruin it by getting all mushy and "mom-like." I intended to stay cool and chill.

"What about you?" he asked, sitting forward a little.

"What about me?"

"Are you happy?" The question threw me off guard. It wasn't the type of thing Aaron had ever asked. Our entire relationship had been based on me worrying and wondering about him, not the other way around.

"Yeah, I think so."

"Really?" His eyes narrowed.

"Yeah. Really."

"What is the thing in your life that makes you the most happy?"

I shrugged. "I guess knowing that you're happy."

He shook his head. "Seriously?"

"What? I'm being honest. You're what I'm most proud of in life. You're my greatest accomplishment. My legacy."

"Oh, my god, you're so cheesy."

"Sorry, but you asked."

He sighed, leaning forward even farther. "No, Mom, I asked if you were happy. You. Not me. Isn't there anything in your life that's just for you? Like outside of me and Dad?"

I thought for a moment. "Yeah, I mean, I guess. I have Christine and we do yoga and go to the gym. Have girls' nights."

"That's good." He smiled, and I was glad I had appeased him.

"Whew." I mockingly wiped the back of my hand on my head. "Glad I passed the test."

Laughing lightly, he said, "No test. Just wanted to make sure you were good."

"I'm good," I assured him.

I actually liked this. Maybe this new season in our lives wasn't so bad. He may not have needed me like before, but we could have real, meaningful conversations like friends.

Friends.

That could be nice.

Somewhere outside, a door opened and closed. Keys jangled. Footsteps sounded in the grass. The noises weren't in the distance. They were close. They were coming toward the shed. It had to be you. I wanted to peek through the crack to make sure, but the footsteps were getting closer. There wasn't time.

For one panicked second, I contemplated playing dead. Making you believe that you had actually killed me after you grabbed the candlestick from my hand and bashed me in the head with it. But no. That would be stupid. What if you decided to dispose of the body? Then what?

You were at the shed now. I could hear you putting the key in the lock.

Oh, god. What was I going to do? I was too weak to take you down.

I thought about the wound on my head. Well, two could play at that game.

Determined, I dipped my hand into the nearest box and rummaged around. At first my hand only felt fabric, blankets, nothing hard. Nothing that could be used as a weapon.

My heart hammered in my chest.

You'd gotten the lock undone. I saw the tips of your painted nails curve around the edge of the door. Pastel pink. So unlike you. If it wasn't for your tacky rings, I would've thought it was someone else's hand. Besides, I recognized the color. It was mine.

My heart leaped in my chest as my fingers closed around something hard. I yanked it out, a wave of emotion hitting me. It was an art project of Aaron's from elementary school. Some clay dish thing. It wasn't exactly what I'd been hoping for, but I figured if I could strike you hard enough it would at least buy me time to make a run for it.

I brought my arm back, holding the dish up. The door started to open.

"Kelly!"

I stiffened.

Raf?

The door stopped. Your hand slipped away.

"Kelly? You here?" I heard him call out in the distance.

I held my breath. Your footsteps retreated. At first I thought maybe you were running away. Like you were worried that you'd been caught. But then I heard the back door open and close.

You'd gone inside.

My entire body went cold.

Rafael had said: "You here?" Not: "You home?" That's what he normally said. But he wasn't calling out for me this time, was he? He was calling out for you.

Wow. You really did have the upper hand.

You even got him to come home early. He hadn't come home at all for weeks and now he was here on a Wednesday. For you.

Did he know I was locked in this shed? Did he know you'd attacked me? I swallowed the emotion welling in my throat. My eyes burned.

How could he do this to me?

I knew things weren't great between us, but this? I glanced around at the tiny shed I'd been locked in for days. I wouldn't wish this on my worst enemy. Had my husband really been okay with this?

Did he know about your connection to Aaron?

I blew out a breath. Wind whistled through the trees. The doors to the shed rocked back and forth in the breeze. One of them flew open and cold air smacked me in the face, stealing my breath.

My chest expanded.

The lock. You'd forgotten about the lock.

I stepped forward. The light was bright against my eyes as I emerged from the shed. Shielding my face, I stared downward. I still had that damn headache, but I couldn't think about that now. I needed to get help. Call 911. Get to the doctor.

I headed as quickly as I could toward the side gate, ignoring the dizziness and pounding in my head. This would all be over soon. I just had to get out of here. Get to a neighbor's house. Use their phone. I'd almost made it to the gate when I spotted you in the window. You and my husband.

I stopped walking. I stared at you two and tried to imagine what you were saying. Were you patting yourself on the back for a job well done? Was he congratulating you?

Anger thrashed in my veins.

Were you talking about Aaron?

I couldn't leave quite yet. Not until I knew the truth. Not until I made sure both of you paid for what you'd done to me, and Aaron. And I wanted to make sure Sullivan was safe.

Turning away from the gate, I stalked unsteadily toward my house. My feet sank into the grass with each step, leaving evidence of my continued existence all over my backyard.

CHAPTER TWENTY-NINE

There was no way I could've made it in the house through the back door without being detected. I wasn't quite ready to make myself known. If you thought you'd killed me once already, I doubted you'd hesitate to do it again. I had to come up with a game plan.

Plus, I really wanted to know what you were saying in there.

Moving away from the window, my gaze swept up the back of the house until it reached the balcony outside of my bedroom. It was one of the major selling points of this house. I had envisioned myself drinking my coffee out there in the mornings, sipping wine at night. But, actually, I'd rarely ever used it.

My heart arrested at the sight of a ladder leaning against the side of the house. About a month ago, Rafael had been out here cleaning out the rain gutters. This was probably the first time I felt grateful that he didn't put something away.

My body swayed slightly as I made my way over to it. Dizziness crashed over me and I almost fell over. I stopped

walking and took a few deep breaths while silently praying I could do this.

You need to get to the doctor, a voice that sounded suspiciously like Carmen's kept saying in my head.

But there was a conflicting voice. A stronger voice. It
was Aaron's, and it said, *Mom, you can do this.*

With what can only be described as superhuman
strength, I moved the ladder to the balcony. It was a tad
unsteady, since the ground was wet, so I tried my best to
shove the legs into the ground before stepping up on it. As
I made my ascent, it wobbled a couple of times, but I made
it to the top unscathed.

There was a plate of half-eaten cheese and crackers and
an empty wineglass sitting on the wooden outdoor table.

It appeared you had enjoyed my balcony.

My stomach growled at the sight of food. I had no idea
how long it had been sitting out here, and it was slightly
damp. Still, I shoved the remaining crackers and cheese
into my mouth with total abandon.

A week ago, I would've found this behavior disgusting,
but starvation does funny things to a person.

I thought I would feel better after eating, but my stomach churned once I'd swallowed everything down. Nausea
washed over me. My mouth filled with moisture. I breathed
in through my nose and out through my mouth a couple of
times until it subsided.

Luckily, the patio door was unlocked. I deliberately
turned the knob, and then quietly opened the door, careful
not to make much noise. The minute I stepped into my room
I smelled you. That floral scent of yours. It fueled my anger.

Clothes were strewn all over the floor. A damp towel
lay on top of the unmade bed.

This place is a pigsty. Rafael's voice echoed in my head. I fought the irrational urge to clean up.

A glass of water sat on the nightstand. Desperation filled me. I hurried toward it. When I rounded the corner to the other side of the bed I almost walked right into the bassinet, where Sullivan was soundly sleeping.

Gasping, I clutched my chest. Thank god I hadn't woken him.

After gulping down the water, I felt a little stronger.

Thanks for leaving me the food and drink, Kelly. That was nice of you.

My lips twitching at the corners, I tiptoed to the door. Holding my breath, I slowly opened it and carefully stepped into the hallway.

"You still haven't answered me." Rafael's growl reached my ears. I was familiar with that voice and it caused me to flinch involuntarily. Pressing my back into the wall, I reminded myself that his anger wasn't toward me. At least, not at this moment. "What are you doing in my home? And where is Kelly?"

"I'm right here," you responded, defiance painting your tone. Without even seeing you I could picture your chin raised, your eyes flashing. Weird how I'd only known you a month and already I could read you so well.

It sounded like you two were in the family room at the bottom of the stairs. I crept forward, keeping close to the wall.

"No, not you. I mean…" His voice trailed off.

He meant me. Not you.

A swell of triumph filled me. So, clearly, Rafael wasn't privy to what you'd done.

"Oh, my god. You're her. You're my wife's new friend, Kelly."

Finally. It's about time he figured it out.

"She told you about me?" You sounded shocked. I wasn't sure why.

"Yeah. I mean, she told me she had a new friend, but I never thought she was talking about you," he answered. "Why would you befriend my wife? What are you doing here, Kelly?"

"I'm here for you. So we can be a family," you said. "You, me and Sullivan."

"Sullivan?"

"Our son," you said.

My insides quivered. Sullivan was Rafael's, not Aaron's. I finally had my answer.

"Th-th-that's not possible." His voice quavered.

"Why? Because you told me to get rid of my child? Did you really think I'd do that?"

"You said you would." Rafael spoke slowly, firmly, methodically. The hairs on my arms rose. How sickening that he would ask you to terminate your pregnancy.

"I couldn't do it," you confessed. Despite my best efforts, I admired your courage. "You should be happy I didn't," you added. "Now you have a son."

"I already have—I already had a son." I heard the sadness in his tone, the shakiness of his voice.

My eyes and throat stung.

"Right. You had a son. But now Aaron's gone, and Sullivan's here." I heard shuffling on the carpet as if you were walking, pacing. "Me and Sullivan. We're your family now. I've given you back the family you lost. I've fixed everything for you."

It was all I could do not to stomp down the stairs and rip the smug look I was sure you were wearing off your stupid little face. I may not have been able to get answers out of you about my son on Sunday night, but I sure as hell would now.

"What do you mean, the family I lost? Where's Kelly?" he asked. "What have you done with my wife?"

Running a hand down my face, I groaned in frustration. Really? He was going to pick now to start giving a damn about me? I was fine. *Ask about Aaron.* Find out what she knew.

"It doesn't matter. She left," you said. "She didn't want you. Not like I do. And you don't need her anyway. I'm your wife now, and Sullivan's your son. We're the new Medinas."

"What do you mean? Did you hurt her? And how did you know about Aaron? Wait… Kelly said she found a picture of you at some party with him. I thought she was going crazy again. I—I—I thought she was making it up." He paused, a strangled sound filling the air. Bile rose in my throat. "Oh, my god. She was right. You knew Aaron?"

I should've felt vindicated, but I only felt sick.

"Of course not. I have no idea what you're talking about. Kelly's crazy. I would never hurt your family," you said firmly. "Your son's death was an accident and your wife took off. I'm here to rescue you. Whisk you away to a tropical paradise."

"You think I'm going to leave town with you? *That's* crazy."

"I'm not crazy." Your tone shifted. "Kelly's the crazy one."

"Tell me where my wife is."

"I'm right here."

"My real wife."

"Come on, you can stop playing the good-husband act. We both know you're not one."

"Did you really think this was what I wanted?" Raf's voice was quieter.

"Isn't it?"

I inched along the wall, moving forward until you both were in my line of sight. Your back was to me, but I could make out Rafael's face.

He drew in a shaky breath, and wiped his eyes. "Where's Kelly? Please tell me what you did to her."

"God, you never cared about her this much before," you groaned in frustration.

"I always cared about my wife."

"Come on, Raf. Why are you talking like this? It's just us here. You don't have to put on an act." Your voice turned strangely seductive as you moved closer to Raf, swaying your hips. "I know you. You want me. And now you have me. So, let's forget about your old family. It's time to move on." Reaching up, you ran a finger up his chest.

"Stop it." He slapped your hand away. Took a step back. "I want to know what you did. Where is Kelly?"

You stood perfectly still for a moment. I couldn't see your face but I imagined your shocked expression. After a few seconds, you shook your head. "You haven't changed at all." Your voice was quieter. Raw. Almost childlike. "You're the same guy who told me to get rid of my child. I thought once Kelly and Aaron were out of the picture, you'd be different. But you're not. You were always just using me, weren't you? You told me you loved me, but that wasn't true, was it? You never loved me. It's always been them, hasn't it?"

"No." He shook his head desperately. "That's not true."

"It *is* true. All you care about is her. You know she thinks I'm an unfit mother? But I'm not. I'm a good mom."

Rafael nodded. "I'm sure you are."

Ugh. He was a better actor than me. I'd never be able to say all of this with a straight face. Then again, he'd always been good at pretending.

"Really? You think I'm a good mom?" Your voice was so hopeful then. Clearly, your need for his approval was huge. Poor girl. You really didn't have a clue, did you?

He swallowed hard, his neck swelling with the effort. "I...um... It's obvious by the way you talk about him that you care a lot about your son." He shook his head. "Our son."

Good. Smart thinking.

"You finally said, *our son*," you said. "She wanted to take Sullivan away from me. Did you know that? I found notes she was keeping."

Aah, yes. The notes.

"Is that why you did all this? Because Kelly was trying to take your baby?"

"No, I did this because I love you. You're all I have." I recognized that timbre in your voice. I'd experienced it before. Your plan was unraveling, and now so were you. "I've lost my grandma and my mom. I want a family with you and Sullivan."

Behind me, Sullivan let out a little cry. I ducked down, hiding behind the wall.

"I'm sorry about your family, but what about—"

Your head snapped up. You'd heard it too. "Hold on."

Sullivan's whimpers increased. *Shit.* I hurried down the hall and into the bedroom, keeping my ears perked in case you came up the stairs.

"Shh," I quietly mumbled to Sullivan as I lifted him out of the bassinet. Inside was a pacifier. With trembling fingers, I picked it up and desperately shoved it in his mouth. He instantly quieted. I stood still.

Silence. My skin prickled. I shuddered. Moved closer to the doorway. Held Sullivan tighter against me. What was happening down there? Swallowing hard, I stepped back into the hall. The conversation from downstairs was too far away and muffled for me to pick up from here. Glancing down, I checked to make sure Sullivan's pacifier was securely plugged in his mouth. He sucked vigorously and my stomach twisted. He was hungry. I wouldn't be able to keep him quiet for long.

Downstairs, I heard footsteps, rustling. I walked forward, cocking my head, struggling to hone in on your words.

"What are you doing?" You spoke loud enough for me to catch it. "Don't move." Your tone was icy, dangerous. Biting my lip, I moved faster. "We're playing by my rules now."

God, Raf, what did you try to do?

Bouncing Sullivan gently in my arms, I kept his face planted against my shoulder, hoping it would serve as a buffer to keep his pacifier in place. I'd made it to the end of the hallway. Feeling brave, I peeked around the wall.

That's when I saw that you were holding a gun. It was aimed right at Rafael. Raf's phone was sticking out of the top of your pocket. He'd probably been trying to call for help. I wanted to stay put and listen to your conversation. My need for answers was so great, I could taste it. But I'd seen what you were capable of. Who knew what you'd do wielding a gun. Chances were, all of us could end up dead.

I remembered Aaron's cell phone. His room was close.

I was certain I could make it inside undetected. Carefully, I pressed his bedroom door open. After stepping inside, I closed it almost all the way, enough to shield the noise but not enough to slam it and alert you. Then I inched across the floor. It moaned beneath my feet, but at least the movement kept Sullivan happy. A black cord wound its way from the outlet in the far wall. I followed where it led.

The cell phone sat on the nightstand, face up.

When I touched it, the lock screen appeared, my last text visible. Unread.

I palmed the phone, put in Aaron's code. It opened to his Messages app, our conversation thread at the top with all my texts. All the ones that had gone unanswered.

I miss you.

I love you.

I wish you were here.

And the latest one where I told him all about you.

It felt like a lifetime ago when I sent it. I don't even know why I did. Sometimes it just felt good to talk to him, even if I knew he couldn't talk back. Our texts had almost become like a diary to me. A way to keep him alive.

Taking a deep breath, I brought up the keypad.

With a slick fingertip, I dialed 911. After the operator answered, I whispered off my address and said there was an active shooter in my home. Heart hammering in my ears, I hung up, praying you hadn't heard me. When I turned around, I half expected you to be standing over my shoulder. I could almost feel the cool metal of the gun barrel against my temple.

But you weren't. The room was empty, and I sighed with relief. I was about to put the phone down when I spotted Aaron's audio-recording app. My insides leaped.

Perfect.

Phone in hand, Sullivan cradled against my chest, I made my way back to the hallway and crouched down. Downstairs, the scene looked tense. You were pacing, careful to keep the gun trained on Rafael. His face was a sickly gray color.

I pressed Record in the audio app and then, careful of Sullivan's binky as I bent, I set the phone down on the ground near my feet.

Raf hung his head. "I'm so sorry. I never should've said that to you."

That's good. Keep apologizing.

"Don't patronize me." You stopped pacing and lifted your chin. From this vantage point, I could make out your profile. A slight sheen of sweat had gathered on your skin. "You're not sorry. You wish I would've done it. Gotten rid of our child."

"No." He shook his head, his eyes pleading with yours. "I don't wish you'd done that. Not now that I know what it feels like to lose a son. I was wrong, okay? I was wrong about all of it. I'm so sorry, Kelly. But, please, I need to know what happened with Aaron."

Sullivan wiggled in my arms. I held the pacifier in place, bouncing him. I needed him quiet just a little longer. Desperation swam in my veins. My need for answers was so great I could hardly stand it. I pitched forward, afraid of missing even one word.

"Aaron." The way you spoke his name gave me pause. If I didn't know better I'd say you cared about him. "Aaron is my one regret in all this." Your lips shook. You bit down on the lower one. "He was nice. A lot nicer than you're being right now." You frowned, your eyes narrowing at Rafael. "I didn't want to hurt him. You have to believe that."

"But you did? You hurt him?" Rafael asked in a way that told me he didn't want to believe it.

"I didn't have a choice."

"So, it wasn't an accidental overdose?"

It was silent for several minutes. I started to think you wouldn't answer.

But then you shook your head, offering a quiet "No. I put the pills in his drink."

Tears slid down my face. My lips quivered.

My son.

My baby.

I met a girl. We're not dating yet. But I like her. She's cool.

It wasn't an accident.

You killed him.

Rafael's hand flew to his mouth, his eyes filling with tears. His face was such a sickly gray, he matched the walls. "You drugged my son? You killed my son?"

"I had to. Don't you get it yet? It was the only way for us to be together," you said, your tone desperate.

"Oh, my god." Rafael staggered backward, his eyes wild. He brought his arms up, running his hands down his face. "I—I don't get it. I don't understand."

"Don't get what?"

"Any of it."

"You said you already had a kid and didn't need another." You shrugged. "So I fixed it."

"Oh, my god. Did you really think you could get rid of my family and just replace them, and I'd be okay with that?" Rafael's eyes flashed. "Were you expecting me to show up here today, find you in my house and run off with you, no questions asked?"

"You think this is how I planned it?" Your voice was stronger now, a fire burning beneath it. "No, I had hoped you would choose me. That you would help me. I wasn't supposed to do any of this alone. That's what I'd been waiting for when I stayed in this shitty suburban town hanging out with your wife and living in a hellhole. That's why I was calling and texting you all the time, but you didn't respond."

"And you couldn't take the hint?"

"You were miserable with them!" Your voice rose. "You told me so yourself. I did you a favor. I thought you would thank me. And Kelly wasn't happy either. That's why I started to think maybe I wouldn't have to kill her. I thought she'd give us her blessing, move on and find a new family of her own."

Raf's mouth dropped. "You were waiting for Kelly to give us her blessing?"

"Or for you to come around." You stepped closer to him. "It didn't have to be this way. I know you, Raf. I know you've always wanted me more than her. You only told me a million times, so why'd you have to make this so difficult? Why did you turn on me like this?"

God, I hated you both in that moment.

I was so tired of listening to all of this crazy shit. I wanted all of it to be over.

Sullivan whimpered, kicked and wiggled in my arms.

I held him so tight my fingers dug into him. He looked up at me with wide, trusting eyes.

Had my son looked at you the same way?

He was the spitting image of you. You and Rafael. I could see that now. He wasn't Aaron's. He wasn't my grandson. He was the reason you'd bashed me in the head and left me bleeding in that shed. He was the reason my son was murdered.

Sullivan clutched my shirt, his fingers grazing my skin. It disgusted me. I held him away from my body. His eyes widened as his legs dangled over the banister. If I held him out a little farther and let go, he'd fall. It was a long way to the floor.

An eye for an eye. A tooth for a tooth.

One son for another.

CHAPTER THIRTY

I watched as Sullivan's body tumbled toward the ground. Everything seemed to decelerate, as if I'd pushed the pause button repeatedly. He was moving in slow motion, his chubby legs and arms flailing as he made his descent toward the floor.

You screamed, falling to your knees in angst. A guttural sound escaped your lips. I thought it would feel good to see you suffer, but it didn't. My mouth filled with moisture, and I gagged.

Rafael looked up at me in horror.

Oh, god, what was I thinking?

Blinking, I came out of my trance.

Heart thumping, I drew Sullivan back into my chest. His pacifier popped out, fell to the ground the same way his body had in my daydream. He let out a wail.

How could I even let my mind imagine that? He was an innocent child. If I had hurt him, I'd have been no better than you.

"I'm so sorry," I mumbled, stroking his head. My lips

grazed his soft skin. He cried into my shoulder. Shame burned through me.

"Kelly?" You still had the gun aimed at Rafael, but your gaze had found me. "How? What? I thought…"

"That I was dead? Dying? Locked in the shed?"

Your eyes widened.

Satisfaction filled me.

"Oh, thank god," Rafael breathed, his shoulders visibly relaxing. Until his eyes raked over my bandaged head. "Are you okay?"

I wasn't okay. Not by a long shot. I wasn't sure I ever would be. But I nodded.

"What happened?" he demanded.

"Your girlfriend tried to kill me…after she killed our son." I made my way down the stairs.

The closer I got, the wider your eyes became. Your entire body trembled and your gaze shot back and forth between Rafael and me. We had you surrounded.

I smiled.

You turned the gun on me. "Stay back or I'll shoot."

"You won't shoot me." I glanced down at Sullivan. "Not with Sullivan in my arms. I mean, that's why you did all this, right? For your son. You took my son so you could give your son a better life?" It was a gamble. I prayed I was right.

Where were the cops? Shouldn't they have been here by now?

"Did you really think any of this would work, Kelly? Did you think it would be worth it?" I shook my head. "Rafael doesn't want you."

"Yeah, I get that now." You raised the gun, a flash of defiance in your eyes.

"Kelly!" Rafael hollered, his eyes catching mine.

In the distance I heard sirens. Air swelled in my chest.

Your eyes shifted wildly, your expression filled with betrayal. "You called the cops?"

"Time's up, Kelly."

"No, *your* time is up." Your finger rested on the trigger. It was all happening so fast.

"No!" Rafael yelled, lunging in your direction.

His arms came around you as the gun went off. I dived to the floor, my ears ringing. Sullivan screamed. I wrapped my body around him, taking the brunt of the fall. When I dared to open them, I frantically searched my body and Sullivan's for blood, bullet holes.

Impossible. We seemed to be unscathed. Where had the bullet gone? The sirens came closer.

You and Rafael rolled around on the ground as he attempted to wrestle the gun out of your hand. Grunting and groaning filled the room. Sullivan wailed in my arms. I scooted toward the couch. When I reached it, I pressed my back into it, holding Sullivan tightly against my chest.

"Shh, it's okay," I assured him, running my hand up and down his back.

Lowering my chin, my lips brushed over Sullivan's head. Behind us I heard Rafael grunt, then the crack of the gun hitting the floor.

Shit. It wasn't over yet.

Carefully, I peered around the couch, keeping Sullivan's face hidden in my bosom and my hands tucked around his ears.

You'd gotten control of the gun again. Rafael tackled you. Sirens pierced the air. Red-and-blue lights appeared outside the front window.

My stomach churned.

It was like last time.

Mrs. Medina? We need to talk to you.

The gun went off. This time it was so loud it practically burst my eardrum. Pain radiated through my head. I couldn't hear anything, even Sullivan. Was he still crying?

Police swarmed the room. It all seemed to be happening in slow motion.

It was like I was having an out-of-body experience.

Who was hit?

Blood pooled in the center of the room, but I couldn't tell who it was coming from. You were on top of Rafael, but both of you were unmoving.

There was blood on your hands.

With Sullivan still in my arms, I started to cry.

CHAPTER
THIRTY-ONE

The sterile hospital scent wafted under my nose, a mixture of alcohol and bleach, and it turned my stomach. The fluorescent lights hurt my eyes. I was tired of the needles, the tubes, the scratchy sheets and squeaky bed. Tired of the nurses, the noise and the police officer's incessant questions.

I had to keep reminding myself that it was better than the shed. Starvation. Thirst.

But not by much.

I longed for my own bed. To be home.

Too bad it was an active crime scene right now.

"Oh, my god!" Christine rushed into the room. "Thank god you're okay." She fell into the chair near my bed and scooped up my hand. Only Christine would show up to the hospital in a little black dress and long dangly earrings. She looked like she was heading out to a nice dinner. It made me smile.

"Hey," I croaked. She smelled like something fruity. Apples, maybe. It was a welcome distraction. I squeezed her hand.

"I cannot believe this happened. It's just crazy."

I tried to laugh, but it came out all scratchy and garbled. "That's one way to put it."

"How's Rafael? I still can't believe he got shot."

"I don't know. He just got out of surgery. But I think he'll be fine."

"Thank god." Christine shook her head. "I knew something was wrong when I came to your house for wine night and you said you were sick. That's why I called Raf, told him I was worried."

"Wait…what do you mean?" I sat up a little, the bed squeaking with every movement. "How did I say I was sick?"

"You texted."

"She had my phone." The pieces were clicking into place. I nodded. I had to hand it to you. It was pretty clever.

"Yeah, but I knew something was off about the texts."

"How?" I was curious what you'd done to give yourself away.

"You ended with TTYL." She laughed. "And I have never known you to use text speech."

I smiled. It's funny, the little things friends know about each other. I leaned back until I felt comfortable. My head still hurt a little. I had needed a few stitches, and apparently I'd suffered a concussion. They'd bandaged me up pretty good, gave me some meds and were keeping me overnight for observation.

A couple of nurses walked by in the hallway, pushing a cart. Its wheels buzzed along the linoleum, one of them squeaking as if it was broken. Machines beeped in the distance. I heard a woman wailing. I tried to tune it all out. I'd had enough drama for one day.

"Yeah, Aaron always teased me about that," I said, in an attempt to stay present, to keep the conversation flowing. "I still remember the first time he texted me 'LOL.' I had to google what it was."

Christine chuckled, but then her smile turned to a frown. Her eyebrows knit together, the skin around her eyes crinkling. That's when I saw what I never noticed before. The dark circles, the frown lines. She'd been worried about me.

"How are you taking it? Knowing what really happened to Aaron?" she asked.

I was grateful she was holding my hand. I needed someone to hold me steady right now. "I don't know," I answered honestly. No one had asked me that yet. So far everyone had only wanted answers from me. Facts. Dates. Times. Thank god I had the recording, so I didn't have to rely solely on my memory. Also, now even if you tried to lie, the police had evidence. They had the truth.

"I haven't had much time to think about it." I breathed in, and the memories of everything you'd said flowed through my chest. It swelled, and I felt it—the pain, the betrayal, the anger, the devastation, the sadness. Then I breathed it out, releasing it all into the air, knowing it would always linger nearby. A mere thought or memory away. "I never bought their theory about him doing this to himself," I finally said. "So, I guess in some ways I feel vindicated. But mostly, I just feel sick…and sad. It was so senseless, what happened to him."

Tears filled Christine's eyes. "It must give you some relief to know she's going to pay for what she did."

The vision of you being taken away in handcuffs with Rafael's blood painting your shirt filled my mind. "Yeah, she's never getting out of prison. I'll make sure Aaron gets justice."

"What about her baby? Do you know where he is?"

"Child Services took him. I did tell them that Rafael is his dad, and I told them we wanted him." I shrugged, feeling sick. "But I don't know what's gonna happen there. I think they have to do paternity tests and all kinds of stuff. The whole thing is a mess, Christine."

Frowning, she held tightly to my hand, lightly running her thumb over my skin. "I'm so sorry, Kel. About everything."

"It's not like it was your fault." *It was yours, Kelly. Yours and my husband's.*

A sob tore through Christine's throat, startling me. She smothered her mouth with her hand. "But that's just it. It *was* my fault."

"What do you mean?" I seriously couldn't take any more surprises.

"I knew something was wrong. I should've gone to the police or forced my way into your house or something. But when I told Raf, he said I was being ridiculous. And, I mean, you have been acting strangely." Her cries deepened. "And, honestly, I kinda thought you were making Kelly up. I mean, because of how you used to talk to Aaron like he was still alive all the time. And remember when you started talking about your childhood imaginary friend like she was real?"

I nodded. "Yeah, but that was right after Aaron died, and I was on a lot of meds then."

"I know. And I should've recognized that you were better. But even Raf thought maybe you'd snapped again. That's why he decided to go home and check on you. He thought maybe you'd taken someone's kid again or something. I hate that we even thought that… I feel like the worst friend." She sniffed. "I'm so sorry."

"Hey." I squeezed her hand. "You have no reason to apologize. I'm alive because of you."

Her head snapped up. Sniffling, she wiped her face. It was so rare to see her like this, mascara running down her cheeks, her nose red. "Really?"

"You knew something was wrong. Even if you weren't sure what it was, you still took action and called Raf. And regardless of the reason why, he came back two days early. If he hadn't, I don't think I would've survived."

"Oh, god, when I think of you locked in that shed…" Her lips quivered again. "You must've been so scared."

The familiar panic clawed at my insides at the memory. I shifted on the bed. "Can we talk about something else?"

"Of course." Nodding, she wiped her face and forced a smile.

A nurse shuffled in, her pants whistling between her thighs. I swallowed hard, wiped my face. God, I must've looked hideous.

"Don't mind me, I'm just gonna check your vitals," she said. As she flitted around me, I leaned toward Christine and smiled. "Any new gossip I should know about?"

"Always." She winked, tossing a strand of hair over her shoulder and shifting in her seat until she got settled.

I was back home now. I'd been released from the hospital a few days ago. Rafael had come home today.

After giving him his medication, I fluffed the pillow behind his head and smoothed down the covers.

"That good?" I asked.

He nodded. His skin was sickly pale, and his face seemed thinner than usual. He hadn't said much. Not in the hospital, or on the drive home, or even once we'd gotten here. We still hadn't talked about everything. Maybe he wasn't ready to.

I had no idea what to say, or where to start.

His cell phone buzzed from where I'd set it on the nightstand.

"Your friends from work keep texting and calling," I said. "Frank, Jon, Adam…some other numbers I don't recognize."

"Thanks." Without answering my unspoken question, he reached for it.

I thought about Keith. You. The pictures. The texts.

Swallowing thickly, I made my way to the window and opened the blinds. Natural light spilled in. I looked down at the shed and felt sick. I couldn't bring myself to go out there, and I hated that you still had any power over me, especially in my own home. The place that was once my sanctuary.

"Have you checked on my dad at all?" Rafael asked.

I turned. "You're worried about your dad right now?"

"He did just suffer a bad fall."

"He did, didn't he?" In all the craziness, I'd forgotten. *He thinks you've been here. That you've visited recently.*

The night that Rafael's dad fell, you weren't home. I thought about our conversation the week before. How you'd asked if Rafael would be home the next weekend. You didn't want that, did you?

God, I was so glad you were in jail and out of my life.

I forced a smile. "Yes, of course I'll check on him. No need to worry about that. We have enough on our plates."

"Kel." His tone was hesitant.

"Yes?" My head snapped up. This was it. He was finally going to talk about it.

Our eyes locked, then his drifted past me. "I… I think you should take that bassinet out of here."

I pictured Sullivan squished inside, the pink blanket wrapped around him. "Yeah, you're probably right. Sullivan's outgrown it. I'll get him a crib."

"No, don't do that."

"But we have to have everything ready for when he comes to live with us."

"We don't even know if that's happening."

My pulse quickened. "Why not?"

"He's probably not even mine. Kelly was crazy. How can we trust anything she said?"

I knew Sullivan was his, but I also knew better than to argue. "Of course. I'll take it out of here right away."

"If I had known…" The words lingered. I stood still, waiting. "…what she was capable of, I never would've…" He shook his head.

He never would've what? Slept with you? Got you pregnant?

"You have to believe me," he continued. "I had no idea she was this crazy."

It was then that I knew I'd never get an apology. In his mind this was your fault, Kelly, just like everything else had been mine. You were just a toy that never should have turned on him.

"I'll go get the tools to take apart the bassinet," I said.

When I reached the doorway he stopped me. "Kel."

I peered over my shoulder, allowing myself to feel the faintest hope. "Yes?"

"Can you get me some more water?"

"Of course." On trembling legs, I walked back in the room and retrieved his water cup. Next to it were all of his prescriptions, labeled with menacing lists of side effects and precautions.

As I left the room, he lay back on the bed, his eyelids fluttering. He was getting tired again.

Even though I'd cleaned my house, the ghost of you lingered. I saw you when I walked down the stairs, my gaze traveling to where you'd stood across from Rafael with a gun in your hand. I saw you in the stain on the couch and near the mantel where you'd inspected my family portraits.

I wished you were dead for what you did to Aaron, to me, to my family. But I guess rotting in jail would have to suffice. I knew what it was like to be stuck in a small space. To be alone with your thoughts. Your memories. The things you'd done to the people I loved were horrific, and I prayed you'd be tormented by them every day of your life.

I knew all the details now, even the ones you hadn't shared with me.

Your real name was Kelly Hawkins. You'd switched the last name to Medina on Sullivan's birth certificate.

You still hadn't admitted to coming over late that night, but I knew you were there. I saw you. I'm assuming now you were here for the cuff links.

There were enough charges against you I was certain you'd be behind bars until the day you died. You would never see the light of day. You'd never see your son. And, most important, you'd never hurt anyone else's child. And that was something that would give me peace. It was the one thing I could hold on to—knowing you were getting what you deserved.

I filled Rafael's cup with water, adding two cubes of ice the way he liked it. Then I headed back upstairs, passing Aaron's room on the way to mine.

Rafael was asleep so I set it on the nightstand, and perched on the edge of the bed.

He hadn't asked about Sullivan since that night. The only mention of him had been today when he told me to get rid of the bassinet. It was like he didn't care about his son at all. The irony wasn't lost on me. You'd done all of this for your son, but you'd made one big mistake. You'd misjudged Rafael.

He wasn't worth it.

He wasn't the kind of father you should've wanted for your son.

I may hate you now, but we were friends once. You were young and idealistic, a romantic. So much like me in my younger years. Rafael was your professor. A man of power. I couldn't solely blame you for your relationship with him. In fact, I blamed him more. He was your Jeremy.

I knew you never had a father. When I saw you talking with him, I think I finally got it. You needed his approval. In some sick way he was a father figure to you. He was someone you had been searching for your entire life.

I would never forgive you for what you did to Aaron. But I knew it had all started with Rafael. He was the one who got the ball rolling. The one who put all of this in motion.

If he had just kept it in his pants, none of this would've happened.

I would still have my son. Aaron would still be alive.

If I had known what she was capable of...

What about what he was capable of?

The lying.

The cheating.

The abuse.

He'd destroyed all of us. Me. Aaron. Even you.

And I was sure in time he'd destroy Sullivan too.

When would it end if he couldn't even own it? If he didn't even realize he was the problem?

I thought of the texts he'd gotten today. The numbers I didn't recognize. Had he moved on from you? Did he have a new mistress now?

He was a predator, always looking for new prey.

When the doctors released Rafael this morning, they told me he wasn't completely out of the woods yet. They made me promise to take good care of him. It's what I'd always done. Taken care of Rafael. Made sure he had what he wanted. A clean house. A dutiful, faithful wife.

Reaching across the bed, I picked up the pillow from my side. It smelled clean and fresh, newly laundered. I'd washed everything before Rafael came home, so he wouldn't complain. Bending toward him, I took a deep breath. He never even saw the pillow coming.

"I'm just cleaning up the mess you made," I whispered in his ear. "I know how much you hate messes."

He struggled a little, but then he stilled, drifted off.

I took care of him all right. I took care of everything.

* * * * *

Acknowledgments

Huge thanks to my literary agent Ellen Coughtrey of the Gernert Company. From our very first conversation I knew you were the right person to champion this book. Your enthusiasm, insight and understanding of the story and its characters blew me away. The story was so much stronger after implementing your ideas and revisions. Some of my favorite scenes came from our brainstorming sessions. You've changed my life, and I'm forever grateful. Also, thanks to Will Roberts, Rebecca Gardner and the entire team at the Gernert Company. You guys are awesome.

April Osborn, I'm so grateful to you. You've been so fun to work with, and your edits to the book shaped it into something even better than I imagined. To the entire team at MIRA, thank you for believing in this book, and in me. You have made my dream come true.

Megan Squires, thank you for reading early drafts and helping me see issues with the story as they arose. And, of course, thank you for working your magic on my author photos. But, mostly, thank you for being such a supportive friend.

To my parents and my entire extended family, your unwavering support means the world to me. I'm so blessed to have each one of you in my life.

Andrew, none of this would've happened without you. You've always put your own dreams on hold so I could chase mine. Know that I see that, and I don't take it for granted. You're my favorite. I love you.

To my kids: Eli, thank you for helping me work out the ending of this book, and also some of the stickier plot points. Brainstorming sessions with you are my favorite. Kayleen, my mini-me, my perpetual cheerleader, my confidante. Thanks for your constant support and encouragement. I love you both with all my heart.

And to God, everything I do is for you.

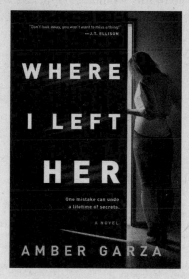